# THE DREAM

Iain Ryan

LAMB HOUSE BOOKS

# Praise for THE DREAM

'Refracting the grim spirit of noir through 1980s Queensland is a natural move, and Ryan launches into building a glitzy, violent and meretricious underworld with flair.' —*Sydney Morning Herald*

'Perfect for fans of Garry Disher, Adrian McKinty and Peter Temple' - ***Books + Publishing***

'Iain Ryan is one of the most gifted writers in the contemporary Australian crime fiction scene' – **Steven Powell, author of** *Love Me Fierce In Danger: The Life of James Ellroy*

'Splendidly gritty' – **Kate Mildenhall, author of** *The Mother Fault* **and** *The Hummingbird Effect*

' The best fictional rendering on the page of Queensland's not so distant criminal past that I have read.' – **Andrew Nette, author of** *Orphan Road* **and** *Gunshine State*

# THE
# DREAM

A NOVEL

# IAIN
# RYAN

# THE DREAM

A NOVEL

IAIN RYAN

# Also by Iain Ryan

Lamb House Books

ISBN: 978-0-6458735-5-9

Buy the books direct from www.iainryan.com

Ryan, Iain. The Dream (Gold Coast Quartet Book 2). Lamb House Books. Kindle Edition.

Cover design by Damonza.

Copyeditor: Deonie Fiford

Proofreader: Camha Pham

# THE DREAM

A NOVEL

IAIN RYAN

# THE DREAM

A NOVEL

## IAIN RYAN

*For my sons*

*We live in the civilization they created, but within us the wilderness still lingers. What they dreamed, we live, and what they lived, we dream.*

— T.K. WHIPPLE

*The constables were convicts and in later times ex-convicts, generally illiterate, and very poorly paid. There was a huge turnover in personnel as constables were dismissed for drunkenness, corruption and neglect of duty. Given the composition of the colony, it was inevitable that constables should be ex-convicts, but higher wages might have attracted a better type. No one was prepared to pay for this and so the choice had to be made from the dregs.*

— JOHN HIRST

# PART ONE
# MONDAY, 27 SEPTEMBER
# TO TUESDAY, 28 SEPTEMBER,
## 1982

# VICTOR

*In dreams, only the parts make sense. There's no seeing the whole story, and our interpretation of the fragments offers very little. They're stitched together and hackneyed. Superstitious. Pseudo-religious. We try to find meaning in our dreams by piecing them back together, but they have no meaning. They're not a story.*

*A dream is about how you live through it. A dream is—*

*'Sir, your medication.'*

*It's Elda, my nurse. Her footsteps on the rug.*

*The blinds of my room are drawn back.*

*I open my eyes and sunlight blinds me. I refocus on Elda with her silver tray and her terrible plastic cup. Behind her, a vivid blue sky in the window, the shimmering peaks of palm trees.*

*'What time is it?'*

*'Eight o'clock, sir.'*

*'Was I sleeping?'*

*'Perhaps. But now it's time to wake up.'*

*'I'm old, Elda. Old and rich and sick. I should be allowed to sleep as much as I like.'*

1

'Take your medication and you can do as you please,' Elda says, like I'm due a quick sip of medicine instead of a dozen pills.

Within minutes, these meds will run rampant in my blood, rendering me delirious and wired at the same time. It's been weeks of this. Day after day in a liminal zone between waking life and unconscious dreaming. Fragments and whole.

I can't complain.

It was sitting here, drifting around in my drug haze, that I came up with the plan that set this whole thing in motion.

Elda clears her throat. 'Is there anything else, sir?'

'No, you can fuck off now.'

'Very good, sir.'

'Wait. Is there anyone on the books for today?'

'You have a call with Allan Watts at eleven.'

'What does he want?'

'I don't know, sir. You told me to schedule it yesterday.'

'I did? Maybe we should schedule my reasoning as well.'

'Sir, you don't tend to enjoy explaining yourself.'

She's right.

I move my wheelchair across to the window. I watch the still water of the canal, the white split-level mansions and empty yards. There are pools beside sea water. Tennis courts by lawns. This is a paradise of my own making. The envy of all.

When I carved this land from the sea, I sold it as Venice-by-way-of-Miami, but it's better than that. Venice is a toilet, and while the Americans may have invented our way of life, they didn't perfect it. The Florida Riviera is a few good beaches and nothing more. The Gold Coast puts it all to shame. We have *twenty miles of unbroken soft sand. We have rolling surf and warm winters. We have money and power and support. A place endowed with nature's blessings and owned by men who can harness such things.*

*I am one of them.*
*I lived and dreamed.*
*I built and conquered.*
*And as feeble as I am, I'm far from finished.*

# BRUNO
## The Pacific Ocean

DETECTIVE BRUNO KARRAS FLOATS in the dark ocean, out past the breakers where the quiet water drifts. It's just him and another bloke further down, the two of them exchanging a distant nod as they wait for the next set. It's a couple of minutes past dawn, too early for everyone else.

Another week in this year.

The year where nothing matters.

Bruno turns towards the shoreline: Surfers Paradise lurks in the distance, grey and calm. The city is a jagged line of high-rises, cranes and scaffolding, all in silhouette.

A place on pause.

Australia in recession.

Everything going backwards.

The sea water swells beneath him. He paddles for a wave and finds himself on the right of the other surfer. Bruno pulls back, lets the other guy have it, then tracks the man's head and shoulders as he travels the wave and dips away. Bruno tries for another two waves from the set, but none of it breaks the right way.

He returns to his spot in the quiet.

He waits.

He thinks about work—the go-nowhere case load assigned to him— and he's still thinking about it when he senses movement in the water, some strange current.

He searches around.

A long shadow passes beneath his feet.

*Shark.*

Bruno swims, thrashing as the swell comes in behind. He stays prone on his board as the wave crests, desperate to keep his legs out of the sea.

'Shark,' he screams, searching for the other guy. 'Shark.'

The wave carries him like a glacier.

Bruno paddles, arms burning. He's still shouting when a dolphin jumps out a few feet away, its glistening black hide slick with water.

*False alarm.*

Bruno keeps swimming, cursing the dolphin all the way to shore. He waits in the shallows and tries, with all his might, to let his pounding heart subside into a crying jag, but the tears won't come.

THE CARPARK by the beach is a quarter full, despite the hour. Bruno towels off by his ute, gives the carpark a quick scan, drops his togs and pulls on a pair of white cotton jocks. He puts the rest of his work clothes on, except his shoes, then slips behind the steering wheel to wax his hair in the rear-view. That's when he notices it: paper tucked under the windscreen wiper. He reaches around and yanks it free.

It's a white business envelope.

His name, written in blue biro on the front.

He holds it up to the light.

No wires. Nothing sus.

He opens it and finds a deck of photographs.

He flicks through them.

A street.

A house on that street.

The same again, but with a car in the foreground.

It's a big house, but nothing outrageous. Some new-money mansion with tapered kerbs and a dry lawn out front. Could be one of a dozen new estates cropping up around the coast.

Bruno keeps moving through the images.

The same house, from different angles.

The same street.

Over and over.

The final image is facedown in the deck. Bruno turns it over and immediately checks his surroundings. He looks at the photograph again and feels absolute dread for the second time this morning.

# AMY
## Surfers Paradise Foreshore

AMY OWENS CHECKS THE GIRL in the passenger seat, taking a quick look out the side of her sunglasses. *No change.* The morning glare must be hell on the girl's eyes, but she still stares out the windscreen, motionless and silent. *Gone*, Amy thinks. She's been like this since Amy picked her up from the hospital. Whatever they did to her in there, it didn't work.

*It's going to be a long couple of days.*

Across the beachside carpark, a white ute reverses, coming out hard. The ute belongs to a local copper. A young Italian bloke. A minute ago, Amy watched him get dressed out in the open, caught a look at his pert arse. The cop tears out of the carpark without noticing them.

This prompts the girl to finally speak. 'What was that all about?'

'The guy?'

The girl doesn't turn her face. 'No, the envelope.'

Amy hits the ignition. 'I don't know. I didn't look.' It's a lie. 'Put your seatbelt on.'

'How far is it?'

'Pretty far.' Amy pulls out onto the main drag, glances at the girl again. 'Hey?'

'What?'

'I said put your belt on.'

THE JOB IS PURE SHIT-WORK: get the girl to Adelaide. She won't fly, so it's a two-day drive instead. Amy ends up with it because the girl's important to Colleen Vinton. *Colleen the Queen*. Colleen is upriver from everything unholy on the coast. Prostitution, porn, gambling, narcotics, police corruption. If it's illegal, or bad for the soul, Colleen owns a piece of it. She owns a piece of Amy, as well. A big piece.

Amy steers them down the coast across the river into New South Wales. The girl doesn't have luggage or dietary requirements, but she has a request. She wants to go to church. Apparently, it has to be her regular haunt. Saint Andrews, of all places.

*Christ almighty.*

When they get there, Amy sends her in alone, opting to stay by the car and smoke. She's not worried about losing her. The girl's moving like she's under-water. She's not running anywhere.

After a time, the girl comes back out with the priest in tow.

It's not just any priest. It's the man himself.

Father Frank Hanlon.

Like Colleen Vinton, Frank's a man with a lot of enemies. Everyone on the coast knows him, especially the people in Colleen's orbit. The two of them are mortal enemies—a real yin and yang deal—and it's a mystery to everyone why Frank still draws breath. Colleen has killed men for much less.

He waves Amy over to the church.

'What the fuck do you want?' she whispers to herself, jettisoning her smoke. Amy tells the girl to go to the car and wait, then walks across to the church steps. 'What?'

'I've got people in Adelaide,' says the priest.

Amy opens her hands. *And?*

'I'll know if she doesn't get there.'

'I think you've got me mixed up with someone else.'

'No, I know who you are,' he says. 'I knew your father back in the day.'

Amy starts back across the lawn.

'You really haven't lived up to your potential, Miss Owens,' the priest says.

*Fuck this guy.*

'Wait,' he says.

She stops. Something about his voice.

'If you ever want to take off the leash, my door's always open. We take all comers down here. I can help you. I've helped plenty of people just like you. You don't have to spend your whole life doing Colleen's bidding.'

'Is that what I'm doing?'

The priest looks past her, over at the girl. 'False idols speak only of false dreams.'

'If you say so, buddy.'

Amy doesn't stop a second time.


THEY DRIVE ALL DAY, stopping only to pee and refuel. It's hard going. The inside of the country is low and dry and monotonous. It's that thing where you can see too much of it at once: trees and grass all the way to the horizon, with nothing further out. No

11

hills or mountain ranges to provide perspective. No waterfalls or alpine greenery. Just dead grass and dirt, all the way to the centre.

By nightfall, they reach the town of Nyngan and hole up in a motel. Amy polishes off two bottles of the house red, but the girl won't drink. Instead, she watches television in the darkened room, getting up every five minutes to change the channel.

'Can you stop that?' Amy snaps, tired.

'Sorry,' says the girl. She turns the TV off.

'You didn't have to do that.'

'It's fine,' says the girl, and then, a full two minutes later, just as Amy is drifting off, she says, 'They wouldn't let us change the channel in the hospital.'

# AMY
## Nyngan, New South Wales

SOMEWHERE DEEP IN THE early hours, the girl starts moaning and whimpering. Her words are mangled, almost distorted—emerging from her throat like a wet cough. 'I see the devil now. I whisper to him . . . The names. Teddy, Eddie, Brian. *Violet*.' She keeps repeating the last one. 'Violet, Violet, Violet . . .'

There's no sense in it.

Amy stands over the girl's bed, praying she'll resettle. When she doesn't, Amy lies down beside her, cuddling the girl from behind, the way her brother Will used to console her back in the bad old days. It seems to work. The girl's voice drops, and her whispering peters out. Amy wants to tell the girl it's going to be okay, but for the life of her she can't remember her name.

The girl's murmuring starts up again. 'Lenny. Joel. Violet, Violet, Violet . . .'

Amy touches her face, and it's slick with sweat.

She stirs. 'Where . . . what?'

'It's okay. You were having a nightmare.'

The girl goes quiet, then she rolls over and

13

touches Amy's cheek— just as Amy has touched hers. The girl gently kisses her on the mouth.

'Go back to sleep,' Amy whispers.

She gets out of the girl's bed, moves back to her own sweat-drenched sheets and stares into the black void of the ceiling.

THE NEXT MORNING, they're back in the car and heading south. It's more of the same. More grass fields and shit towns, all dry as a match and devoid of mystery. Even the radio doesn't work out here.

The girl stays quiet for two hours, but Amy knows she's working up to something. She's not as zombified today. Whatever they gave her in the mental hospital is wearing off.

Amy is so bored she gives her a nudge. 'What's your name again?'

The girl says nothing.

'They told me, but I forgot. Do you know my name?'

'Amy Owens.'

'Okay.'

'You work for Colleen Vinton. You take dirty pictures for her. I know who you are. I remember you.'

Amy keeps her eyes on the road. 'It's not all I do.'

The girl doesn't comment.

'I do background checks, find people, dig stuff up. It's not all . . . So we've met before?'

'At Tropical Touch,' says the girl. It's one of Colleen's brothels.

The road bends, but only a little. The landscape stays the same. It looks like fucking Mars out the window. Amy lights a smoke and sucks on it.

'They took my baby away,' says the girl.

'What?'

'They took my baby. That's why Colleen is sending me to Adelaide. I had a baby before I went to the hospital. They gave it to some cop. Colleen said it was for my own good, but . . .'

Amy exhales. 'You can't tell me this stuff.'

'Because of Colleen?'

'Fuck yes, because of Colleen.'

'You do whatever she says?'

'I do what she pays me to do.'

The girl looks over at her. 'I've got money. What if I paid you?'

'To do what, exactly?'

'Find my baby.'

'What are you going to do with a baby? How old are you? Nineteen? Twenty? When you get to Adelaide, you can start over.'

'Start what over?'

Amy lets it go. She wipes wet hair from her brow.

'What do you reckon?' says the girl.

'Tell me your name first.'

'Sarah. Sarah Utton.'

'Who's the father?' Amy says, but then shakes her head. '*Fuck.* Don't answer that. Forget I asked.'

'Can you help me?'

'No, I can't.'

'Just . . . *no*?'

'That's right, Sarah. Just no.'

# MIKE
## Surfers Paradise

MIKE NICHOLS WATCHES THE Gold Coast tilt and turn from the back seat of a helicopter. His stomach churns, but it's all down there. The dream. The diamond life. Paradise in the making. Seeing it at scale, ranging out from the edge of the ocean, brings a hint of euphoria out of his hangover.

The pilot puts them down in an airfield in Coolangatta. There's a car waiting. The car takes him to a tall apartment block on the foreshore of Point Danger. 'It's the penthouse,' says the driver.

Mike finds the intercom, hits the biggest number on there.

'Who's that then?' says a voice.

It's a voice Mike has heard in a hundred interviews. The nasal whine of the Queensland north filtered through private schooling.

He plays it safe and straight. 'It's Mike Nichols, sir. I have a ten o'clock appointment with the minister.'

'That's me. You'll have to let yourself in when you get upstairs.'

The gate buzzes open.

THE PENTHOUSE IS ALL WINDOWS, and the windows are filled with the ocean and the sky. Against this backdrop, the minister is sprawled out on a chaise lounge like a long, thick slug. In the backrooms of parliament, they call him the *God Minister*. The all-knowing one. He has a huge portfolio. He sees all, but he's no benevolent deity. The God Minister strikes his fist into the earth all the time.

Today, the minister is dressed for the office, despite the fact his right leg is plastered from the knee down. The *Courier Mail* reported that he fell from a ladder, but the rumour mill says he took a spill down the back stairs of a brothel up in the city. 'I'd offer you a cuppa,' he says, 'but this fucking thing.' He waves at his leg. 'It's a damned nuisance. Itches like the clap.'

'I'm fine without, sir.'

'Good, good. Sit down, you're making the place look untidy. Now Roger Pearse tells me you've been bringing in a lot of big fish lately.'

Mike nods. His gazetted role is Public Liaison for the Queensland National Party. It's a wining and dining gig. Lots of late nights with big business, lots of getting everyone in the mood and greasing the wheels of industry. In reality, he's a party planner and a bagman for the state government.

'I want you to come work for me,' says the minister.

Mike takes a second. 'I have a few projects for—'

'Fuck Pearse. Do you wanna hang out with the big dicks or not, son?'

'What do you have in mind?'

'Tell me what you know about Fantasyland.'

Mike clears his throat to give himself a moment. 'I only know the gossip, sir.' Fantasyland is a half-built amusement park about half an hour's drive inland. The place is owned by Noah Winters and his family. Cement magnates from Townsville.

'What might that gossip be, son?'

The minister looks over his glasses and waits.

A test.

'It's behind schedule. Way behind. The talk is that the whole thing is getting shaky. Money trouble left and right. Noah Winters is the one driving it into the ground. They reckon he's lost his mind.'

The minister shifts his gaze.

*Passed.*

'It *is* behind schedule,' the minister says. 'They keep telling me it's the bloody recession, but my gut says otherwise. Lots of people I know

are up to their eyeballs in it, invested to the hilt, so I want you to look after it. The official opening needs to be announced in the next couple of weeks. Make sure it opens on time. You reckon you can handle that?'

'How much discretion do I have?'

The minister laughs. 'I think you're going to have to get your hands dirty on this one, son. Go with the Lord. If you can do this for me, there's a sizeable drink in it for you.'

Mike knows enough to make the ask. 'What sort of drink?'

'Twice what Pearse is paying you, and that's just the beginning. Show me what you can do and we'll talk more.'

'When do I start?'

'There's a site visit tonight. You're going in my place.' The minister scratches at his leg with the end of a plastic ruler, then slides it down into his cast.

'That looks painful, sir.'

The minister grins. 'It is.' He scratches some more and says, 'She wasn't worth it.'

# BRUNO
## The Paradise Hotel

BRUNO SCANS THE FRONT BAR, sorting Criminal Investigation Branch detectives from the lunchtime tradies and bar flies. There's not much in it. He does the rounds, asking questions about the photos and the mysterious house depicted. No one has any answers. A Homicide bloke asks Bruno why he's *breaking up the session with this bullshit*, and Bruno tells him the truth, 'Because no one is back at the station.' Giving up, Bruno orders a schooner from the tab and settles in.

An hour later, his old partner Detective Lana Cohen rolls through with her new workmates, the Robbery Squad. *The Robbers*, as they're known, have a full plate at the moment. A local crew is knocking over Gold Coast banks at a rate of one a week and the last two robberies involved fatalities. Now the state media have latched onto it and the pressure has dialled up. Lana slips away from her lot and sidles up to Bruno by the bar. She gives him the once-over. 'You're looking more and more like one of the boys, Bruno.'

'If you can't beat 'em.' He drains his glass and motions to the barman for two more.

Lana winks at a passing constable. 'Fancy a smoke?'

'I'm trying to quit,' says Bruno.

'Is that a yes or a no?'

'I guess I haven't quit yet, so there's no harm in it.'

They take their beers and cigarettes to a table outside and spark up in the sun. September is hot already, but there's the whisper of a breeze coming in off the ocean.

'How's the big time treating you?' says Bruno, tapping his smoke into a stray glass.

'It's going,' says Lana. 'They have me following up leads with the bank staff. Rank and file work. Pete Reynolds doesn't give a shit, though. Half the time he's off doing Christ knows what.'

Lana is partnered with Reynolds. It's a punishment posting. Reynolds is an old enemy: a bent copper who used to run the Gold Coast CIB with Ron Bingham and Mark Evans, back in the Strike Force Diablo days. Diablo was a serial homicide case that went pear-shaped a couple of years back. Lana came across the border on secondment for it, and Bruno was the guy helping her get acquainted.

'I thought you'd be old mates with Reynolds by now,' says Bruno.

'Piss off.'

'Well, let me tell you, things are hotting up in Missing Persons.' He hands a few of the photographs over. Only the images of the house. 'Someone popped these under my windscreen wiper yesterday.'

Lana looks through them. 'Creepy. Whose house is this?'

'Well—'

'There's a licence plate in this one.'

'There are actually two different plates visible. I ran both. The first one, that yellow Cortina, belongs to a family in Beenleigh, so that's a bust.'

'This doesn't look like Beenleigh,' says Lana, tapping the image.

'The second one gave me a house here in Southport. Pohlman Drive.'

Lana shrugs, doesn't know it. 'You run the deed?'

'The house belongs to Phillip and Marion O'Grady.'

'Should I know who they are?'

'Phil O'Grady was a magistrate up in Brisbane. I've given evidence in front of him. He must have retired down here.'

'What's the deal? Are the photos a tip-off?'

'I drove past the house a few times yesterday. No one's home. But the lights were on last night. I don't know what's going on.'

Bruno's mind flashes to the last photo in the deck, the one he's *not* showing her.

*A while back, as everything was going to hell.*

*Some strange autumn afternoon.*

*The loading dock of a shopping centre.*

He swallows it down.

Lana hands back the photographs. 'What did Bingham say?'

Inspector Ron Bingham is the boss.

'He thought it was a bunch of nonsense but told me to look into it.' Lana winces and shakes her head. This is their lot at the moment, and they brought it on themselves. At the end of Diablo, Lana and Bruno put Inspector Bingham offside. They went around him to get Lana posted on the Coast, and it wasn't a clean deal at all. Lana had photos of Gold Coast

23

coppers stepping into a brothel and she had Bruno trade them up the chain for a job. Bingham was the last to know and he wasn't chuffed. But Bruno and Lana solved a few cases when they hit Homicide together the following year, and that kept the Inspector at bay, until Bruno's father got sick.

He needed time off.

Then his father died and Bruno took a longer stretch.

*Had to*.

And Inspector Bingham was lying in wait the whole time. He took the gift of Bruno's absence and started meting out the punishment.

Lana demoted to Robbers, a dead-end at the time.

Bruno found himself filed in Missing Persons.

The union stayed mum.

Everyone knew what was happening.

Lana holds up her glass. 'For our sins,' she says.

Bruno taps his glass against hers.

'Amen.'

# BRUNO

## Pohlman Drive, Southport

AFTER THE PUB LUNCH, Bruno sits in his car until dusk, watching the house on Pohlman Drive. There's nothing doing. The street is dead as a doornail.

Bored, he walks to the payphone box on the corner and drops a coin in the slot.

The call connects. 'Hello?' It's his brother, Danny.

'It's me,' says Bruno. 'You got a shift tonight?'

'Yeah, I'm on the way out.'

'Can you feed the cat? I'm tied up.'

'I think I can handle that,' says Danny.

'Did you have someone over last night?'

'Maybe.'

'I thought I heard voices, that's all.'

'It was just some girl from the bar.'

'Don't bring sluts back to the house, okay? Go to their house.'

Danny laughs. 'Jeez.'

'I'm not joking.'

'I know you're not. That's why it's funny. How

are you a bloody copper when you're this fucking charming?'

Bruno looks back up the street at the house. 'Just smart, I guess. Look . . .' Bruno scratches at something on the phone booth's glass beside him. 'Just be careful with who you bring home, okay? There's a gun in my room.'

'I know there is,' says Danny.

They're both thinking the same thing. But they wait it out.

'Well, brainiac,' says Danny. 'I better get going.'

'See you in the morning.'

'Yeah. See you then.'

His brother hangs up first.

DANNY MOVED HOME when their father got sick. Danny did the muck work with that, took their father to his appointments and doled out the medication. It didn't work, but someone had to do it. Their mother was long gone.

There was five years between them, but with Bruno's job—seeing what he saw every day—it was more like ten. Danny was still loose and free. Good-looking, easy to talk to. He tended bar down at Seagulls on the border and had no plans for the future. He was still a bit of a kid.

After the funeral, Danny's only concession to the grief was moving in with Bruno. He didn't want to keep on living in their dead father's house, and Bruno didn't blame him. Having him around again was the best part of a bad era.

. . .

BRUNO DROPS another coin into the slot on the payphone. While the call is going through, he unfolds the photo, the one at the bottom of the deck. He's still walking around with it.

A voice answers the call. 'Yeah?'

'It's me. Someone took photos of us.'

'Who's this?'

'Back in April.'

'Back in April? What are you talking about? How'd you get this number?'

'I'm a cop,' says Bruno.

The line disconnects.


BACK IN THE CAR, still brooding, Bruno presses his fingers into his brow, trying to massage out a headache. It's almost dark now. The house sits across the street. Suddenly the lights blink on inside, upstairs and downstairs at the same moment.

The exact same moment. *They're on a timer.*

Bruno writes it down, then walks over and hits the doorbell, hearing the chime echo through the interior.

*Futile.* No one's home.

He stands in the dark alcove of the house and smokes a cigarette. He's still standing there when a kid comes past on a BMX bike. The kid stops at the house, opens the letterbox and pulls out the mail, then gets back on his bike and rides off.

Bruno creeps back over to his car, gets in and follows. He finds the kid a minute down the road, riding fast now. They round the corner of Queen Street and head west. Keeping back, Bruno watches as the kid ducks down a side street and winds through the suburbs. Eventually, they come to a park reserve, a place where the creek runs under the street. The kid cuts down a dirt track into the scrub by the water.

Bruno gets out and jogs after him, down a track that takes him to a part of the exposed creek bed, the water barely a trickle across the sand. It's shallow enough to ride through and the kid is long gone. Bruno crosses the creek and looks around. There's another suburban street up on the opposing bank. Litter threaded through the underbrush there: chip packets, shop flyers, a pile of old tyres. Heading back to the car, he notices something. It's a fresh white rectangle snagged in some creek-side grass. A letter. Bruno makes his way down the creek bed and fishes out the envelope.

*Phillip O'Grady, 15 Pohlman Drive, Southport.*

Bruno walks further downstream and finds more. Thirty envelopes caught in the nearby brush, all of them in varying states of soggy decay. All of them have the same address, all sent to the O'Grady family, and all here because that kid is dumping them in the creek.

# AMY

## The Mayfair Hotel, Adelaide

AMY GETS SARAH UTTON to Adelaide. She's going to be fine. Arrangements are in place. And Amy's boss Colleen isn't in the habit of sending people all the way across the country to get knocked. That's not her style. With her, the bodies tend to wash up where everyone can see what happens when you step out of line.

Amy checks into her hotel, hits the foyer bar, and waits it out. She has no interest in the city. No plans for dinner.

Time passes.

Some businessman buys her drinks.

Then a tourist.

Then another business guy. His name is Tony.

Tony is a rep for a tiling company.

Tony tells her he's in shape.

Tony slips his wedding ring off when he's in the bathroom and buys three rounds of drinks in a row. He seems absolutely devoid of life or ambition. 'To Adelaide,' he says.

Later, the barman kicks them out as the after-dinner trade files in. They hit Tony's room and the minibar and then the bed and it's no good for either of them. Amy experiences the whole thing like a curious bystander. It's not Tony's fault. Tony tries a little of everything. And Tony—who *is* in shape—can't come either.

'Can't you tug me off?' he says.

Amy holds up her right hand in front of his face and clenches it into a fist.

The bones creak and pop audibly.

'Bloody hell,' says Tony, fascinated.

That's about it, Colleen Vinton style.


BACK IN HER OWN ROOM, the night doesn't get any better. Amy relives old mistakes, sees siblings and parents and funerals, gasps in horror at bad memories arriving for reasons unknown. She paces the room and thinks about Sarah Utton and her missing baby. She thinks about her dead brother.

It's a load of shit.

*Start what over?*

Sarah was right. Smarter than Amy ever was.

*But why think about it?*

Amy shouts at herself to stop. She sucks beer and turns on the TV. More sports coverage, more aerial shots of QEII stadium. The Commonwealth Games is about to start back in Brisbane and the entire city is holding its breath. *Our moment to shine*, says some dickhead on the screen, waving away blowflies. Amy couldn't care less. Her mind drifts elsewhere.

She shivers in the aircon.

Feels the dread building even more.

*Fuck it.*

Amy grabs the gun from her luggage and loads a

bullet from the case, spins the barrel, watching herself in the bathroom mirror, half-naked and looking straight-up possessed. With absolutely no ceremony, she puts the gun in her good hand, places it under her chin and pulls the trigger.

*Snap.*

Pulls it again.

*Snap.*

She doesn't look any different.

No tears, no emotion, no—

*Snap.*

Not long now. She's already lost count.

The phone rings.

*Snap.*

'Fuck.'

It keeps ringing.

Amy picks it up. 'Yeah?'

Colleen's voice slides out of the receiver. 'How's the City of Churches, darl?'

'It's okay.'

'You get the girl there in one piece?'

'Yeah.'

'That's good.' Colleen sparks up a smoke on the other end and waits. Eventually, she says, 'That's my good deed done for the year. Did she say anything about the baby?'

'No.'

A lie, all instinct.

'That's a relief. If you knew who knocked her up, bloody hell . . . you'd have to stay down there with her.'

'No thanks. Is there something else I can do for you, Col?'

'You in a hurry, darl?'

'No, I just . . .'

'I get tired of this shit sometimes.'

Amy waits her out.

On the line, Colleen exhales a lungful and says, 'I have another little job for you tomorrow. I want you to go and see a copper in Brisbane, on your way back from the airport. Ray Blintiff. Do you know Ray?'

'Only by reputation.'

'Well you know he's a prick, then. That helps. He's got some work for you.'

'What's my end?'

'It's all yours,' says Colleen. 'I just need to stay in the good books with the Licensing boys. You know how it is.'

Amy knows. She signs off. She finds herself back in the room with the gun in one hand and the phone in the other. Amy looks down and almost laughs.

# MIKE

## Fantasyland, Gold Coast

MIKE SCRATCHES AT HIS shirt collar. It's a warm night, but the crowd is dressed up to the nines. Fifty black suits and gowns collecting dust from the carpark gravel. No one minds, particularly. Everyone is liquored up. Even the pre-party drinks are top shelf.

The crowd chatter cuts, washed over by a blast of feedback from a nearby PA.

Over the mic: 'Ladies and gentlemen, welcome to Fantasyland. Sorry about the delays!'

'Too right,' screams some drunk guy.

That gets a laugh from everyone.

Mike flashes back to the God Minister. *Just make sure it opens on time.*

'Yes, yes,' says the voice from the PA.

Mike pops his head above the crowd and locates the speaker. It's Buddy Winters—the big man's son, heir to all this.

'Tonight, we're going to show you what you've all been waiting for, and trust me, it'll be worth the wait. So grab another drink and make your way to the train, please.'

Mike follows the herd and finds himself boarding one of two small convoys. It's not really a train. There's no track. It's a small motorised cart hooked up to a string of open-air carriages. Mike finds a seat and the bloke in front of him immediately turns around and says, 'Is this the fucking Pac Fair train? My kids love this thing.' He looks at Mike. 'How'd they get hold of it?'

Mike shrugs.

A woman slips into the seat beside Mike. 'Evening,' she says, but doesn't introduce herself. The woman is tall with a long face and shoulder-length black hair cut into a rigid line around her shoulders.

'I'm Mike.'

'Sadie,' she says. 'Where did you get that drink?' She cranes around, looking for a waiter.

The bloke in front turns around again and tries his luck. 'Luv, do you reckon this is the Pac Fair train?'

'Who cares?' Sadie says. 'Do you have a light?'

Both men fumble to find one.

THE TRAIN TAKES them on a tour of Fantasyland and locks them into an hour-long pitch for how successful it'll all be and how they *just need more time*. In the darkened night, lit only by floodlights, the park has an abandoned and haunted vibe. The attractions are gaudy and half-built. In the Australian section, there's a shantytown of bush huts and a little colonial village with a town square. The train stops in the square for drink refills and to watch a re-enactment of a gunfight between escaped convicts and mounted police. As the convicts retreat, one toff near Mike lobs a tinnie onto the battlefield and hollers, 'Let 'em alone!'

From there, it's on to the roller-coaster and the swimming pool area, then a paved shopping district that looks like something out of an American cartoon. They also visit Royaltyland featuring a replica of Buckingham Palace and a fake royal family: actors smiling, a Prince Charles with prosthetic ears, a demure meter maid Princess Di, a tottering Queen Elizabeth played for laughs. 'Down there will be the games arcade and the miniature golf course,' says the guide. 'In phase two, we're planning a hotel over here, with a five-star restaurant. Soon you'll be able to stay in the park for as long as you wish. Just gotta get it built.'

The tour ends in the empty dodgem car arena, with the party clustered around a little podium. Behind the podium is a pink neon sign displaying the Fantasyland logo, washing out the scene in stark, futuristic light.

After a time, Noah Winters steps out into the glow. This is the founder, the old man who all this is riding on. Seeing him here tonight is not particularly encouraging. He looks terrible: haggard, hunched, frail. He's tall and broad, but they can all see that his hair has turned white and he has thick bags under his eyes. Winters bends down and taps on the mic. 'I'd . . . I'd like to thank you all for coming. Fantasyland is my life's work. It's everything and, mark my words, it *will* be the premier amusement park in the Southern Hemisphere when I'm done with it. That's my promise to you. When I settled here twenty years ago, God told me that this vacant land would one day amount to something, and that I was the one responsible for making it happen, and when God talks, I listen. When I heard that . . . when I heard that, I—'

*Is he crying?*

The rest of the Winters family fidgets. His son Buddy edges closer to the podium, visibly wincing at the old man's blather.

'And I said to myself, I can dig this out myself. Why, all I need is—'

Buddy claps his hands together. 'Thanks, Dad. We really appreciate all you've done for us. The park's looking great, isn't it? A round of applause for Noah Winters!'

The crowd gives a half-hearted response. Everyone can see the make-shift bar and booze off to one side. It's time to wrap this up.

'Okay, stick around,' yells Buddy. 'There are brochures, there are t-shirts. We have a sales stand over there.'

The aides rush in and whisk Winters Senior away. He looks pissed off, like he's about to fight someone.

Buddy stands cover, a smile plastered on.

Cocaine eyes beaming.

*This will not be easy*, Mike thinks to himself.

Something is vastly out of whack here.

# MIKE

## Fantasyland, Gold Coast

WITH THE OFFICIAL PROCEEDINGS
DISPENSED, the party goes up a gear. Mike is in the
zone: sinking beers and talking shit. He collects gossip
and factoids. He sets up callbacks and makes intros.
He knows people. There are entrepreneurs and politicians, media people and shonky cops. A few athletes
and film stars. Mike gets into the ear of some of the
bigger players. Buddy Winters invites him to lunch.
Dennis Benson, a local yacht builder, gives him a light
in a dark corner, asking if Mike is the minister's new
man. Benson's a square-john-looking bastard, neat as
a pin. While they're talking, he's joined by another big
fish: Allan Watts. Allan owns a few Surfers Paradise
hotspots and he's the opposite of Benson: loud, shirt
open, sweating like a glassblower's arse.

'Argh, fellas!' screams Allan, giving them each a
hug. He takes Mike around the shoulders. 'How's the
minister's sore foot, mate?'

Mike deflects.

Over in the DJ booth, the Steve Miller Band crossfades into 'If You Want My Love' by Cheap Trick, and the volume grows thunderous and reverberant.

'Can I ask you two a question?' shouts Mike.

The men are all ears.

Mike looks around. 'How would you fix this mess?'

Both smile.

Allan puts a hand on his shoulder and says, 'Mate, do you fancy a bump?'

THEY DO the coke in a large washroom by the unfinished merry-go-round. The drug loosens Allan up even further, but Benson just sits on a closed toilet pedestal and takes it all in, as stern and intent as ever.

'So, fellas, let's get down to business,' says Allan. 'Or did you two lure me back here to fuck me?'

Benson adjusts his glasses. 'Steady on.'

Allan moves his jaw around. 'So, ah, Mike, what does the minister want with this flaming mess?'

'He's looking to get it back on track.'

'I didn't think he had a piece?' says Benson.

'I don't know the details.'

Benson stares into space. 'And it's your job to do what, exactly?'

'Whatever I can. What do you blokes need?'

'A fucking miracle,' says Allan. 'This is not a warning, mate—well, not from me anyhow—but you need to go very lightly with this stuff. I don't know if this is something someone like you can just waltz into. No offence.'

'I can be pretty resourceful,' says Mike.

'Not if you're fucking dead, mate.'

'Christ,' says Mike. 'What are you talking about?'

Benson finally looks at him. 'The last one the minister sent disappeared.'

'He was a cunt,' adds Allan. 'Jason Hooper. You know him?'

Mike does. 'I thought he was on long service leave.'

'Oh yeah, he's on leave alright. He's having a long spell from walking around,' says Allan. The man moves closer. 'We like you, Mike. You should have stuck with Roger Pearse.'

'I can still hook you both up with Pearse, but . . .'

'But what?' says Benson.

'Bring me further in on this, and I can be even more helpful. I need to look busy, and you both know the minister will just send someone else if I blow it.'

Benson gets up. 'He's got a point.'

'It's your funeral, mate,' says Allan.

It's all lies.

Bluster and lies.

Everyone hedging their bets. In Mike's experience, you can never come in the front door on stuff like this. You have to look like you're barely trying.

'Let's go.' He grabs Allan's coke baggie off the sink. 'Can I set you up for this?'

'Keep it,' says Allan, standing in the corner. He's staring at a folding contraption, something he's lowered from the wall. Allan squats, looks at the levers under it. 'What the hell is this thing?'

'It's a change table,' Benson says. 'For babies.'

'A baby can't reach this high,' says Allan.

'It's for the mothers.'

Allan shakes his head. 'If you say so.'

Halfway back to the dance floor, Benson asks if they're coming to the afterparty.

It's news to Mike. 'I thought this was the afterparty.'

Allan whistles. 'Oh boy.'

HOURS LATER, deep in the thick of it, Mike finds himself wandering around another part of Fantasyland. The afterparty is on the rooftop of a moulded fibreglass mountain, some giant prop for the log ride that towers over the rest of the park. At the summit, the mountain is partially cratered and open to the night sky; the maw paved with timber decking. Down inside, the afterparty rages. 'Welcome to the mouth of the volcano,' says some pissed idiot.

It's a wild scene. Open kegs and a naked string quartet. Half-dressed hookers every which way. Flesh jiggling, loud laughing, some strange industrial sound from below, cranking away, gushing water. People fuck out in the open. Mike spots Sadie from the train getting fingered by a local footballer.

It's getting late and it's all pretty hazy to Mike.

Nothing feels real.

He spots something going on down the far end of the deck. A crowd stands around watching some guy dressed up as Ned Kelly in flagrante with Princess Di from Royaltyland. Mike spots two women standing off to the side of the spectacle, fully clothed. One of them—a bright redhead in a short black dress—has something in her hand. Mike's not sure what it is, but it sparks something in him that cuts through the booze. He circles round. 'What have you got there?' he says.

The redhead smiles. 'It's just my smokes, darl,' and she holds up her pack.

It's not a brand Mike recognises. Up close, the

woman is beautiful. Crisp blue eyes set against porcelain skin. She's a little older than him: mid-thirties, maybe early forties in better light.

'I'm Mike.'

The woman doesn't give an inch. 'How are you enjoying the party, Mike?'

'Bit much for me, if I'm honest.'

'You do look a bit hot and bothered.'

'I *am* bothered. I'm here for work and, ah, I don't feel much like working at the moment, let me tell you.'

'Do you like my friend?' says the redhead.

The woman beside her smiles.

'She seems nice,' says Mike. 'Bit young for me.'

'You like older women?'

Mike figures he should just go for it. 'I think you're the most beautiful one here.'

'That's very flattering,' says the woman, taking a drag on her smoke.

'It's meant to be, but I'm not lying to you.'

'I can see that,' she says. 'Oh, well.' The redhead sighs, murmurs something to her companion, then she takes Mike by the hand, leading him away. They walk along the deck and then down a steel service stairway to a thin gangway that hugs the contour of the mountain. Around the way, out of sight, the redhead leads him to a secluded bench. Fantasyland sprawls out below, a half-moon in the clouds.

'This is nice,' says Mike.

'Shut up.'

She unzips his fly.

The rest doesn't take long.

When it's over, the woman gets off him and straightens out her dress. She slips a missing shoe back on.

Mike takes a minute to recover. He's still sitting there with his pants around his ankles when he hears a little click. He looks over and the woman has her cigarette packet held up to her face like a camera.

'What's that?'

'Oh, darl, just a little souvenir. Nothing to worry about.'

And with that, she's gone.

# BRUNO
## Pohlman Drive, Southport

BRUNO PLAYS IT BY the book. He files for a search warrant on the house. It's a long shot—he's petitioning off the back of his anonymous photographs and a kid stealing mail—but he gets lucky: the magistrate signing off on the warrant knows the O'Grady family. 'Phil O'Grady's a good egg,' he says. 'A bit of a law-and-order guy, actually. Loves cops. He's not going to get his knickers in a knot if this turns out to be nothing.'

It's 8 pm by the time Bruno has the warrant in hand, but going home for a quiet night in isn't on the cards. He tries, mind you. He heads home and makes himself dinner and hits the hay, but there's no sleep to be had.

By eleven, he's back on the streets. He drives to Pohlman Drive and has a good look around the yard with a flashlight. At the back door, Bruno notices some loose brickwork by the stair and in the mortar line, a glint of metal in the beam of his light. He lifts away bricks and there it is. The spare key.

When Bruno steps inside the O'Grady house, the lights are on. He's in the rear kitchen.

'Hello?' he hollers.

The kitchen is spotless. No dishes or dust. He opens the fridge, and it's still running. Empty but cool. Closing it, he notices a fridge magnet for a local cleaner. Bruno takes the number down.

The rest of the house is in a similar state. It looks like a display home. Everything neat, clean, orderly, vacant.

A static dining room.

A bare-bones study.

He finds bathrooms, bedrooms.

There's a doorway and a stair down to an empty basement under the house: a plain white vacant room with a concrete floor.

Back up on ground level, he locates the garage, a black BMW parked inside. The other spot is empty. Bruno runs his hands over the paintwork of the car and there's a little dust there. He writes that down.

Up on the second level, Bruno yells out again. 'Hello? Anybody home?' But the place is silent. There's freshly steamed carpet in the hall leading off to the bedrooms. The place is so devoid of life that it gives Bruno the creeps. He has to splash water on his face in the bathroom just to settle himself. He desperately wants a smoke.

Bruno makes his way into the master bedroom and gives the place the once-over. The walk-in robe is full of clothes, drawers and shelves heaving with personal effects. At the back of the robe, there's luggage stowed under a line of coats. He kneels down and studies the bags and finally breathes out. There's a missing slot from the luggage row. It's big enough for two suitcases.

*They're on fucking holidays.*
*This is all a mix-up.*

The elation quickly turns to annoyance. He walks back out to the king-size bed and lights up that cigarette he's fanging for.

Bruno sneers, angry at himself.

But there's something else, too. Some subterranean feeling. His interior is churning—has been, constantly, since his father died. He's uneven.

*Did I want this to be a murder case?*
*Am I fucking disappointed?*
*Am I that desperate?*

'Pathetic,' he whispers.

Bruno ashes his smoke on the carpet, and that is almost that, except that the carpet is so clean and crisp that he feels bad about the ash on it and kneels down to rub it away. That's when he notices that the weave is brand new to touch. Down at that angle, he also notices that the bed is new, as well. The sheets starched white. He lifts them up: the mattress label is pristine. Scraps of plastic cling to the castor wheels at the bottom of the bedhead.

Bruno pulls the bed away from the wall.

Nothing under it.

He peels up the mattress.

It's clear.

He turns on his torch and uses the beam to zero in and focus. He works back and forth, up and down, studying the room.

*There.*

A slight discolouring on the wall, where the bedhead normally sits. Bruno gets down on hands and knees and rips the fresh carpet back from the wall and finds it: a small pool of dried blood on the exposed flooring.

# PART TWO
# WEDNESDAY, 29 SEPTEMBER
## 1982

# VICTOR

ONE OF THE struggles of getting old is holding on to power. You spend your whole life in the thick of it—building, selling, reaping rewards and destroying enemies—and then at the end, you're forced to sit still and brood. It's pitiful. I'm not suited to it at all.

In some ways, death can't come fast enough.

Until then . . .

There is one last project.

A reason to open my eyes.

My son, wherever he is, stolen by a young witch.

IN THE AFTERNOON, I watch home movies, shot on super 8 film. In the dark, my life literally flashes before my eyes. Most of it disgusts me. My former wives were not auteurs. There are too many records of Christmases and birthdays. So much cake and children running back and forth. It bores me. The only films I like are the ones that show days at the beach. In those, the city can be glimpsed in the background. Over the course of years, the place rises up like a wave. Glorious. A triumph.

49

*But there aren't many of those movies, and I've played them all to death. Reviewing them involves my nurse Elda moving things back and forth, which she finds tiresome. There are days now where she simply refuses and in my weakened condition there is little I can do to persuade her. She's a fool, but one cannot trouble one's nurse too much. So instead of the beach movies, I watch the other home movies. The films of the woman. They're longer, engrossing me for hours on end. The dirty pictures of the concubine I invited into my world. A ghost captured in flickering light. I gorge on her, then and now. The flesh is weak, right till the very end.*

THE PHONE *in the study snaps me from a daydream.*

*I wheel myself over.* 'This is Victor Owens.'

'Just calling to make sure you're still alive.'

'You can't get rid of me that easily, Allan.'

'We're nearly there, mate. I can't let you croak just yet.'

'How's business?'

'The money's coming in.'

'I should hope so.'

'We're getting there. That's the main thing.'

'You have to dream big to win big, Allan.'

*He laughs.* 'There's big and then there's . . .'

'Yes, son?'

'This is diabolical. We're bloody well up to the guts in nutters, Victor. These blokes are . . . it's more of a nightmare than a dream.'

'It's all the same thing.'

'Is it?'

'It's how you look at it. One should take the good and the bad with everything. My clean money and your *dirty deeds. My noble enterprises and your sinful busi-ness. It's all light and shade, Allan. It's all the same when it's over. The future forgets everything that came before. It's about to be a new day, my friend.'*

*'Well, right now it feels like bloody midnight.'*

*I laugh at that. 'Allan, that's just because you're still asleep.'*

# AMY

## Brisbane Airport

AMY KEEPS HER WAYFARERS on in the terminal. It's early and the twenty-minute wait at the luggage conveyor puts her on edge—all these businessmen standing by, talking football and finance and about their children and the economy. They look at Amy like she's a virus, and she feels the same way.

HER BREAKFAST DATE is Detective Senior Constable Ray Blintiff. Ray's a real piece of work. A terrifying thug who tries to hide it under neat hair and crisp collars. It doesn't play. Blintiff is the second-in-command in the Licensing Branch, and the Licensing boys run Brisbane. They're gangsters in uniform. Today, Ray's waiting for her in the cafeteria of the Queen Street Coles building. He's already halfway through his bain-marie fry-up, and he cuts a strange figure in the room: two feet taller than the old biddies around him, so big he can barely squeeze his legs under the table. He takes one look at Amy and says, 'Christ, kid, you look terrible. Rough night?'

'I was in Adelaide.'

'Say no more.' Ray dabs at his mouth with a serviette. 'Take those sunglasses off. You're scaring the grannies.'

Amy takes a long look around the cafe, then sits across from him. 'I thought you fellas were supposed to be making good money these days.' Ray laughs. 'I love this joint. My mum used to bring me here when I was a kid. You should get yourself something. My shout.'

'Sorry, can't stay long. Colleen said you had some work for me.'

He lays down his fork. 'Word from on high is there's a bloke from down your way who has some police files he shouldn't have. Not sure what he's playing at, but it's not a good look. Anyway, we need that stuff back before we let this bloke go.'

'What's his name?'

'Bill Webber. He's a Black fella, works in Gold Coast CIB.'

Amy leans in. 'So, what do you need? Do you want the files back or do you want dirt on him?'

'Either works. Both, if you can swing it.'

'Who's paying me?'

'*I'm* paying you, sweetheart.' Ray produces an envelope, lays it on the Formica tabletop. When Amy reaches for it, he places a hand over hers. 'You have nice eyes, kid. You know that? I've never noticed them before.'

Amy pulls the money loose. 'Thanks, Ray.'

'You're completely welcome.'

They're all the same.

*A pig is a pig is a pig.*

Except you absolutely cannot fuck around with Ray Blintiff.

## THE DREAM

Ray kills people who do that.

# MIKE
## Coolangatta

MIKE WAKES IN A white room, sprawled out on a bed, still in his Fantasyland outfit. He has no memory of getting in last night. There's a door across the room. He opens it and finds tall pines and a blue ocean.

There's a phone on the bedside table. Mike gets reception on the line. 'Where am I?'

A motel in Coolangatta, apparently.

Down on the border.

Coolangatta is a small place.

The God Minister can see this motel from his penthouse.

No doubt.

AFTER THE SHAKY START, Mike hits the morning hard. He's thirty-two years old next month and still has the constitution of a teenager. A room service bloody mary and two coffees take care of his hangover, except . . .

*The photo.*

*His pants around his ankles, wet dick centre frame.*

*'Oh, darl, just a little souvenir. Nothing to worry about.'*

Mike smiles at the memory, despite it all. He replays vivid images of the redhead. Can't keep her out of his mind. But if there's one rule in politics it's this: everything is *always* something to worry about. Worrying is half the job.

Mike gets on the phone and starts making calls. No one will give up the woman's name. Everyone says the same thing: they didn't see her.

She's an apparition. The only person who gives him a hint is Allan Watts, who sounds like he still has a load on. 'Buddy, you don't want to know who that was. Trust me on that one.'

But he wants to know.

*Has to.*

THE BIG-TICKET ITEM of the day is lunch with Buddy Winters, heir to Fantasyland. Mike doesn't know what to expect. The meet is happening in the Playroom on the shore of Tallebudgera Creek. The place is a grimy rock club.

Mike knocks on the glass out front.

Allan Watts opens up.

'I should have known,' says Mike. 'Let me guess, you own a piece of this shithole?'

'Hey, *hey*, this is Australian culture, mate.' Allan waves a hand at the posters plastered to a nearby wall. 'We've got No Fixed Address performing this week-end. Chisel on the way. It's all happening.'

Mike could give a fuck. Pop music is low-life trash. Inside the venue, the place is empty except for a half-dozen men and one woman standing by the bar. Most of the men are familiar faces in the murk. The mayor. Dennis Benson. Buddy Winters. They call these blokes the White Shoe Brigade. They're the money down here on the coast. The men who keep development cooking, or did before the recession.

To start the meeting, they take their beers and stand in a circle. 'Good party last night,' one of them says.

Buddy Winters ignores it. 'Can we move this along?'

They come in closer.

Buddy stares, dead-eyed, as he starts, 'Look, right at the top, I want to say I'm doing everything I can. I'm pushing things as hard as they can go right now.'

'No, you're bloody not,' says the mayor. 'You're killing me with these delays. My phone is running white-hot, day and night.'

Allan chimes in. 'Same here. I understand that shit happens and that these things take time, but I've got—'

'It's my father,' says Buddy. 'He's . . . he's having trouble.'

Everyone stops.

'What sort of trouble?' says Allan, quietly.

'Head trouble. The situation is affecting him. He's not coping.' Buddy takes a pull on his beer. 'I know this thing has been dragging on, but . . .'

'Out with it,' says the mayor.

'It's the boat. He's fixated on the boat.'

A ripple of confusion circulates.

'The pretend ship?' says the mayor.

'Yeah, the fucking HMS *Whatever-it-is*,' says Buddy.

'It's the *Endeavour*,' says Dennis Benson.

'Yeah, that bloody thing,' says Buddy. 'The old man is losing his mind over it. It's just . . . He's not himself. He says he won't open the park until they can do the landing re-enactment properly and he won't listen to me or anyone else.'

The mayor puts his drink down. 'You're telling me we're all about to lose our shirts because your dad's pretend ship doesn't work?'

'The ship is fine,' says Benson. 'It's finished. That was my contract.'

Buddy turns to one of his aides, the woman. 'It's the canal,' she says. 'The canal is the real problem.'

'*The canal*. The canal looks fine to me,' says the mayor, sputtering. 'I pissed in it last night. How is the canal the problem?'

Buddy keeps his eyes on the ground.

'It's too narrow,' says the aide, facing off with the mayor like it's just another day at the office. 'The *Endeavour* can't round one of the corners. It keeps getting stuck. It's a bit too long.'

Benson lifts his head. 'It's not too long. It's the length you ordered.'

'It is a *bit* long,' says the aide. 'But the canal is also significantly more narrow than planned. It doesn't work. Further excavation is underway. We've broken—'

'Dad's doing it,' says Buddy. 'That's the problem. Since the recession, Dad has taken it upon himself to dig the canal out to keep expenses down. He's using an excavator. He dug the thing originally, if you remember? It took years. He's fucking stuck. Fixated. We have to do something.'

'Something fast,' quips Allan, mainly to himself.

The room goes quiet.

Mike sips his beer and studies the scene. 'The minister wants to help.'

'Can he drive an excavator?' says the mayor.

'He is an excavator,' says Mike.

They all know it.

It's what this whole meeting is leading to.

# BRUNO
## Pohlman Drive, Southport

BRUNO IS DEAD ON his feet. He wanders around the O'Grady mansion, giving the Science Investigation Bureau space to work, praying for leads.

None are forthcoming.

The O'Gradys have a son named Samson. An only child. There are photos of him spread around the house and clothes matching his description in an upstairs bedroom. Samson is in his mid-twenties. Good-looking. Preppy with sandy blond hair, long at the back. Bruno puts calls through to the station to try and dig Samson up, but his last known address is right here on Pohlman Drive. That puts the potential body count at three.

Around 2 pm, the SIB wrap it up. 'Someone probably died up there,' says one of the scientists.

Bruno rubs his eye. 'That's the sort of joke that puts you offside with my lot.'

'Okay, well, there was a lot of blood at some point. I mean, a *lot*. That's all we know for the moment.'

'Enough blood for two people?'

Bruno figures they were killed in their bed.

'I'd say so,' says the scientist. 'We'll run more tests.'

'What about the other bedroom?' Presumed to be Samson's room. 'There's residue in there too, on the walls.'

'Weapon?'

'If I had to guess, I'd say it was a knife. If it was a gun, I think we'd have signs of that by now. The walls haven't been repainted, so yeah, a knife or an axe. Maybe a hammer. Something that really doused the place.'

'How old is all this?'

The man makes a ring with his thumb and index finger and gently loops it over his nose.

*Fuck knows.*

Bruno rubs at his face again. 'Whatever we're paying you, it's too much.'

THE INSPECTOR KICKS loose three uniforms for the neighbourhood canvas. Bruno has dispatch call them over and they head out.

They return with neighbourhood chatter and not much else. More dead ends. No one has seen the O'Gradys in weeks.

'They're on a cruise,' says one of the uniforms.

The other cops confirm it. That's what the entire street thinks.

Bruno found plenty of material about cruise ships in the house. There's a departure date marked on a calendar by the fridge and there's every chance the O'Gradys really are on a cruise right now, out there on the open ocean as policemen comb through their house and home.

*But if that's true, who died upstairs?*

'What about the kid on the BMX?' says Bruno.

The uniforms all shrug.

One of them says, 'There's a hundred kids riding bikes up and down the street all day.'

'Do all of them pinch people's mail?' says Bruno.

'The old biddy across the street said she'd keep an eye out.'

*Great.*

'Can we go, Bruno? I've got real work to do.'

'Yeah, sure,' he says, and that's that.

BACK AT THE STATION HOUSE, Bruno is called into the inspector's office. He finds his boss, Ron Bingham, standing by the window, shades open an inch, staring out at the men in the bullpen.

'You wanted to see me, sir?'

'Sit.'

Both of Bingham's chairs are piled with paperwork. Bruno clears one. 'If this is about—'

'Just shut up and sit down,' says Bingham.

Bruno waits in silence.

Pete Reynolds comes to the door next. He's older than Bruno and looks completely weathered and worn. *Corrupted* is the word that comes to mind. Pete's always in need of a shave and a haircut, like he can't be otherwise. 'Look, Ron,' he says, 'if this is about the squad car the other night, I can—'

'What car?'

Reynolds spots Bruno sitting in the darkened office. 'Ah, nothing. Don't worry about it.'

Bingham huffs out a tired breath. 'This won't take long. Pete, I need to put you with Bruno for a few days. He thinks he's found a murder scene.'

'I've got my hands full with Robbers,' says Reynolds. 'I can't spare anyone. It's a fucking madhouse at the moment. They're going to knock over another bank any day now.'

'Are you listening to me, Pete? I'm assigning *you*, personally. Brian Seigler can stand in as lead with Robbers while you work both cases.'

Reynolds stares, open-mouthed. 'What is this?'

Bruno starts to answer, but Bingham shushes him. 'Shut up, both of you. *You*,' Bingham points at Bruno, 'whatever *you* did, it's already landed on Brisbane's radar. The deputy commissioner called me and whatever is going on with . . . who are they?'

'The O'Grady family. Phillip, Marion and Samson.'

'Whoever they are, they have friends in high places, and now we need to get to the bottom of it posthaste.'

Bruno says, 'It's a missing persons case. That's my—'

'Don't talk to me,' says Bingham. 'Talk to him.'

'I don't want to fucking talk to him,' says Reynolds.

'Tough shit,' is Bingham's answer.

BRUNO AND REYNOLDS take it out to the carpark where they each light a smoke and eye each other off.

Reynolds caves first. 'Go on. Talk me through it.'

'I got an anonymous tip on a house in Southport. Found blood in the upstairs bedroom.'

Reynolds waves his hand. *Continue.*

'That's it. You want to swing by and take a look?'

'What's there to see?'

'The crime scene. Two people are missing. Maybe three.'

'An empty house, then. Who's the *maybe* victim?'

'The son. Samson. Can't get a hold of him. There's blood in his room as well.'

'The son. If I run him down, will you let me get on with the bank case?'

'Works for me. What's this about, you reckon? Bingham didn't have to make you do this.'

Reynolds just looks at him and Bruno sees it then. Somehow, by investigating this, Bruno's tripped a wire somewhere. He's stirred up the Joke, the system of graft and corruption that has its hooks in the Queensland Police. The rumour is that it goes all the way up. Some say it's orchestrated from up there, with only scraps trickling down to dirty bastards like Reynolds.

'You want my advice?' says Reynolds. 'Make this go away as quickly as possible. If the deputy commissioner is calling Bingham, you've already fucked something up pretty bad, so the faster we handle this, the better.'

'It'd be nice to just do my job sometimes.'

'You don't need to tell me,' says Reynolds, grinding out his smoke and heading back inside to the Robbery Branch.

# AMY
## The Back Streets of Surfers
## Paradise

AMY MAKES HER WAY to a nondescript building back from the foreshore. Five storeys and decrepit, a place not long for this earth. On the top floor, there's a brothel called The White Light. It's one of Colleen Vinton's daytime haunts. Say what you might about Colleen, she's not above slumming it with the girls. She likes to show her face.

Today, Colleen is in the lunchroom, seated at the table with a sandwich, her bare feet up on an adjoining chair. Everyone else has cleared out. It's just her and *The Mike Walsh Show* on a black-and-white TV. Taking in Amy, she says, 'I'm hungover to buggery. You want this? I can't eat it.'

Amy ignores the food. 'I saw Blintiff. He wants me to find some copper.'

'Oh yeah. Which one?'

'Bill Webber. You know him?'

Colleen shakes her head. 'What's he done, darl?'

'Stole some files, apparently. Blintiff was cagey. You okay with it?'

'As long as he paid you up-front?'

'He did.'

'The Licensing boys can be tight pricks. If they give you any trouble, let me know. You do the other thing?'

The copper at the beach, the photos under his windscreen wipers.

'Yeah, he got 'em.'

On the TV, Dame Edna Everage swans onstage, waving and smiling. A cacophony of clapping blasts out. Colleen stares at the screen.

Amy asks, 'Is there anything else?'

Colleen twitches as if caught out. 'Ah yeah. Yeah, there is.' She takes her feet down and sits up a little. 'What do you know about Fantasyland? It's that new theme park out at Nerang.'

'Nothing much.'

'All the big boys have a piece of it, but the whole thing is going to hell. There's a bloke involved called Allan Watts. Local businessman. You know him?'

'Sure. I know who Allan is.'

'Well, take a look at him for me.'

'Anything in particular?'

'A little bird told me he's having money trouble, but he's also everywhere I bloody go at the moment. He's making some sort of move and I want to know what it is.'

'Okay, I'll see what I can turn up.'

'Do that.' Colleen settles back in. She drags her sandwich closer, turns back to the telly. 'He is right up the chain, so go easy.'

Amy nods, makes to leave.

'Allan used to pal around with your father. I wonder if that might be a way in.'

'My dad?'

A wave of dread washes through Amy.

Colleen isn't looking at her. 'Yeah, Victor. You know, the guy who knocked up your mum.'


DOWN THE FOYER of The White Light.

Into the empty stairwell.

Grimy walls revolving, her own echoing footfall on the timber stair.

Down, down, down.

Amy's clenched fists are the only outward sign of the torment brewing inside her. She needs to keep it bottled up. Colleen will have cameras in here, watching. Because Colleen Vinton may look harmless— some broad watching daytime TV—but there's no one in this world with a better antenna for human suffering. Colleen lives off it.

It's her currency.

*A total fucking vampire.*

Amy feels pale.

# MIKE
## Cavill Avenue, Surfers Paradise

MIKE PUSHES THROUGH THE AFTERNOON. It's muck work, currying favour and making calls. By his own estimation, he's moving in the right direction. Knock-off drinks with the boys in the local council put a pin in Noah Winters's DIY canal project. *We can't have that old fella driving an excavator into the drink, can we?* Work will cease on that tomorrow, taking one big problem off the table, just in time for another.

One of the council blokes knows something on the down low and wants five minutes with the God Minister in return. The minister oversees the Local Government portfolio, in addition to Main Roads and a few other things. 'Can you get me in with him?' pleads the council bloke. 'I really need it.'

Mike says, 'I can try.'

'Great.' The council bloke looks around and leans in. 'You need to have a chat with Jack about Fantasyland.'

'Is that it?'

'You'll see.'

The bloke seems serious, and unfortunately Mike knows who this Jack is. Jack the Bagman. He's an ex-copper who works as a cut-out for the higher-ups in the Queensland Police. He's big-time. The sieve through which all dirty money flows. Roping him into anything is like summoning a demon.

The council bloke knows it, too. 'I'm not fucking with you on this. I wouldn't do that. Not with those fellas. I just really need this one-on-one.'

'So what is it? What's your problem for the minister?'

And the bloke tells him. It's some nonsense about parking meters.

That's the trouble with being the God Minister: he hears the prayers of everyone.

AS IT TURNS OUT, Jack the Bagman is on the coast. 'Hard at it,' he says on the phone, but when Mike catches up with him, he's half-a-dozen pots into a session at the Burleigh Surf Club, surrounded by men Mike doesn't recognise, all rough-looking bastards. They barely glance at Mike, and Jack doesn't make introductions. He just says, 'Son, let me drain the lizard and we can take this downstairs.'

Outside on the boulevard, it's all long shadows and afternoon glow. The beach is emptying out for the day. Mike has a house back in Brisbane—and a family, or the remnants of one—but he figures he could get used to this. It's beautiful. Where everyone wants to be.

'Here we are,' says Jack, sidling on up. 'You know, when I got your call, I nearly told you to piss off.' This is the Jack that Mike has heard about his whole career. The likeable, normal bloke who is anything but. Dirty deeds doled out with clean hands and a cheery smile.

'What changed your mind?' says Mike.

Jack laughs. 'The lord above.'

*The minister.*

'I'm trying to get Fantasyland back on track. Your name came up.'

'Well, Mike, this is the part where I politely thank you for your time and tell you to leave it alone.'

'We can skip that part. How are the police involved in Fantasyland?'

'I can't talk to you about that. If the minister wants to know, he can ask someone else. He's still the Police Minister, right?'

'I think so. And he *is* asking.'

'This is well above my pay grade, mate. Yours too, I reckon.'

'Who should I be talking to, then?'

'Do you know what you're doing?' Jack takes a long look at him, registers something. 'I might be able to get you in front of the deputy commissioner, but, with all due respect, I don't even know who you are.'

'That's because I'm good at my job. Send it up the line. Vet me.'

'Okay, well, one lackey to another? Tread carefully. Don't barge into this next bit like you have with me here today. Deputy Commissioner Sorensen isn't someone you want offside.'

Mike says, 'I can go easy.'

'I should hope so. The last guy couldn't.'

Jack pushes off.

'Hey, hang on. Why *is* this so tricky? The minister is Sorensen's boss, isn't he?'

The blood drains from Jack's face. 'Are you fucking serious? No one is Sorensen's boss. No one.

The *commissioner* doesn't even hold the reins with Sorensen. You need to be very, very fucking careful, son. Christ almighty.'

Mike watches him go. As Jack disappears into the surf club, Mike notices the second-storey balcony area above. Three men stand there, watching him. They're the men Jack was drinking with, and now they're staring down at him like crows on a wire.

It works.

Mike's rattled.

# BRUNO
## Heron Avenue, Mermaid Beach

BRUNO HEADS HOME FOR A SHOWER. Whatever happened to the O'Grady family isn't getting solved without sleep. In the living room, his brother Danny sits in front of *Sale of the Century* with a beer. Bruno grabs a XXXX Bitter and joins him, pecking at the lukewarm fish and chips on the coffee table.

'Rough day?' says Danny.

'Just a day.'

'Gracie called.'

Their sister. The youngest.

'What did she want?'

'She wants to know when we're going to start cleaning out Dad's place.'

'What did you tell her?' Danny smiles a little, keeps his eyes on the TV. 'I told her I'd drop the keys round whenever she's ready to get started.'

Bruno can't be fucked with this tonight.

He takes a sip of his beer.

He closes his eyes.

. . .

YEARS AGO, when Danny was nine and Bruno was fourteen, the two of them got caught in a rip during a swim. It was Danny's fault. He went out too far and Bruno—already a cop in some capacity—went out to tell him to come back in. They both got swept away.

It wasn't a big deal. Both of them were strong swimmers, and the lifeguards were on hand. It was really just about staying calm, and Bruno was always calm.

'What do we do now?' said Danny, dog paddling in the water, the shoreline receding in the distance. 'I can't remember.'

'Save your energy.'

'I feel like we should try to swim up a bit.'

Bruno could already see the lifeboat coming down the beach. 'They're on their way.'

For minutes, they remained in the current. The water flat and quiet.

'Mum's going to be pissed,' said Danny.

'One thing at a time.'

Mum was at home. She hated the beach.

Danny craned his head, searched the shore. 'What do you think Dad's going to say?'

'He's probably still asleep.'

They'd left the old man passed out on the sand with the newspaper spread across his face.

Danny laughed. 'Jeez, I hope so.'

But Dad wasn't asleep. He was wide awake and red-faced. He gave them an earful when they got back to shore.

The boys took it. It was fair enough.

He *had* told them a hundred times.

And yet he never told their mother. No, their dad watched them get washed out to sea and never said a word.

No one did.

No one wanted to worry her.


'AL PACINO,' shouts Danny, pointing at Tony Barber on the TV. 'Holy shit, I could have the car, mate. I'm good at this.'

Bruno jolts awake, half-asleep in the chair. 'What?'

'Go to bed.'

'I'm okay.'

'Go on.'

Bruno slowly drags himself up. He goes to his room and opens the closet. There's a safe in the floor and Bruno lifts a steel box out of it, then opens the box with a key from his belt. He puts his service gun inside. Then he takes the photograph from his jacket —the one that came with the deck of house shots— and he places that in the box with the gun and locks it in. He tries to sleep but finds he's so tired that his mind is playing tricks on him. Bruno checks and rechecks the safe a half-dozen times before he finally passes out.

# AMY

## Bulcock Street, Coolangatta

DETECTIVE CONSTABLE BILL WEBBER eats dinner alone in a Chinese restaurant on the high street of Coolangatta. Amy snaps photos of him from across the street. She picked up his trail an hour ago, coming off shift at the Surfers Paradise police station. From the get-go, Webber isn't what she expected. He's lean. A tall Māori bloke in his early thirties. Good-looking for a copper, or would be under better circumstances, because he is up to something. Something *bad*. Amy can see it all over him: half a beard, slumped shoulders, a blank stare. He's a walking ruin.

After dinner, Webber hits a nearby squash court where he plays loose and angry, talking very little during the games.

Amy returns to her car for a smoke. She turns the radio on and off. Reads a few pages of a paperback: *If There Be Thorns.*

She avoids the rear-view. Knows she looks just as ruined as Webber.

Amy casts her mind back to earlier in the day:

*Allan used to pal around with your father.* That's what Colleen said.

A couple of hours of walking around with it has settled the thought in Amy. She can approach it in her mind without her nerves acting up. There's a grim satisfaction about this ability to mute herself. She can usually quash her thoughts. What happened in Adelaide—the hotel suite, the gun pressed under her chin in the mirror—is an outlier, a weird surprise. Normally, *this* is who she is. A woman who can see the centre of the problem, can watch the black hole spinning, and feel absolutely nothing.

It's what Colleen pays her for.

BILL WEBBER LIVES in a high-set brick place, built into the incline of San Michele Street, Tugun. Amy watches him go inside. The house lights come on one at a time. It's too early to peep his windows. Cops are security conscious—even when they're walking around in a daze. She can't go anywhere near the place while he's home. This is a waiting game.

Tonight, it pays off. Webber isn't inside an hour before he comes back out, dressed head to toe in black, carrying his squash bag. He gets into his personal car and backs out.

Amy tails him through the coast and out onto the late-night highway. It's quiet this time of night, so she hangs back. He heads north for half an hour, then turns off at Ormeau, halfway to Brisbane. It must be way out of Webber's jurisdiction.

They drive into the rural gloom, away from the highway and the streetlights, and into the scrubland of Cedar Creek. Amy loses sight of him—his taillights disappear—but she keeps driving, scanning the road shoulder.

*Come on.*

Cursing, she spots his car, her headlights illuminating Webber as he steps out from behind the wheel. She passes, keeps moving before circling back with her lights off. She spots the car again and pulls into a nearby driveway.

Webber is parked in front of a lonely, dark farmhouse.

She hears shouting inside, echoing through the empty night.

Amy grabs her camera and runs towards the house.

Over the fence.

Delicately up the stair.

More shouting.

She rounds the verandah and creeps to a dimly lit window.

Takes a look.

A vacant room, curtains half-drawn. Through the doorway, in an adjoining kitchen, she can see Webber, white pupils beaming out of the eyeholes of a balaclava. Amy lifts her camera, winds the lens, years of muscle memory quelling the adrenaline, keeping her hands steady.

The camera clicks.

A naked old man at Webber's feet. Must be mid-seventies, at least.

*Click.*

The old man is bleeding. Webber straddles him and punches him repeatedly, bright blood spraying the side of the oven.

*Click.*

He keeps going.

*Click.*

Webber doesn't speak, doesn't question the man.

*Click.*

He just beats the shit out of him until he's unconscious or dead.

*Click.*

Webber gets up.

Amy can hear him walking straight along the hall to the front door and down the steps.

Footfall in the gravel.

His car engine turning over.

Amy creeps to the edge of the house and watches Webber pull a swift U-turn—headlights washing over her parked car—but he doesn't stop, doesn't slow down. He just gets the car pointed the right way and floors it.

She waits a minute before making her own exit. On the way out, she pinches mail from the old man's letterbox. Back in the car, she drives the opposite direction to Webber.

That's enough for one night. She doesn't help the man in the house. Can't. If he's dead, or dying, then he's dead or dying, because that was a Queensland copper back there and this changes everything. She's already overexposed. There's no telling how dangerous this is now.

# PART THREE
# THURSDAY, 30 SEPTEMBER
## 1982

# VICTOR

MY NEIGHBOUR'S *dog barked all day, and there was no punishing the thing. It was too big. An oversized kelpie-cross with a mouth the size of a child's head. You can't trust a dog like that, not that breed. They're all part dingo. The only people who have a dog like that in their house are men who share the same frailty. That's how I came to know Allan Watts. Through his dog, and what it told me.*

*Allan moved into the street a couple of years back and everyone could immediately see he was out of his element. No one minded too much. It's the Gold Coast. It's all new money. But Allan was especially green. He had a stupid red sports car. Gaudy lawn furnishings. A pool that lit up at night. He had a speedboat and parties. And to top it off, he had the dog that barked all day.*

*We got to talking over the fence, at first about the barking, and then about other things. This was back when I could get around. Allan came over for dinner and we played pool and drank together. It became a regular thing. Later, I invested in a few of his restau-*

*rants and it paid off because I recognised Allan for what he is: a man with a suppressed hunger.*

*I can't say I ever felt the same affection for his dog, though. Luckily, I didn't have to put up with it for long. Allan's wife didn't take too kindly to his new mistress, and she left him, taking the cursed pet with her.*

*Some things just don't fit in a new place.*

*Other things adapt.*

# MIKE
## Coolangatta Beach

MIKE WATCHES HIS CHILDREN paddle in the shallows. His son, the oldest of two, is turning eight next month, just old enough to see how unhappy his parents are. His sister is easier to deal with. She's still carefree. Everything's a surprise to her.

His wife is Sonya.

High school sweethearts. Married at twenty-two. Separated three months now.

Sonya doesn't show for the drop-off at his weekly visitation. She sends the nanny instead: Marta, the Polish teenager, from next door.

'That boy is too skinny,' Marta says today, shielding her eyes as she looks at the water.

'I was like that as a kid,' says Mike.

'My mother says she doesn't feed them enough.'

'She feeds him. Christ. How is your mum?'

'Terrible. Sore hands.' Marta makes her hands into claws. 'It's called something.'

'Arthritis.'

Marta doesn't seem convinced. 'She used to be a florist. That's what did it.'

'Moving flowers around wrecked her hands?'

'I guess so.'

Mike's son runs up the beach. 'Dad, can we go in the surf?'

'Sure. Give me a minute.'

The boy sprints back to the water.

'It's too cold for them to be swimming,' says Marta.

'Never.' He takes his shirt off. 'Dare I ask how Sonya is? I haven't laid eyes on her in weeks now.'

'She's unhappy.'

'She's always unhappy. Is there anything else?'

'You mean gossip?'

'No, I mean does she need anything?'

Marta chuckles, nods at Mike's Speedos. 'She needs a husband who can keep that thing in his pants.'

Mike wants to say something more, but that's about the shape of it.


SONYA KICKED him out after the second affair. Getting caught once was bad luck. Twice is sabotage, and both of them knew it. The weird thing is, Mike still loves her. Sonya gave him the kids. Sonya gave him everything. And now she won't take any part of it back. Not a stitch, not a cent. That's how he *knows* things are different now.

It's a message.

She's not going to forgive him anytime soon.


MIKE'S SON floats beside him in the water, out past the breaking waves. The boy doesn't say a word. He isn't big on talking, never has been, even before all this.

'You like it down here, mate?'

He nods.

'I love it,' says Mike.

It wasn't like this when Mike was little. There were no weekend trips to the beach with a Polish nanny. Mike grew up in Inala with wall-to-wall dead-shits. Nothing dramatic—no unjust beatings or abuse —but no big plans, either. Just the slow grind of working-class poverty in an unclean house.

'I want to move us down here,' Mike says.

'Mummy doesn't like it.'

'She'll come round, mate.'

Marrying Sonya was trading up. She was from good stock. Well-spoken, extravagantly educated, great-looking. Her father was in car dealerships, but Mike wanted more than his father-in-law's hand-me-downs, and once Mike started getting it, he couldn't stop himself. The National Party of Australia made him more than all that. It was his golden ticket, not the marriage. Turned out the Nationals had plenty of political talent back then—a lot of smart kids and farming money—but the government needed something else to hold on to power. They needed men like Mike who could get along with anyone and didn't give a fuck about the rules and regulations. Loose units to keep the figureheads clean. It was the perfect place for Mike. All he had to do was go where the wind was blowing, a strategy that had served him well his entire life.

# BRUNO
## Surfers Paradise

THE STATION HOUSE IS DEAD. A few stray CIB detectives, asleep on their feet, talking about an armed robbery overnight. *Number Six.* Not a bank, this time, but the ocean-front house of a jeweller. A dawn raid, unknown takings. Two casualties: a husband and wife. The husband was dead on arrival, the wife now lay in the ICU at Southport General. It's the same crew, according to the boys.

Everyone is assigned and mobilised.

Everyone.

The Robbery Squad dragging in bodies and overtime.

But Bruno doesn't get the call.

He's still in the sin bin.

BRUNO DRIVES BACK to the O'Grady house and takes another walk through. SIB is finished with the crime scene and the place is empty, just a collection of sharp echoes and the debris of evidence collection. Bruno pulls a stool across the kitchen and plants himself at the bench like he lives there. He uses the family's phone to chase the O'Grady travel agent, but the number rings without answer. Next, he puts a call through to Main Roads and waits on the line for a make and model for all vehicles belonging to the family. They confirm the dusty black BMW in the garage and provide a lead on the missing vehicle: a five-door, dark blue Holden Commodore registered to Samson O'Grady. He notes down the plates.

Wondering what else to do, he turns to a dark green garbage bag on the bench. It's full of mail. Some of it is from around the house, the rest is from the creek—ink smudges and wrinkled paper. Bruno starts sorting. Plenty of junk to start: Boys Town prize home brochures, golf club solicitations, bullshit about a local park. There's a bit of mail for the son, Samson. His school alumni newsletter. A flyer from the local radio station. There's a book about gardening sent in a brown paper package. Bruno keeps at it, opening everything: utilities bills coming due. Marina board correspondence. An overdue account with a financial planner. There's a second invoice for a motor shop service on the missing car. Then there are Phillip O'Grady's porn catalogues. Housed in plain white envelopes, the stuff looks high-end. Pages and pages of glossy smut magazine covers. Lots of eight-millimetre film reels for sale, and even a page of VCR tapes. It's vanilla X-rated stuff. Lots of fake tits and big hair.

Bruno opens his notebook, writes *perv* on a blank page, then makes a note to recheck the house inventory for film-screening equipment. He continues sorting. Two wedding invites. Someone's fiftieth birthday shindig. A postcard from someone called Lisa, sent two months back, *Welcome to Niagara Falls*. Bruno opens a dozen window-faced letters from the local council and various coastal businesses before coming to an envelope containing a handwritten note. *We've located several irregularities with your checking account. Please call us on your return.* The note is pinned to the front of a bank ledger of some sort, dated weeks back. Various numbers and dates on the ledger are marked in red biro. The letterhead reads, *Alfred Simmons, Deputy Manager, South Beach Building Society.*

'Now we're talking,' says Bruno. And he's just about to do away with the whole process when he finds one more letter in the bag, something slimy and stuck to the bottom with Christ-knows-what. It reads: *Australian Customs* and *Notification of Seizure.* He scans the rest. Looks like ol' Phil has had one of his mail-order fancies confiscated at the border.

Bruno underlines *perv* in the notebook.

# AMY
## San Michele Street, Tugun

AMY EMERGES FROM A soft sleep, sprawled out on the rear seat of her car. The interior is as hot as an oven and it pushes her out onto the footpath where she squats by the car's rear tyre and sucks down luke-warm water from a canister. Wiping her mouth, Amy recalls dim memories of last night's stake-out. The old man. His house in the sticks. And Bill Webber, the policeman, doling out his violence. Webber's house is just up the street. Amy has come off a long night of watching it, made all the worse by the constant desire to drink this mess away.

Amy gets flashes of the Adelaide hotel room:

*Half-naked and looking straight-up possessed in the bathroom mirror.*

*Gun in hand.*

*Snap.*

Quivering now. She tries to tamp it down.

*Shit.*

*Shit, shit, shit.*

This mess she's in is almost worse.

She forces focus.

The quiet street reappears.

Amy polishes off the water, then grabs her pocket camera and a leather-bound bible from the boot of her car, taking both up the street.

Webber's carport is empty. Amy knocks on the front door, ready to tell Bill about her lord and saviour, just in case he's inside. But there's no answer. She checks the windows and knocks again.

Nothing.

Amy opens her bible and fishes out the lock kit from the cavity inside. The entry alcove provides all the cover she needs. The lock pops on the second try.

'Anybody home?' she calls.

The interior is decked out like a bachelor pad. Bill's got a black leather couch, a gaudy white rug and a big TV. There's a *Mad Max* poster on the wall.

She sets her watch alarm for five minutes and gets to work.

Sweeps room to room, starting with the master bedroom in detail.

Standard police-issue stuff in his wardrobe.

Empty nightstands.

Panadol and shaving gear in the ensuite bathroom. No meds.

Amy keeps moving.

The spare room has a set of dumbbells.

The study has nothing, not even a desk.

She takes an interior stair down to the rumpus and goes through to the garage. Not much to see there either until she inspects a tool shelf lining the far wall. There's a box on the shelf covered in an old towel. Amy pulls the towel free and finds a safe.

She takes a polaroid photo of it.

And that's time. Her alarm bleeps.

Out the back door.

A quick look at the backyard.

She sees a concrete block incinerator down further, goes to it and touches it. *Still warm*. He came home and burned the clothes.

Back on the Strip, Amy uses a payphone she likes, tucked away in the nook of a hallway in the Imperial Hotel. She calls the Surfers Paradise police station and asks after Bill Webber. *Out in the field*. She hangs up and drops another coin in the slot.

Dirty Doug picks up on the first ring. 'Yeah?' he says. 'Who's this?'

Dirty Doug is a PI. He works out of the Redlands, up near the city.

'It's Amy from Southport.'

'What do you want?'

'Can you still pull police records?'

'Sure. Two hundred a pop.'

No one knows how Dirty Doug plies his trade, but the nickname is probably well-earned. Amy gives him Webber's name and date of birth, then the name and address of the old man Webber assaulted. 'Be careful,' she says. 'I'm pretty sure that last bloke is recently deceased, so there might be eyes on it.'

'What are you looking for?'

Amy spots a familiar-looking woman up the hallway of the hotel. The woman sees Amy and turns back. 'I've gotta go,' she tells Doug. 'Just give me anything out of the ordinary, okay?'

In the front bar of the hotel, Amy takes a stool beside the woman from before, watching her probe the depths of her handbag. Without looking up, the woman says, 'I thought that was you.'

'Yeah,' says Amy.

Her name is Angela Clarke. She's Amy's stepsister.

'Figured this was still your local. I can get this one, Angie.'

'It's a free country.'

Amy orders a bloody mary and a lemonade, then watches her sister shakily light a smoke.

'What's wrong with you?' says Amy, unable to stop herself.

'Christ.' A single tear rolls down Angela's face. She wipes it off with the back of her hand. 'I didn't expect . . . I didn't expect *this*, is all. You're like a bad penny.'

'Keep your fucking shirt on.' Amy pushes the cocktail over to her sister. 'You're going to need this.'

'Why? Oh Christ, what have you done?'

'Nothing.'

'Amy, I swear to god, if—'

'Jesus, Angie. I've got a question about Dad. That's all. Bottoms up.'

'Oh, it's *just Dad*.' Angela takes a deep slug of her drink. No straw, straight from the glass. 'Is he dead?'

'No, not that I know of.'

'Fuck,' says Angela. 'I could have sworn that was why you were here.'

'Sorry.'

Another tear rolls out.

THEY TAKE their second round out to the garden where the sun and the booze seem to chill Angela out a little bit. Amy's mother split when she was a toddler. Their father, Victor Owens, remarried eighteen months later, bringing her two step-siblings: Angela and her brother, Will. The marriage didn't last. The new stepmother fled the country—such was Victor's effect on people—leaving the three of them with a revolving cast of carers. None of them lasted long, either. For the most part, it was three kids in a mansion with a madman.

'I'm still working for Colleen Vinton,' says Amy. 'She's got me looking at a local businessman. Allan Watts.'

Angela slides on a pair of black sunglasses. 'Sure. I thought this was about Dad?'

'I'll get to that. What can you tell me about Allan?'

'Well, if it's on Colleen's dime, you need to pay me.'

Angela's a journalist for the *Gold Coast Bulletin* these days. A shill, by all reports.

Amy stares at her lemonade. 'Yeah, okay.'

'Where do you want me to start?'

'Can you just . . .'

'What?'

'Just tell me what you know and I'll leave you alone,' says Amy. 'That's how this works. This doesn't have to be . . .'

'You've already upset me, Amy, so it's going to be how it is.'

'I'm sorry.'

'No, you're not.' Angela takes a sip of her drink. 'Let me see. Allan Watts. Allan is . . . well, he's smarter than he looks, but not much.'

The rest comes out like a press briefing, or an obituary. Allan got his start in Hobart. He's a country kid. No family connections, but he's bright enough for a business degree and diligent enough to make his way in the Tasmanian banking sector. 'He looked after logging interests, for the most part,' Angela says. Like everyone else, he took a shine to the Gold Coast in the seventies, but unlike everyone else, he had the seed money to spend up big. He invested in a local restaurant, then another. 'And ever since then, he's one of the crew. In with the big boys. The White Shoe Brigade do all their work over beers and tits, and Allan is their office manager, their concierge. He brings people together, sets the party. And they've richly rewarded him for it. Not bad for a dickhead from Tassie. Is that enough?'

'It's a start,' says Amy.

'What's Colleen's angle? I thought she'd have a bloke like Allan by the balls already.'

'She probably does. I think she's trying to catch him out.'

Angela tilts her head, studying Amy from behind those dark glasses. 'She doesn't like it when people pull on the leash, does she?'

'No,' says Amy. 'She certainly does not.'

'How's the hand?'

'It's like this,' Amy says, giving her sister the finger.

'Still sore then.'

'Colleen thinks Watts has some connection to Dad. That's the clincher.'

'Well, he does. Of course, he does. Dad has money invested in the Silver Fish. That's one of Allan's spots. I think there's money of his in Clydes, as well.'

'How do you know all this?'

'I looked it up.'

'Just looked it up?'

'Haven't you ever thought about trying to hurt him?' says Angela.

'Not by looking through his financials.'

'And that, dear sister, is why you're living your sad little life, and I'm living mine.'

That's the end of the discussion, but they sit there a while anyhow. Two sisters with a shared history and not much else.

As Amy gets up to leave, Angela turns her face to the midday sun and blasts out a lungful of smoke, like she's won an argument or something. 'Goodbye, I guess,' she says.

Amy doesn't even bother.

# MIKE
## Surfers Paradise

MIKE GETS A CALL from Jack the Bagman at 12.30 pm. 'Do you still want that dance with the devil, son? Because Deputy Commissioner Sorensen is going to be down your way this afternoon. He's having a few drinks at the Silver Fish for a friend's birthday. Maybe you want to pop by?'

'You going to be there, Jack?'

'You never know your luck. Just remember what I said, be on your best behaviour. And you tell that minister of yours that he owes me one. That's the only reason we're talking about any of this.'

'I take it I checked out?'

'That you did,' says Jack. 'I gotta say, I'm actually a little impressed. To a man, they all told me the same thing.'

'Yeah, what's that?'

'That you're a devious little prick. I hope it's true, knowing where you're headed.' Jack hangs up.

Mike immediately gets back on the line, punching numbers.

The God Minister answers. No secretary, no

assistant. Mike briefs him. The minister huffs at the mention of Jack and the Queensland Police. 'Use every means possible.'

'I will,' says Mike.

'I'll take care of you if it turns ugly.'

THE SILVER FISH restaurant is on the fifth floor of an Esplanade high-rise down on the Strip. It's upmarket: tan tablecloths and orange carpet.

Today, hot sun blasts in through the wall-sized windows, barely restrained by the aircon. The place is almost empty. Recession vacancies, all the way.

The lack of customers doesn't stop the knob at the front counter asking Mike for his name twice. Mike coughs it up and gets nowhere. *Not on the list.* The knob scurries off and returns with Allan Watts.

'Well, well, well,' says Allan, making a show of considering Mike. 'Far be it from me to turn away God's only son. Come on, then.'

They make their way through the tables.

'Is this one of your spots?' asks Mike.

If Allan hears it, he doesn't bother answering. 'You better not embarrass me with these fellas. Just a warning, they're in a fucking mood.'

Allan takes him to a secluded corner table. Seated around it are a dozen men in suits, all wearing them like plainclothes coppers. As he seats him, Allan makes introductions, just the lower-level stooges. Mike feels a short, sharp flicker of fear creep in. At the end of the table are the big boys, in the flesh: Police Commissioner Terry Lewis, deep in conversation with a young male aide. Next to Lewis is Inspector Harry Bower—known to everyone in Brisbane as *the Old Bloke*, a notorious CIB powerbroker—and across from Bower is Deputy Commissioner Arthur Sorensen.

A hand clamps down on Mike's shoulder. 'What a nice surprise,' says a familiar voice. Mike jolts around to find Jack the Bagman grinning at him. 'Didn't know you were in town, mate,' he says, with a wink. He leans in, beer-breath in Mike's ear. 'Here we go, Mister Big Shot.'

Mike laughs, like he's hearing a joke from an old friend.

'Softly, softly,' says Jack, and moves on.

After a round of beers and prawn cocktails, one of the nearby detectives swaps seats to get next to Mike. 'We've met before, right?' he says. Mike has already forgotten the man's name, but he's about Mike's age and looks a little out of his depth as well. 'I think it was at a party in West End,' the detective says.

Mike flags down a waiter and motions for another. 'Did I behave myself?'

'Not one bit. We were on the . . .' and the detective taps his nose.

'Right.' Mike leaves it alone. He tries to join another conversation, but the other cops around him have absolutely no interest in him. They mainly talk about casework. They're all bent out of shape about the Commonwealth Games. The city is awash with drunken brawls courtesy of the temporary late-night drinking hours. There's road closures and the Aboriginal protests. As the lunch lurches on, beers become bourbons and the social order loosens a bit. The men stand up and move around.

Mike spots Jack talking to Sorensen and Commissioner Lewis and makes his move. He sidles up. They all give him the nod, polite enough, but nothing more.

'Jack here tells me you're working for the minister?' says Commissioner Lewis.

'Yes, sir.'

'What does he have you doing, apart from spying on me?' Lewis says gently, all smiles.

Mike laughs and takes a quick look at the other two. 'Well, ah . . .'

Sorensen leers, gorging on the awkwardness of it.

Jack plays dead.

'It's all right, son,' says Lewis. 'We've all been there.'

The feigned kindness makes it worse.

Fighting every urge to back away, Mike swallows a mouthful of beer and does the opposite. He steps closer to the trio and comes right out with it. 'The minister wants Fantasyland back on track. I don't know why. But he has me down here, sniffing around the coast to help out.'

'And it brought you to us?' says the commissioner.

'Yes, sir, it did. All roads lead to Rome.'

Lewis looks away, giving Sorensen his turn. 'Tell me more about these roads?'

'Maybe it's all talk?' says Mike.

'Maybe it is,' says the commissioner.

Jack points across the room. 'Sorry to interrupt, fellas, but . . .'

A girl in a gold lamé bikini weaves her way towards them. In her hands, she has a large brown cake with dark chocolate icing. The thing is shaped like a police truncheon.

Commissioner Lewis looks on serenely. 'Pity the premier isn't here. He'd have loved this.'

# MIKE
## Surfers Paradise

THE YOUNG BUCKS RUNNING with Sorensen and the police commissioner slow down as the afternoon closes out. The men are all drunk by then. They put the feelers out for a palate cleanser. *Is anyone carrying? Who's got the gear?* A boozy Mike feels the air buzz around him, like a miracle is about to happen. He slips a hand into his jacket pocket and brings out the leftover cocaine from Fantasyland. 'I can pick us up,' he says.

Everyone's eyes light up.

'Mate, *you* are under arrest,' says one of them, scoring a laugh.

Mike does a line in the Silver Fish bathroom with three CIB detectives and an office clerk. He regales jittery men with political intrigue and who's fucking who in the Nationals. Back at the bar, he orders gin and tonics. 'This will liven us up.'

And just like that, he's in. It's only the ground floor, mind you—the old boys aren't having any of it —but it's enough. The detectives start talking to him. They tell him about brothels in the big smoke and illegal casinos, and which pubs have the biggest counter meals, and which undercover cops have the best weed. They talk about another party tonight and tell Mike he's invited. There's also an *after*-afterparty and, 'Yeah, we can probably get you into that too, mate, if you can sort us out with some more of this marching powder. It's going to be a long one.'

Mike doesn't look the gift horse in the mouth. He immediately goes and buys an eight ball of coke from Allan in the Silver Fish's kitchen. Allan knows the drill, but he's shocked all the same. 'You're good at this,' he says. 'Beating me at my own game.'

'I live to serve.'

They do a line together.

'You know,' Allan says, 'some of those blokes out there are drug police, right?'

Mike's feeling good now. 'I know.' He wipes his nose. 'I can sell ice to Eskimos when I'm like this.'

THE FOLLOW-ON PARTY is in a tavern upstairs from the Silver Fish. It's more of the same, but the cast expands. Commissioner Lewis and Deputy Sorensen have retired elsewhere, leaving their men to mingle with the regulars. Mike keeps the day going at light-speed, working every angle, fishing for cop scandal, Fantasyland juice, and the lock on an invitation to the *after*-after shindig. That is where the real action will be.

To shore it all up, he sneaks off and uses the bar phone to get a connect on some working girls. Half an hour later they arrive, chaperoned by a familiar face: the redhead from Fantasyland. The one with the cigarette-box camera.

*The photo.*

*'Just a little souvenir.'*

The redhead walks right up to him, her eyes fixed on his eyes. 'Hello, stranger.'

Behind them, the CIB boys cheer.

Glasses get clinked.

Fake giggles echo.

The redhead takes in the scene, then looks back at Mike. 'This is interesting. I hope *you're* paying.'

'It's covered,' says Mike. 'You wouldn't have a little souvenir you'd like to give me, would you? I'm a bit worried about it.'

She smiles at that, gently leans against him. 'Maybe there's a little souvenir you'd like to give me?'

*Jesus.*

'Little?' he says.

'I'll need to have another look at that photo.'

Mike checks in with the detectives. They're all coupled up, drinks in hand.

'Come on,' says the redhead. 'It won't take long.'


THEY ROLL around on the floor of an apartment in the same building. The woman tells him it's what the place is for. Naked, in the fading dusk, Mike drinks her in. Her pale thighs wrapped around his waist, hair splayed out, bright red and iridescent against the cream shag-pile carpet. She moans and touches herself while they do it, completely uninhibited.

Mike feels *big*.

The woman is everything, all-encompassing.

And when it's over, she hangs around this time. She walks to the bathroom nude, a hand cradling herself. On the way back, she grabs a bottle of white wine from the refrigerator and pours it into two coffee cups.

'What's your name?' Mike says.

'Oh dear.'

'Are you offended?'

'No. I just thought you had more pull than that.'

'Maybe I do? Maybe I like the mystery?'

She rolls over onto her stomach. 'The *only* thing men like is mystery. I'm Colleen.'

'Colleen what?'

'Vinton.'

'Uh fuck. I walked into that, didn't I?'

He knows the name. Knows it well. *Colleen the Queen*. She owns the Strip. Has the local pollies in her pocket. Fingers in the Gold Coast police. The driving force behind the first legal casino they're building down here. Rumour has it that Robert Emmery—the casino's frontman—is her puppet. She works independent of the Brisbane mafia, but she's still plenty dangerous in her own right.

'How does that grab you?' she says.

Mike shrugs. 'I'm in politics.' He collects his coat from the floor. 'I might have a bump.' He chalks up the powder on a hardcover copy of *Noble House* and they each do a line.

'Is this Allan's stuff?' asks Colleen.

He nods.

She grabs her purse and takes out a photograph. 'Here. For services rendered.'

It's the picture of Mike with his pants around his ankles. It's as unflattering as he imagined. Drunk off his arse, his flaccid dick is fleshy and alien under the flash. On the back, Colleen has stapled the film negative. 'Thanks,' he says, pocketing it. 'Have you been carrying this around?'

'I recognised your name when the order came in.

112

Unlike you, I know who I'm sleeping with. Why are you down here?'

'I'm working on Fantasyland.'

'Figures.'

'Does it?' Mike runs a hand through her hair, teasing out a long strand. 'Are you involved with it?'

'Not as involved as I want to be. It's the biggest game in town at the moment. What's your angle?'

'I need to get it back on track. I'm working for the minister.'

'The minister of what?'

'Everything.'

'Oh. So we're both playing with fire, then? Do the Nationals think partying with the Brisbane police is the best way to get Fantasyland back on track?'

'I don't get paid to think. I just go with the flow.'

'But it doesn't stop you thinking, does it?'

Mike laughs. 'Colleen, are you working me?'

She slides over. She straddles him.

Mike runs a hand over her thigh. 'I want this to happen again, but if you're working me, I figure we should just get it out in the open right now.'

'No, I'm not. But maybe I should be? Maybe we can work each other?'

Colleen moves back and forth.

'How much trouble does that get me into down the way?'

'I think you like trouble,' she says, slipping him inside.

# BRUNO

## Surfers Paradise

BRUNO WALKS INTO THE South Beach Building Society ten minutes before closing time. It's an old-school bank building with clean marble floors and high ceilings. Polished and prim. It doesn't really gel with the rest of the Strip. It's not for the battlers and the dreamers. This is a rich person's bank. Tonight, two young guards are stationed by the front door, something they're keeping locked. Inside, there's an older guy on duty. The young bucks let Bruno pass, no questions asked, but the old guy pegs him for a cop immediately. 'We all good?' he says, coming across the foyer, hand out.

'Just following something up,' says Bruno. 'Is Alfred Simmons around? I believe he's the deputy manager.'

'Al's out back. I'll bring you through.'

Al has a big office with an L-shaped couch in one corner and an aquarium built into the wall. He looks exactly as expected: pudgy, late fifties, suited up and busy. Standing beside him at his desk is a much younger woman. Al turns to her and says, 'Who's this?' as Bruno walks in.

'I don't know,' says the woman, picking up a manila folder and coming round.

Bruno doesn't wait for a negotiation. He opens his ID wallet and says, 'I'm from the Gold Coast Criminal Investigation Branch. I only need a few minutes.'

'Can it wait?' says the woman.

Al's watching on. He looks tired. His eyes are bloodshot.

'That's not how this works,' Bruno says.

'It's okay,' says Al. 'Can she stay?'

'She can do whatever she likes.'

'Take a seat, kid. But can we make it quick, please? I'm not messing you about. I've got somewhere to be. I'm trying to get out the door.'

Bruno opens his notebook. 'I'm looking for a client of yours. Phillip O'Grady.'

'Sure. I know Phil. He's away. On a cruise, I think. Doreen, weren't the O'Gradys in here a couple of weeks ago getting traveller's cheques?'

'That's right,' says the woman.

'I can't go into details about what's happening,' says Bruno, 'but we have a letter from you, Mister Simmons, that outlines irregularities with the O'Gradys' bank account.'

'That's right.'

Bruno waits for more, but Al doesn't offer anything else. 'I've had a look through those bank statements you sent through the mail. It looks to me like someone is running down their accounts.'

'It looked that way to me too.'

'And you didn't think it was Phillip and his wife doing it?'

'No, I didn't.'

'Do you know who was cleaning them out?'

'That's a private matter. I can't discuss things like that.'

'I don't think the O'Gradys are on that cruise ship. So, what's this private matter?'

'Have you seen the automatic teller machine outside, Detective?'

'What about it?'

'Have you used one before?'

'No. I don't want to talk to a machine.'

'Well, Phil O'Grady doesn't share your distaste for them. You use a key card and a PIN number. It's like a secret code. I think someone has Phillip's card and his PIN.'

'When was the last withdrawal?'

'I don't know exactly. We've cancelled the cards. Doreen, could you take him out and have Frederick bring up the records?'

Bruno stays seated. 'Who do you think has this card of theirs?'

Al looks at the papers on his desk. 'I couldn't say.'

'I think you could.'

'I really can't say, Detective. Is that all?'

Bruno stands up. 'It'll do for now.'


OUT IN AN OFFICE behind the front counter, Bruno waits at the desk of a German man called Frederick. Frederick isn't big on conversation. When Bruno asks how he's faring with the O'Grady records, Frederick says, 'Do you want to take over?'

He doesn't.

To kill time, Bruno wanders around the bank. He watches the tellers standing behind the long counter, finishing up with the day's last customers. An old biddy fusses with a deposit slip. Down the hall, Doreen drags the vacuum cleaner out of a closet.

'Here,' calls Frederick. 'Come, please.'

Bruno turns.

Bright lights across the rear wall.

Behind him, a man hollers.

The whole building shudders as what sounds like lightning erupts through the foyer, the force of it spraying glass and dust. The blow knocks Bruno over as the overhead sprinkler system sprays the room. Flashes erupt in the water.

*Gunfire.*

Screaming.

The bank tellers scramble for cover, ducking beneath the counter and nearby desks.

Bruno reaches under his jacket, but a gloved hand grabs him by the neck and rams his head into a filing cabinet, knocking him to the floor. A man with a shotgun steps around. Black balaclava. Blue sports tracksuit. 'Get your fucking faces down,' he screams.

Bruno and the tellers all press themselves to the floor.

Another man appears, jumping over the counter and landing on the wet carpet. The second one is armed and dressed in the same garb. He drags Al Simmons from his office down the hall and yanks him off into another part of the bank.

A voice shouts, 'One minute,' from across the room.

Bruno forces himself calm.

*Three assailants.*

*At least two armed.*

*They don't know I'm armed.*

Shouting in the hallway, a way off. Al's voice.

118

The sprinkler system keeps on drenching the place. They're all soaked to the bone. Water pooling on the floor.

*No sirens yet.*

For a horrible minute, nothing happens. Everyone thinks about dying.

The masked man by Bruno shuffles his feet, lifts his gun.

'Two minutes,' yells the other voice, agitated now.

'Okay,' says the one near Bruno.

It's followed by more screaming down the corridor.

Al Simmons reappears, the second man behind him. Bruno gets a good look at the assailant this time. White skin through the eyeholes of his balaclava. He has Al by the throat.

'I don't have it,' whimpers Al.

The man throws him down, fifteen feet from where Bruno lies.

'Please,' says Al, a shotgun in his face.

The gun fires and Al's face evaporates, turning the wall behind him black and red.

A teller behind Bruno starts shrieking.

Doreen appears out of nowhere, sprinting from the hallway where she's hidden herself. She clears the counter, into the foyer. The man who shot Al follows her out, poised, gun raised. He fires again and Doreen yelps.

Bruno springs up, gun in hand, pressing the muzzle into the man closest to him and firing twice.

A voice screaming, 'Go, go, go.'

More shots, the rounds sparking the filing cabinet by Bruno. Bullets ricochet.

Bruno spins and fires blindly across the room.

*Snap, snap, snap.*

He ducks and reloads. 'Come on. *Fuck.*' Absolute panic in his voice as something catches his eye. Bruno glances over at the body of the man he's just shot. *He's moving.* His hand is reaching for the discarded shotgun by his side. Bruno pounces, but the man has the gun now. They tussle, arms heaving, fighting for the shotgun. Both have their hands on it. Bruno presses down with all his weight, the gun fires and the man's body goes limp.

It's over.

Bruno doesn't look.

The sprinkler rain keeps coming.

There's a teller sitting five feet away and she's holding her throat, blood silently bubbling out.

'Stay down,' he says.

Bruno pads around for his police revolver, spotting it under a nearby desk. He pushes the bullets in and comes up, scanning around.

*Move.*

He runs down the counter and around.

There's water everywhere, carnage everywhere.

Gun smoke.

Flashing lights.

Ringing ears and submerged sirens and moaning.

A banged-up Ford utility sits in the centre of the bank foyer, engine running, high beams in the mist.

*It was a ram raid.*

The young guards are standing back, too stunned to move.

The older one is keeled over, injured.

Doreen's dead, blasted apart at the shoulders. The wet ground around her running pink.

Bruno feels it all at once, the sudden press of adrenaline, insanity, fear.

He hears fake silence.

## THE DREAM

He scans the room. He keeps his gun up.
He moves out onto the street.
Police cars arriving, jumping the kerb.
Regular people coming out of hiding.
A helicopter overhead.
It's not good.
They're gone.

# AMY
## Surfers Paradise

AMY IS IN HER apartment when she hears the radio call-out. It comes in over her illegal police scanner. *Robbery in progress at the South Beach Building Society*. It's half a mile away as the crow flies. She figures Bill Webber might show and hits the footpath, hearing alarms ringing. A thin column of smoke rises up over the Strip.

An ambulance roars past.

Fire engines.

Minutes later, she's standing across the street from the mayhem.

A giant hole in the bank where the doors used to be.

A burning ute dragged onto the street.

Women in blood-soaked dresses.

Bodies in the glass.

Dazed cops, pale faces.

Bill Webber appears from the throng. He looks around, like all this mayhem is just more of the same. Amy locks onto his face—that thousand-yard stare of his—and feels an odd heat coming off him.

*Who is this fucking guy?*

Webber steps into the bank through the jagged hole. He crouches by a body on the floor, then gets up and disappears into the shadows.

ALLAN WATTS OWNS a place on the Esplanade and Amy hasn't had a look at him, face to face, since Colleen put her on the case. She takes the lift up to the Silver Fish restaurant where the dinner trade is filling in. If the crime scene down the road is news, it isn't bothering anyone up here.

Amy sits at the bar and nurses a coke. Down the other end of the room, a dozen men are piled up around the entryway to the bathrooms. Some of Colleen's girls are with them. The men are cops. That stink is all over them. Not local guys, though. *City cops.* Five minutes in, one of them peels off and comes over. A sweaty body piled into a blue silk shirt. 'Hey, babe,' he says, hammered.

Amy shakes her head and tells him to get lost.

To his credit, he takes the hint.

She stirs her drink and thinks about how her father owns a piece of this place. Something about it doesn't figure. Old Victor's a toff. It's hard to imagine him in here, sitting shoulder to shoulder with cashed-up coppers and callgirls. In fact, it's hard to imagine him *anywhere* these days, except in that haunted house of his. He's weak now and doesn't want everyone knowing it. Amy can't remember the last time she saw him out in public. It's a blessing.

Two Japanese women come into the bar and try to chat with her about the coast. 'Girls, it's been a day,' Amy says, by way of *piss off*.

To ward off everyone else, she reviews the day's notes: her photos. That safe in Bill Webber's garage. A follow-up with Dirty Doug. Her sister.

Amy takes an iced water to the public payphone in the corner and calls a man called Mr Sally. He's a shonky locksmith from Main Beach. A real piece of shit.

'Yes?' Mr Sally says, but it's just the machine playing tricks.

Amy shakes her head. 'I have work for you. Call me back.'

She hangs up and lights a smoke. Still standing there by the phone, she clocks Allan Watts walking through the bar area carrying a tray of beers like the world's most expensive wait staff. Amy slips in behind him, trailing Allan through the dining area to a small unmarked door. Amy waits a beat, then follows him inside. There's a quiet hallway beyond. Doors leading off, a glass portal on each. All of them dark except for one down the far end.

Amy makes her way over and looks in.

Men in a private lounge. She knows the faces.

Police Commissioner Terry Lewis.

Deputy Commissioner Arthur Sorensen.

Inspector Harry Bower.

It seems Allan Watts is hosting the absolute apex of the Queensland Police Force in his private room. They sit in front-row seats up against the window glass, watching the Strip go to hell in the streets below.

Harry Bower points down at the South Beach Building Society and says something.

Lewis nods robotically.

Allan tops up Sorensen's drink and the man

barely notices, so intent is he on the scene below. Red siren lights flash in Sorensen's glasses. He sneers at the world outside. Amber flame-light across his face.

# MIKE
## Surfers Paradise

MIKE KISSES COLLEEN GOODBYE in the elevator and comes back through the tavern upstairs from the Silver Fish. It's night outside, black sky in the ocean-front windows. There's some commotion out on the Strip, but the Brisbane detectives still kicking on from lunch don't give a fuck. They're gearing up to leave for the next party. They all give Mike plenty of stick for disappearing on them, all of them except for two Consorting Squad detectives who zero in. One of them says, 'Are you fooling around with Colleen Vinton? Jeeeeez, mate. You're game.'

The other one clucks away, acting bewildered. 'You better get a doctor to check you out, mate. Your dick might be about to drop off.'

'He needs a bloody head doctor, more like.'

And so on.

Mike's thoughts are elsewhere. He can still smell Colleen's perfume on his clothes. 'Where did Terry and the others get to?'

'What do you care?'

'I, ah . . .'

It's a misstep.

*Too busy thinking about the girl.*

'Nah,' says one of the Consorting guys, grabbing Mike around the shoulders. 'You're all right. We can get you a few minutes with the big boss. Don't wet your pants.'

THE GROUP STUMBLES OUT of the restaurant; a raucous, drunken mass. They weave their way onto the downstairs footpath. Ties are loosened, sweat stains seep through shirts. The working girls prop the drunker men up. It's a scene, but they have a shuttle bus waiting. As the policemen climb aboard, the passenger window comes down and Jack the Bagman is right there, pointing at Mike and saying, 'Nah, not him.'

'He's okay,' says one of the men. 'We like him.'

'He's not on the list.'

'What fucking list?'

One of them goes over and confers with Jack.

Jack shrugs and the window goes back up.

Mike's in.

THE RIDE across town is enough to get everyone fired from their jobs. The detectives do Mike's blow in the shuttle bus. They knock back beers. One of them fucks in the back seat, causing general disagreement. *That's poor bloody form, even by your standards, Ray.* One man sits painfully close to Mike and as the bus hurtles through the night, the guy describes—in great detail—a horrific murder case he worked back in May. 'Never seen anything like it,' he says, taking a pull on his stubbie. 'They buried him alive, mate. Imagine that.'

THE AFTER-AFTERPARTY IS in a manor house in the distant hinterlands behind the Strip. It's a big, isolated property. A long, paved road leading in, past a lake and tennis courts. The main dwelling is a collection of timber buildings nestled on the property's high point.

The shuttle puts them out onto a sprawling lawn where Mike is relieved to see that other party guests have arrived. There's three dozen civilians like himself, all milling around. He recognises a few faces: a famous musician, two or three media people, a couple of political operators. They're all monied up to the gills. Tuxes and bow ties. Women in cocktail dresses. Uniformed help. It feels like the big time and, as the detectives spill out of the bus, Mike watches the other guests register their arrival with caution.

This new crowd proves easier going for Mike. He slips into conversations. He chats with people at the bar, lighting cigarettes and flagging down staff. Everyone's talking about the Commonwealth Games and where they're seated for various events. There's plenty of Fantasyland gossip as well. *Out of money, we hear* and *Noah Winters is batshit crazy* and *that son of his can't hack it.*

No one knows if Sorensen is involved.

Everyone assumes so.

There's a tense energy circulating. The tug of something.

*Getting closer.*

A gaunt woman with long white hair tells Mike that, 'The recession is a nightmare.'

Her husband nods along. 'We had to cancel our trip to Hamilton Island. It's belt-tightening all round, isn't it, luv?'

The woman is appalled. 'At this rate, we'll be eating Christmas dinner at the yacht club.'

A helicopter shudders over, low in the sky. They hear it land on the far side of the house.

The party moves inside and ramps up a notch.

The drinks flow faster. Open bar, top shelf. Mike feels the toll. He hides in a bathroom and takes a big bump of his own gear just to stay lucid.

On the way out of the bathroom, a younger guy tags Mike, smiling. 'Did I just . . .' The guy pauses. He has long sandy hair and bright brown eyes.

'Did I just what?' says Mike, but he knows. The guy was listening at the door.

'I could use a pick-me-up, is all.'

'Oh, could you now? Who are you?'

The guy holds out his hand. 'I'm Jamie.'

'What are you doing up here, Jamie?'

'Bit of this, bit of that.'

The guy is all of twenty-five and every inch of his clothing clings tight to his frame. There's a practised sheen to him. Mike knows another hustler when he sees one. 'Step into my office,' he says.

In the bathroom, the guy snorts back the blow without hesitation.

'You been here before, Jamie?'

'Twice. These parties are a drag, but the money's all right, darl.'

'Who do you work for?'

Jamie smiles. 'Wouldn't you like to know. How about you? You're not a cop, are you?'

'I might be.'

'No, I don't think so,' Jamie says. 'I saw you

working the room out there.' Jamie wipes his nostrils and plants himself next to Mike, both of them leaning against the vanity on either side of the bathroom sink. 'It's a funny old world, isn't it?'

'I'll say.'

'Maybe we can meet up sometime, away from all this?'

Mike smiles. 'Maybe.'

'Is there something else then?'

It's a leap, but Mike takes it. 'How'd you like to make some real money?'

'What do you have in mind?'

'I don't know . . . I've found myself in a sticky situation up here. I'm in the door, but I don't know what I'm looking for.'

Jamie pulls a packet of smokes from the front pocket of his blazer. He teases one out and lights it. 'You know who owns this place, don't you?'

'The Deputy Commissioner of the Queensland Police.'

'Among others.' Jamie looks at the ceiling and blows smoke up there. 'What's on offer?'

'What do you need?'

'Really?'

'I work for a higher power, someone with deep pockets.' Mike pulls out a wad of brown fifties and peels off ten. 'There's more.'

'Keep going then.'

Mike counts off another twenty and hands them over.

'This is a down payment,' says Jamie, pocketing the cash. 'I want another grand on the other side of this.'

'Christ, you better have something to show me.'

'This is not my first time at the rodeo, darl. Give me an hour. And . . .'

'What?'

'Do you have a car?'

'Why?'

'You'll need a fast way to get out of here.'

# MIKE
## The Gold Coast Hinterland

JAMIE WANTS TO MEET up later.

*We have to pick our moment.*

Mike checks in with the CIB men. They're a slathering mess, draped across a set of leather couches in one of the living rooms. Two of them are asleep, the coffee table in front of them is covered in half-eaten party food, empty bottles and album sleeves. 'Rio' by Duran Duran blares out of a nearby stereo. Mike deposits his leftover powder in one of their shirt pockets and bids them goodnight.

From there, he circulates.

He finds a heated pool and a bar outside. Plenty of people are around. A bain-marie of food. He talks politics with two old men as they watch the steam come off the pool water. Some finance guys stand on the other side and Mike slides in, hearing about football, fine dining, as well as a stream of complaints about some dickhead in the banking sector. He keeps moving. He schmoozes the staff. He eavesdrops and gets his arse pinched by a sixty-year-old woman. Mike stands in the corner and thinks about his kids and

Sonya and pushes down the immediate urge to leave, to go home, to beg.

Instead, he takes a smoke break in the rear garden, down the lawn from the throng. He's standing there for a few minutes when a man appears out of the crowd and wanders over. Mike feels he should recognise the guy, but he can't place him.

'Chris,' says the man, giving him the nod and firing up a joint.

'This is some shindig,' says Mike.

'Is it?'

Chris is built solid, but he's tall to balance it out. He has a dark brown Tom Selleck moustache and is well put-together, like everyone here, but there's something else about him.

'How do you fit into all this?' says Mike.

'I work with some of them.'

*A cop.* Mike can see it now.

Chris takes another drag. 'How about you?'

'Politics, but, you know, behind the scenes.'

Chris is close now. 'You like guys, Mike?'

'What?'

Chris steps around and looks at him, head on. He places his hands on Mike's biceps and blocks the light. 'I don't know. I can usually spot it a mile off.' Chris peers into Mike's face, his own face in the shadows. 'Maybe you're not supposed to be here.'

Mike tries to step back, but the man has a hold of him.

'You sure you don't fuck men?' says Chris.

'What are you—'

Chris grabs him by the balls.

'Stop. *Stop!*'

'Steady,' says Chris. He lets out a slow, deep breath. 'Steady on. I'm a policeman. You don't want

to make a scene down here, buddy. It's all good. It's all
. . .' Chris explores, moving his hand around. He still
has Mike's bicep. It's gripped so tight it hurts.

Mike pushes him back, but it makes it worse.

Chris squeezes with his lower hand. 'Uh, uh.'

Mike starts to panic. He flails a punch.

The grip on his balls unlocks and Mike crumples,
kneels in the grass about to hurl.

'Definitely not a poof, then,' says Chris, standing
over him. 'Hard to know sometimes. Sorry about
that. No harm done.'

Mike finds his breath.

The night feels immensely still.

Up at the house, the music cuts mid-song. A
droning version of 'Happy Birthday' drifts down.

'I think they're about to cut the cake,' Chris says,
walking away.


AN HOUR LATER, Mike is still collecting himself.
He's fucking loaded now, slipping into blackout
drunkenness, and can't seem to right himself. He
keeps to the edges of the house, almost scared to go
out into the yard again.

Jamie finds him pressed against a wall beside a
large indoor house plant. 'What are you doing?'

'I don't know. I think it's time to get out of here.'

'You still want to see something?'

'What is it?'

'The room,' says Jamie.


JAMIE HAS some speed he's scored from another
guest, and on Jamie's advice, Mike does a little to
wake himself up. He doesn't like the sound of this

*room* Jamie mentioned, but as they walk around the house and through the gardens, the guy renegotiates the offer, asking for more money.

'I can pay,' slurs Mike, feeling like it's a positive sign. But in truth, he wants it to be over. Only the feeling that he's come too far to turn back keeps him moving.

'Down here,' says Jamie.

They cut around manicured hedges and through a rose garden. No one is out this way. Tall lights appear up overhead. Jamie's taking him to the tennis courts. They walk down a set of concrete steps, along and around the courts to a small, covered shed built under the tiered seating. There's a door cut into the corrugated steel wall and Jamie pulls a set of keys from his pocket and tries one in the door's lock.

No luck.

He tries another.

'Fuck.'

'Where'd you get these?' says Mike.

'These,' Jamie says, 'are what you're paying for.' He holds them up to the moonlight and separates one out before slotting it into the lock and popping it open. 'Here we go.'

The inside of the shed smells like lawn clippings and mildew. There's a steel-frame shelving unit on castor wheels and Jamie unlocks the wheels and moves it aside, revealing the inner doorway. He reaches into the darkness beyond and hits a light switch.

Soft light pours out.

A carpeted stairwell, a timber-lined interior with wall lamps.

Jamie goes first. 'This is where the really fucked-up stuff happens.'

'You've been down here before?'

He nods.

Down in the basement, Mike counts off three rooms connected by a short hall.

Jamie goes straight to door number two.

It's a small cinema room. A screen and projector with seating. On the far side of the cinema, behind a wall-length velvet curtain, Jamie finds another door and unlocks it. This is a storeroom. There are shelves full of film canisters beside five grey filing cabinets.

'If you're looking for something, this is probably where it is,' says Jamie. 'There's a lot of trouble in here. You better be good for that money.'

The films have names on them.

Dates.

Locations.

Brisbane, late seventies, early eighties.

They're all men's names.

Mike tries the filing cabinets and finds paper files. He pulls one out at random and finds a collection of forms.

He looks through.

Official complaints lodged on official police stationery.

Internal Investigations memos and paperwork.

He spots names he recognises.

Magistrates.

Cops.

Politicians.

Priests.

Mike opens another drawer.

More of the same.

There must be thousands of them. This must be—

A loud scraping sound rumbles through the room.

*The door above.*

'Oh god,' says Jamie.

Mike sweeps the room, looking for anything he can grab. He spots a piece of foolscap paper taped to the wall. Names and dates and numbers. While Jamie's back is turned, Mike grabs the sheet and stuffs it in his pocket.

'What was that?' Jamie has his arm. 'Fuck.' He drags Mike out of the storeroom and pushes him into a corner of the cinema. 'Stay there.' Jamie drags the velvet curtain across Mike, hiding him from view. 'Don't move until I come get you.'

The lights go out.

Voices echo.

People enter the room, loud and reeking of booze. Mike can feel their footsteps through the floor. Someone murmurs a hello to Jamie and Jamie says a quiet hello back.

'Find your seats, find your seats,' says a voice.

It takes a minute to settle the room, but Mike is lost to his own void-like fear. He's still in the corner, covered. But someone is close. Someone is going to move the curtain. *I'm in a coffin standing up. I'll never see my kids again.* All the drugs and alcohol in his system are scratching under his skin, like bugs crawling.

Music comes on. Soft funk.

Dialogue, awkward and brittle.

Mike can't breathe. His face is burning up.

He delicately pulls back the curtain and looks.

A white screen.

A woman in an office, unbuttoning a green skirt.

All the seats are full.

Mike slips out and, as his eyes adjust, he notices

another five or so men standing along the rear of the cinema, not four feet away.

No one looks his way. No one notices his sudden appearance.

*Where is the fucking door?*

He waits.

As the fucking starts onscreen and the moaning soundtrack gets louder in the room, he notices a brief slice of vertical yellow light across the way.

A figure slips through the doorway.

Without thinking, Mike follows.

Across the line of men, through the beam of the projector and to the door.

Into the hall, gently pulling the door shut behind him.

Along the hall to the stair.

'Hey,' says a voice.

Mike turns.

Chris stands at the terminus of the hall in a doorway. He has paper towelling in his hands.

Mike walks faster.

'Hey.'

Up the stairs, through the shed and out into the open air. As soon as he's outside, he runs.

No direction.

No thinking.

Just sprints for it.

He hears the clang of the shed door opening behind him.

*'HEY!'*

Mike runs to the cover of the thick gardens adjoining the tennis court. Shrubbery and branches whipping his face and shoulders. A minute later, he breaks out the other side of the garden into an undulating orchard on the side of a hill.

He doesn't stop running.

Gunfire behind him now, an echoing retort.

Shouting. Male voices. Heavy footfall.

He comes out of the orchard into a long sloping field and sprints into the night.

More gunfire in the distance.

His legs give out and he falls.

Gets up, keeps going. In pain, chest barely working.

There's something ahead. Two hundred metres out. Lights in a line. A road dotted with garden lamps.

A car is driving along it.

Mike sprints down to the road and, by some miracle, the car slows a little. He runs alongside it, screaming, 'Help, help!'

The driver brakes.

The passenger door snaps open.

Mike gets in, terrified.

Another gunshot across the night sky. The rear window of the car caves, spraying glass across the back seat. The driver screams and the car shunts forward, speeding up. It's a dark sedan, hotted up, fast.

'Hurry,' says Mike, hiding below the window line.

More shots.

Gravel spraying.

A world-tilting slide sideways and then nothing, just the engine at full throttle and the wind blasting in through the broken window.

A minute passes. 'You can come out now,' says the driver.

Mike looks over.

It's Jamie behind the wheel.

'Thanks.'

Jamie looks over, dazed, in shock. 'You've gotta

pay for that window,' he says. 'You've gotta put that on the tab.'

# PART FOUR
# FRIDAY 1 OCTOBER
## 1982

# VICTOR

THEY CALLED us the *White Shoe Brigade. We reclaimed the water, subdivided the land, raised the high-rises, and for what? For them to insult us for our shoes? It was laughable. The pettiness of small people.*

*There was Bruce Small and Eddie Kornhauser, as well as Dennis Benson, Keith Williams and the Skase lad. We are the true architects of the coast, the true designers. We had help, of course. Sir Joh and the God Minister oiled the gears of government, and the banks and investors did their part. But we built the shopping centres and suburbia, the resorts and apartment buildings. We built the coast.*

*The only thing stopping me is age. But I struggle on, changed but also the same. One must play the hand one is dealt, and when old age arrives, bringing all its entropy and weakness, one must adjust. An old man cannot be bold in his action. He's too slow. Instead, he has to be bold in his mind. He has to lean into his experience, his network and servants. He has to be cunning and forget niceties and grace. Those traits are for the young. The old must be shrewd and ruthless. And the good news is, people mistake the weak for the broken, the ageing for the dead. Even I am guilty of this.*

*Elda brings me my phone. 'It's him.'*

*I hold it to my ear.*

*'It was a bit of a fucking disaster,' says Allan.*

*I hand my tea to Elda. 'Can you reheat this?'*

*She moves slowly, waiting for me to talk further.*

*I wait her out, then say to Allan, 'I saw the papers. Poor Seth. Were there any civilian casualties?'*

*'Not really. One of the guards copped it.'*

*'What did you come away with?'*

*'It wasn't all it could've been. I'm going to need more from you. I think your share is going to have to come up.'*

*'Let's wait and see it. How did your guests react?'*

*'Hard to say. You know how it is with those fellas. Even with the inner circle, you can never be sure who knows what with coppers. But fuck me, it was a bit bloody tense. We could see the bank from the back windows of the Silver Fish and, let me tell you, Sorensen didn't look too pleased. He's definitely got his nuts in the machinery of all this, like you said.'*

*The side of my face burns. I need to have the volume so loud it's percussive in my ear. 'And the boys?'*

*'They're rattled, but they're okay. Seth always was the weak link. Sunny isn't keen on slowing down any time soon. Can't now, can they? They're going to see it through. Weirdly enough, I think we're okay.'*

*'Let's not count our chickens before they're hatched. Anything else?'*

*'Some dickhead from the minister's office is sniffing around. Reckons he's here to help. You don't suppose the God Minister is coming in, do you?'*

*'He does like to sit back and have others do his*

bidding. But he'll be sniffing out a result rather than an investment. He's not coming in. It's not his style.'

'His underling is an efficient fucker. I think he's in bed with Colleen Vinton.'

'That's concerning.'

'Yeah, it is. So what about the money? We're coming up short.'

'Tell Sunny there's wiggle room, but not a lot.'

The call ends.

Elda comes back, takes the phone. 'You need anything, sir?'

'I'm cold.'

'I'll fetch a blanket.'

'It's the bloody medicine.'

*It's the pills and syrups and the treatments and the rest. But it's also death. Death creeping towards me. I hate that it's cold. In my lighter moments, I joke to myself that, after these final weeks in my medicated winter, the heat of hell will be a respite.*

*It's just a joke. I know what's coming is neither hot nor cold. Pretty soon the temperature won't matter. Pretty soon all that will remain is my money and my bloodline, and the plans I've set in place.*

# BRUNO
## Stationhouse, Surfers Paradise

AFTER THE ROBBERY, BRUNO'S night was long, involving a detailed statement at the station followed by a doctor coming in to fix the two-inch gash in his scalp. Someone patched him up back at the bank, but he needed proper stitches after the fact. The doctor told him it was either shrapnel or a near-miss from a bullet. Afterwards, Bruno slipped away to an empty meeting room and crashed.

In his sleep, he saw dark visions.

The bank manager and blood splatter.

Giant pools of water filled with broken glass.

A woman cut in two through the shoulders.

Then: Lana Cohen standing over him saying, 'Easy now. Easy.'

Bruno is lost. 'Where am I?'

She helps him up. 'You're still at the station. You're in the meeting room. It's morning.'

'Is this the old Diablo homicide room?'

'Yeah. Come on, let's get you out of here.'

'I don't like it.'

'Yeah, I know,' she says, smiling. 'It's different

now.' But then Lana stops smiling and brings her face closer, her eyes studying his. 'I think you need something to eat.'


THEY'RE BACK at the building society by 8.30 am, for a proper walk-through with the Robbery Squad. The footpath outside the bank is taped off but there's people all around. Half the squad are still on shift. Their eyes track Bruno as he steps inside. He's the guy who met their prey. He's the guy who could have closed the case, but didn't.

The room smells of petrol and death. Moisture lingers.

Lana stays close. 'The bodies are gone,' she says.

Bruno looks at a taped-out silhouette on the ground. *Doreen*.

Pete Reynolds breaks off from the others and comes over. He nods at Lana, studies Bruno. 'There's a lot here,' he says. 'How are you doing? You okay?'

'I'm okay.' Bruno momentarily flashes back to their last conversation. Reynolds griping in the carpark about the missing O'Grady family. It's light-years away now, like it happened last year or the year before.

'You feel like leading us through it again?' says Reynolds.

Bruno starts at the start. They go to the bank manager's water-logged office where he tells them about the meeting. He reads the notes from his notepad. 'Someone was making strange withdrawals from the O'Gradys' account. I was following up.'

'I'll come back to that,' says Reynolds.

They step out into the hall.

'Alfred Simmons,' says Lana, standing over the outline's feet. 'Your bank manager, yeah?'

Bruno nods. The wall beside the outline tells the story: shotgun wound to the head, close range. 'I saw it happen.'

'You remember what was said?'

'They were looking for something and Simmons didn't have it.'

Bruno details the rest, feeling bloodless and disembodied as he speaks. He tells them where everyone was standing, how they were dressed, and then how the fight went down. 'I shot one of them, twice I think, but he kept moving.'

'They were wearing vests,' says Lana. 'Ex-military stuff.'

Reynolds shows Bruno a polaroid of a bloody, water-soaked bullet-proof vest. The dead bank robber's hand is in the frame. 'You actually got a shot into him, but it wasn't enough to put him all the way down. That's how you two ended up in this tussle over the shotgun.' Reynolds gives an exasperated wave towards one of the outlines on the floor. A spray of black blood fans out from the outline's head. 'It's a shitshow. No face, no ID. Prints could take weeks.'

'It would've been great if he robbed the place with his wallet in his pocket,' says Lana.

'It would be something,' grumbles Reynolds, in no mood.

They move to Doreen's outline.

'This is the part I don't get,' says Reynolds. 'Why shoot this poor bird? You sure she didn't just cop it in the crossfire somehow?'

Bruno's surprised to find himself quite sure. A lot of the memories are blurry, but he can recall the choreography of it. 'After they shot Simmons, she burst out of somewhere and took off.'

Lana points at a nook between the rear counter and a large mailbag. 'From there?'

Bruno nods. 'I guess.'

'And she runs out there,' says Reynolds. 'And around here and then, as she's fleeing across the room, the guy opens up on her with the shotgun? Same guy as the manager, right?'

'That's right. The one who shot Simmons shot her.'

Reynolds steps it out, holding up an invisible gun. He tracks across the room to where Lana is standing. 'I dunno. He's a violent bugger, this bloke. Could be anything, I guess.'

Lana looks at the scene and says, 'His blood's up. She's running. He panics and shoots her just because she's moving when he's told them not to.'

'It fucking fits, unfortunately.' Reynolds rubs his temples. 'He didn't say her name or anything, did he?'

Bruno shakes his head.

'Okay. Lana, leave him with me. Go find Webber. He's bloody taking his time with the cars. I want their way in and out locked down before any of us go off shift, okay?'

She touches Bruno's arm on the way out.

'Come with me,' says Reynolds.

DOWN UNDER THE BANK, there's a room filled with safe deposit boxes. It's not dank or musty. The place is done up for clients, with a polished timber floor and recessed lighting. The handles on each safe box have a gold finish. In the centre of the room, there's a plain table and two antique chairs. As

Reynolds and Bruno come in, two SIB men stop what they're doing. Reynolds waves them out. He waits in silence as they go.

'See this,' Reynolds says, watching the stair. One box is missing. Reynolds scratches at his neck. 'What I'm about to tell you is highly confidential. It can't leave this room. These recent robberies, this sort of stuff is what they're all about. We're not dealing with a regular smash and grab wrecking crew. They're not desperate junkies. They don't take the money off the tellers. They go for stuff like this. High value, precise. It's all targeted. They know exactly what they're pinching.'

'What did they get from here?'

'Dunno. Waiting on a warrant to open it. They're bloody smart enough to close the boxes after them, so we don't know what the scores are.'

'Jesus. And the bodies?'

'Very similar to what you saw last night. They shoot people without hesitation, but it's always like an execution. These blokes are killing specific people, by the look of it, and they know a lot about what they're doing. They get in, they get out, they kill key witnesses, they don't take any risks.'

'That explains the vests. Why are you telling me this?'

Reynolds points at the empty slot on the wall. 'Because you were here, and I know you're working this other thing about the missing family. This is their box. Do you have some information you'd like to share with me?'

'I don't suppose you've found the O'Gradys' son yet?'

'I made some calls. No one has seen him.'

'He's dead, I reckon. I think they're all dead.'

Bruno stares into the wall of safe deposit boxes and finds some small, untapped reserve of determination. He straightens up. 'I've got some leads, but if you want in on my case, you need to work the thing with me. Otherwise, you can go back to chasing your own tail down here.'

Reynolds can't believe what he's hearing. 'Mate, this is serious. I've got three dead people upstairs and one in intensive care. If you have information, you need to disclose it.'

But it's not like that.

Reynolds is dirty. To the boys in on the Joke, everything they do is above board. There's no *real* corruption. It's all harmless. All their secrets and windfalls. But when the proper police work needs doing, everyone outside their little system is supposed to just wade into their swamp without caution.

'Do you remember what you told me, Pete? You told me to make this go away as quickly as possible, and now you've got three dead upstairs and one in intensive care.'

'Yeah, well, that was yesterday. This is today.'

'Sure. Are you in or out?'

'Do you really have something that might help me?'

'I have the start of something.'

'What do you need in return?'

'Right now? A ride to Brisbane.'

'Oh fuck off. Really?'

'I need to go to the airport, but I'm in no state to drive. I'll tell you the rest on the way.'

# AMY

## Beach Road, Surfers Paradise

AMY OWENS COMES AWAKE SLOWLY, like she's being dredged up from the bottom of a lake. She finds herself on her living room couch. Clothes sweated through. The TV playing.

She gives it a minute before moving.

Lights a smoke, hands on autopilot.

Amy pushes herself upright and an icy wave of fear jolts along her nape. Someone's in the room. She feels it before she sees it: a man in her deckchair by the balcony doors. He has a paperback open on his lap.

'Who the fuck?' she hisses, hand fumbling for her handbag.

'Oh, you're up.'

She knows the voice.

Mr Sally. The shonky locksmith she called yesterday.

'I let myself in,' he says. 'I thought you'd have better locks, doing what you do. With what you have over there, you may as well leave the door open.'

She rubs at her face. 'What are you doing in here?'

Mr Sally shrugs. 'You called, so here I am.'

'Okay, give me a second.' Amy goes to the kitchen and pours herself a glass of water from the tap. It's warm as tea. 'We could have done this over the phone. I need you to open a safe.'

'Is it here?'

'Is what here?'

'The safe.'

'It's too early for this.' Amy grabs her handbag off the couch. She withdraws the polaroid of Bill Webber's garage set-up. 'Here.'

Mr Sally glances at the image. 'What's the budget?'

'Colleen Vinton's eternal gratitude.'

'What's that worth?'

'Let me find out.' Amy calls around for Colleen and gets her on the third try. Before Amy can get a word in, Colleen quizzes her on the other job: Allan Watts. *What's Allan up to? What's his game?* Amy stalls. 'Give me another day.' Then she tells Colleen about Mr Sally and his haggling.

'He wants *what*?' says Colleen. 'Put that fucking nonce on the phone.'

Mr Sally takes the receiver and listens. His facial expression remains unnaturally still, like he's hearing hold music. When it's done, he replaces the phone and says, 'I'm at your disposal, it seems.'

This scares the shit out of Amy. Only a psycho would react to Colleen Vinton like this. Amy gives him Bill Webber's address. 'He's a cop, so don't take any chances.'

'Great,' says Mr Sally, with a yawn.

'Can you get out of my apartment now?'

'With pleasure.'

. . .

AN HOUR LATER, Amy is out the door too, on her way to find Allan Watts. He has a place on the river, down where the Strip tapers off into monied suburbia. The glare outside is pure, white hell, but otherwise the day is mild. On the walk across town, Amy stops at a restaurant for coffee and strikes gold. There he is: Allan having brunch with a girlfriend. They have a small, grey dog with them, sitting at the table in its own seat. Amy watches them eat. They don't really talk to each other much. It's quite a scene, actually. The girlfriend tenderly feeds her dog from a separate fork. Allan smiles when looked to, but otherwise sits there sullen and tired, obviously recovering from his big night at the Silver Fish hosting the police commissioner and his cronies. After a while, Allan gives the dog a pat and turns a cheek to the girl, then darts out. Amy follows.

Allan runs errands. A stop at a real estate agency. Flirting with the local florist, placing an order. Picking up fancy booze from the bottle shop. He checks in on the Silver Fish.

From there, Allan heads to another restaurant where there's a party waiting. Allan plies his trade, glad-handing the group, calling in waiters and drinks. Amy watches him take a call at the bar. He hands the phone back to the bartender and orders a shot.

Something's up.

He's flustered now.

No goodbyes to the party, just out the back door, down a service alley and into a side street where a car is waiting. He disappears inside and the car takes off.

Still standing there cursing, Amy catches a break. A cab comes around the corner. She hails it. 'Follow that silver Falcon at the lights.'

'For real?' says the driver, but he's clearly into it.

'I'll pay you double if you can do it,' Amy says.

ALLAN'S CAR puts him out at a grimy workman's pub down in Miami. It's absolutely not his sort of place, but he disappears inside without hesitation. It takes Amy a couple of minutes to find him in the crowded interior and when she does, he's with a fair-headed man. The man is younger, dressed in footy shorts and a chambray shirt, sleeves rolled to the elbows. Whatever this meeting is about, it's not going according to plan. Allan motions about with his hands, clearly frustrated. From her spot across the room, Amy snaps off quick photos with her 'tourist camera', a thin black Kodak Ektralite. She walks closer to them, trying to listen in, but they've got the Commonwealth Games blaring on the TV.

Allan is pointing at the man, beet-red in the face.

The other guy shrugs.

A steak is delivered to the table, and the man takes it, but as he's readying to eat, he does something truly strange: he shoos Allan Watts away. Just shoos him with his fork hand, like Allan is an annoying mosquito.

Weirder still, it works. Allan storms off.

From a front window, Amy watches him jog back across the street to his waiting car. They tear off.

There's no cab waiting this time. Amy goes back to the dining area and the other man is gone.

His meal is sitting there, half-eaten.

# MIKE

## Coolangatta

MIKE SITS IN THE God Minister's living room and waits for him to finish his lunch. Mike broils in the eerie domestic strangeness of it all. There's a glass coffee table covered with documents. Two armchairs matched to the couch's maroon velour. A fancy gold clock under a glass dome. The place is painfully quiet, and he can hear the minister in the adjoining room, talking on the phone as he pushes a knife around on the chinaware.

Mike has nothing to distract him from his thoughts.

Crashing the party last night was sloppy.

People know his face.

People know his name, probably.

Bad people.

The worst kind.

At least no one can touch him up here.

The housekeeper snaps him out of it. 'Would you like some more tea while you wait?'

'I'm good.'

He nearly got himself killed. Shot at by Christ-knows-who at the estate of a crooked copper. The deputy commissioner, no less. And then there's the bunker and the callboy Jamie and all the rest of it.

The police files.

Piles and piles of files.

Mike reaches into his pocket and retrieves the one piece he could snatch up: the page of foolscap paper listing names and dates and numbers. He runs down the list and shudders for the tenth time. He knows more than a few of these names.

Lawyers and judges.

Media people.

Financiers.

Trouble.

*Deep shit.*

Ten minutes later, the minister slowly hobbles out. His crutches look ready to snap under his bulk. He's so wide and tall, he takes up two seats on an aeroplane apparently. 'Mike. I didn't know we had something booked for today.'

'We don't. It's an emergency.'

'I see.'

He doesn't sit.

Mike comes forward on the couch and looks up at him. 'I've been doing what you asked and . . .'

'Yes?'

Mike tells him everything. Everything except the page with the names.

The minister takes it all in without comment. His eyes widen, briefly, at the mention of Deputy Commissioner Sorensen's secret filing room, but the rest washes over him. It's all just information.

'I'm worried,' says Mike.

'Why, son?'

'They're cops.'

'I'm the Minister of Police. They answer to me.'

'Do they?'

'Of course they do. Just carry on with the Fantasy-land job. If the hold-up with the park is purely money-related, and it sounds like it is, well, I can step in, I guess, but . . .'

'What is it, sir?'

'I'd have thought a man as resourceful as you might have his own ideas. Whatever upside you take from this is all yours for the keeping. Do as you please with the details. I just want the thing to open on time.'

'Uh, okay . . . okay,' says Mike, and the words are coming out, but it's just sound in among the other noise in his head.


MIKE STUMBLES BACK down the hill. He walks along the cliffs by the ocean and tries to let the vast open vista calm his nerves. It doesn't work. In fact, the contrast just drives the point in even harder. *This is bad. This is unnatural. This is going wrong. Turn back.* But some spark deep inside him fires to life. It suddenly seems obvious what to do next: *keep moving, stay alive. Win.*

Back in his motel room, he throws together his stuff.

Unsure of when he'll get another chance to call home, he picks up the phone.

His wife, Sonya, answers.

'Can I talk to them?'

Without a single word, she puts his son on the line. 'Dad?'

'Hey, buddy.'

'What's going on?'

Mike covers his eyes, breathes through it. 'Nothing much. Just wanted to say hello. What are you doing?'

'Watching TV.'

'What is it?'

'The cartoons,' and his son tells him the station.

Mike turns on the TV in his room so they can watch it together. 'Who's that?'

'He-Man. Watch this.'

He-Man zaps his cat with a sword and turns it into a giant green beast.

'Not bad,' says Mike.

The cartoon show segues back to the host, a feral-looking puppet, like something you'd find in a bin. The puppet announces a guest.

Mike misses the name, but his son shouts, 'Yes!'

A man in a police uniform appears on the screen. He sits down beside the puppet. There's an overlay of text: *Constable Chris*. The policeman smiles out at the kids watching and Mike feels nothing but pure and complete terror.

It's Chris from Sorensen's party.

The man who grabbed him.

On the screen, Constable Chris is telling everyone about bike safety. He's strapping on a helmet and the fucking puppet is strapping on a helmet, too.

'Turn it off,' yelps Mike.

'What? No.'

He screams, 'Turn it off!'

His kid is crying.

He hears his wife moving around, flustered in the background.

Mike stares into the haze of the screen and feels the world tilt.

# BRUNO

## Pacific Highway, Beenleigh

BRUNO SLEEPS THE FIRST twenty minutes of the drive to Brisbane. He stirs as they cross the Logan River. As soon as Reynolds notices he's awake, he says, 'You ready to explain yourself?' The man sits hunched over the wheel, wound up like a rubber band.

Bruno reaches for his workbook. 'Give me a sec. What's with this traffic?'

'The Games,' says Reynolds. 'Everyone's going to the Games.'

Bruno turns pages, forces his head clear. 'Someone was making unauthorised withdrawals from Phillip O'Grady's bank account. That's why I was at the branch yesterday. I found a handwritten note in the O'Gradys' mail from the manager who was shot in the robbery, Al Simmons. Simmons had noticed irregular outgoings and let Phillip know.'

'And what did Al have to say for himself yesterday?'

'Not much. That someone had Phillip's ATM card and was using it without him knowing.'

'Sounds like the son,' says Reynolds.

'Definitely an option.'

'Is that it?'

'Does your bank manager send you personal notes?'

Reynolds rolls his shoulders. 'No. Don't think I've ever met my bank manager. But then again, I'm not a rich cunt like this O'Grady guy. You think Simmons and O'Grady were into something together?'

'Simmons knew the O'Gradys were away. He's checking their financials personally. And now he's dead, executed by your robbery crew because he wouldn't hand something over. Meanwhile, the O'Gradys are missing.'

'Okay. That's certainly not nothing. Why are we headed to the airport? We checking flight manifests?'

'Nah. Phillip O'Grady had a package held up at customs. Figured we'd take a look.'

The traffic slows. They crest a hill and see a line of cars snaking out.

Reynolds curses under his breath. 'Why do you need me for this? We could have sent a uniform to do it.'

'You wanted in, you're in.'

Reynolds keeps his eyes on the road.

'You really want to know?' Bruno touches the wound on his head. 'Your lot are involved in this, I reckon. That's why you were assigned in the first place. I just want to solve the thing, but . . .'

'What?'

'It's getting messy and I don't want to end up transferred to Cunnamulla when it's over.'

Reynolds keeps driving. No comment.

Two minutes later he says, 'Cunnamulla's not so bad.'

'You reckon?'

'There are worse places.'



THE BUREAU OF CUSTOMS initially gives them the runaround. There's talk of sending them to the city office, but then calls are put through to various managers before a woman in a Federal Police uniform looks at Bruno's ID card and Phillip O'Grady's notice, and nods her head. The Fed brings them out back to a garage area where a baggage handler and a motorised cart are waiting. The handler takes them across the steamy black tarmac to a large white shed on the periphery of the airport grounds. There, he guides them through an unmarked door into a shabby foyer with a flimsy counter and cheap pale plasterboard walls. It looks like a film set. There's an open ceiling exposing the steelwork of the shed's roof. The corrugation above cracks and plinks under the heat outside.

There's a bell on the counter. Reynolds gives it a light tap.

A customs agent in a Hawaiian shirt appears.

Reynolds dead-eyes him. 'Is it casual Friday?'

The agent doesn't answer. He just glances at them blankly. 'What is it?'

Bruno shows the man Phillip O'Grady's notice and puts his police ID card down alongside it.

The man reads the notice and slides it back.

'We want to have a look at the seized material,' says Reynolds.

'All right then.' The agent leads them out of the pretend foyer and into the shed proper, which is about half the size of a football field. As they walk through, they pass rows of shelving, each containing numbered cardboard boxes. The agent doesn't check the aisle markings. He just strolls along, all-knowing.

'You familiar with this case?' says Reynolds.

'Chapman handled it,' says the man, as if that means something. 'Down here.'

'Is this all seized material?' asks Bruno.

The agent laughs. 'Welcome to Queensland, mate. Fun is outlawed, remember?'

The agent selects a box dated *5 September 1982* and points to a demountable office parked against the warehouse's far wall. 'I'll leave you to it,' he says, and walks away.

'What do you reckon?' says Bruno.

Reynolds looks around the warehouse like the answer might be posted somewhere. 'I don't know.'

The whole thing feels off, but they take the box to the demountable. The office is light on furnishings, just a card table, two folding chairs, and a bench along one wall. The bench contains a television and a VCR, a film projector and a few bits of kit that neither of them recognise.

Reynolds plants the box on the table and opens it. 'Videotapes,' he says. 'Do you know how to work that thing?'

'I've seen it done.'

Bruno turns one of the tapes in his hands. No label or case. He takes it to the VCR machine and slips it into the slot, then turns the TV on. The screen pops and fizzles to life. Bruno presses the glowing green button on the VCR and stands back to watch.

*A man in a brown business suit makes his way through the gate of a suburban house. Plenty of yard and garden. The front door opens and a couple invite him in. The three of them are good-looking. Not quite movie stars but in shape, young, presentable. They talk in German.*

'Can you fast-forward this shit?' says Reynolds.

*They race through the rest of the conversation. Lots of smiling and laughing in the blur. The Germans stand up and their clothes fly off. The guest and the woman start fucking, with the man watching on. Then it's the man and the woman with the guest watching, occasionally reaching in. Then it's both men at different ends of the woman.*

'Crikey,' says Reynolds. 'You don't see that every day.'

'Yeah,' says Bruno, wiping sweat from his neck.

*The threesome go at it in different rooms, a flickering montage of obscene positions. They walk through the house, nude bodies on the carpet, hands holding hands, through a door and down a stair into the basement. There's a brace down there, a full-sized wooden cross. The guest is strapped to it and lashed with a black leather whip.*

Reynolds peers at the screen. 'Now we're talking.'

*They let the guest down and the man cradles him, soothes him. It turns into more than that. The two men lock mouths. Their hands searching each other out as the camera zooms in close.*

At this exact spot, the VCR clips back into regular speed. Sound fills the room. The two detectives watch the men go at it in real-time, too shocked to move.

Reynolds starts shaking his head. 'Bloody hell,' he says. 'Can you turn that off?' There's real fear in his voice.

'Sorry, sorry.'

The screen snaps to black.

Still flustered, Reynolds turns to the box and

looks at the other tapes. There's two more. He hands one to Bruno without a word.

They only watch snippets of it.

It's the same actor, similar terrain.

But different too: mixed couples, more fetishes.

A little bit of lesbian stuff.

*Plenty* of men fucking men.

A lot.

'I feel crook,' says Reynolds.

# AMY

## Beach Road, Surfers Paradise

AMY LIGHTS A SMOKE and inhales—thoughts firing, as she clenches and unclenches her hand—then exhales and thinks about her sister. One aspect of yesterday's conversation keeps repeating.

*'She doesn't like it when people pull on the leash, does she?'*

Hard to know what Angela's heard, but even if it's absolutely nothing, it still stings like a bastard. To know any of it and do nothing—to never mention it until now—is rough, even by the Owens family standard. Then again, Angela may have landed a surprise hit. They're both finely tuned to each other's tender spots. They both know how to inflict pain casually and calmly. Both schooled by the master, dear old Victor.

Amy can't let it go.

*Does everyone see me like this now?*

*Does everyone see me as my own sister sees me?*

A stronger, darker feeling lurks underneath. She wants a drink, but that's the problem talking. It's been years now of living and drinking and working in this cesspit. The weight of it has set in her like concrete, and yet somehow—through all the dirty work, all the stake-outs and surveillance shots of cheating husbands and troubled souls—through all *that*, Amy has learned the one fundamental thing about human nature: repetition is survival.

Beat by beat, hour by hour.

Stay in the moment, survive the day.

You have to ignore the tally, the history.

Forget it all, piece by piece.

One moment at a time.

Until . . .

You can't.

AMY CAME into Colleen Vinton's orbit from a long way out. She grew up posh: manicured gardens and housekeepers. A private school education. Victor was a monster, of course—the great vanquisher of mothers—but no one could accuse him of being cheap. He gave them luxury and money and expectations. In Amy's youth that stuff papered over a lot of cracks.

Amy and her siblings also had each other. A strange collection of people. Will was the oldest, the one who looked after the others. Angela, the big sister. Both of them from a different father, orphaned by their mother in Amy's house, and tolerated by Victor for reasons forever unknown to any of them. A desire for control, probably, for keeping up appearances. As ramshackle as the Owens family was, it held together like superglue. Until . . .

1964: Will goes to Vietnam. Signed up to get away from Victor.

Six months later: Angela disappears into a journalism cadetship.

Amy toughed it out alone with Victor till '66. Straight from the mansion to the dormitory, living at the University of Queensland in Brisbane. It was a deep dive into student politics, free-form fucking, pot smoking, booze and zero oversight. By some miracle, she stayed steady. Two years of good grades. A major in Photography, because *fuck the old man and his business brain*. Those undergraduate years were the best of her life. Amy had an eye for it. A calling, as one of her lecturers said. She was free to pursue it. And for a long time, Amy liked the way the world looked through the lens of a camera.

Then, like a clock resetting, Will came home from the war. Honourable discharge. Erratic, unwell, with an arm that didn't work. Worse still, he was completely fucked in the head. A shell of what was there before. Will could barely operate. He couldn't fend off Victor like he used to.

Amy started going home on weekends to see him.

Her grades started declining.

Will sweated through the night, whispering to ghosts.

Angela flitted in and out, called more than visited.

Victor lurked. Working in the other wing of the house. Busy. Always busy. He had an empire to found and remake. Land to reclaim from the sea. Victor helped build the Gold Coast. He and his cronies raised the Strip.

None of it helped Will, though. Money and connections couldn't fix him.

Nothing could fix him.

No one.

Finally: one cold Saturday night at home on the

coast, things didn't feel right. Amy got out of bed, padded through the halls.

*Just a feeling. A weird sense of disorder.*

Will wasn't in his bed.

Not in his bathroom or the living room.

She yelled out.

No answer.

Where is he?

*Where . . .*

He was in the kitchen, covered in blood. Stabbed himself a dozen times with his good arm.

He's dying when she touches him.

Dead before she can get to the phone.

'It's a bad way to go,' is how the detective put it, afterwards. 'Takes a lot of determination to go out like that.'

Victor had nothing to add. Just sneering disgust.

A week later, drunk off her face on the night of the funeral, Angela took little-sister Amy to the jet-black centre of it all. 'Will told me once that Victor used to goad him when it was just the two of them. He told me Victor said only a coward would keep on living in the state he was in. He said, *Dad wants me to die now*.'

It was true. Amy didn't need to ask or investigate.

It was exactly Victor. He was pathologically opposed to weakness. That pathology had defined their entire lives. It created the void they grew up in. Their mothers were weak creatures too, you see.

*Forget it.*

*Beat by beat.*

AMY HITS HER APARTMENT. Paces and thinks.

There's work to be done. She calls around looking for Mr Sally and gets him at home. 'How'd you go?'

Mr Sally doesn't answer, but she can hear him moving around on the line.

'You there?'

His breath in the receiver. 'Twenty, fifteen, eighteen, fourteen, five, twenty-five. I've reset the chamber, so start by turning the dial anti-clockwise to that first number.'

The combination to Bill Webber's home safe.

'Thanks. What's in there?'

'I didn't look,' says Mr Sally.

'That's the correct answer.'

'Am I free to go now?'

'You need to take that idea out of your mind.'

He hangs up.

Amy gets back on the line and calls Dirty Doug, her records guy. He's much happier to talk to her because Colleen has already paid him. Dirty Doug is absolutely the last guy in Queensland you want to short-change. He's the orb of all knowledge. He can be trusted to fuck you back if you cannot hold up your end.

'What's Colleen's money getting me, Doug?'

Doug reads his notes in a monotone drawl. 'Detective Bill Webber is about as clean as they come. No complaints, good credit, not a piece of dirt on him. He's a capable officer who spent his entire career away

from the Joke. Hard to even put him beside it, actually, except for his stint on Strike Force Diablo back in '80, but there were a lot of regular cops working that thing. He's assigned to the Robbery Squad these days. Were you looking for something in particular?'

'I was looking for anything at all.'

'He's an orphan. Parents died in a botched home invasion.'

'Boys' homes?'

'No. He was taken in by a neighbour. Nothing sinister there. Good grades. Went into policing early. Cadetship. I can keep digging?'

'Nah, I think I'm good. What about the other bloke?' She means Webber's victim from Cedar Creek.

'Wally Stewart. A former nightclub promoter from down your way. Bankrupt now. Didn't have five dollars to his name when he passed. I know a copper looking at his case, so I know that your bloke was beaten half to death, then had a seizure of some kind. No criminal record, but he's not all the way clean. Lots of gossip and shit-talking. Liked them young, apparently. Never married, no kids. There's dropped solicitation charges from back in '78. He and some bloke called Christopher Cole nearly went down together, but it got thrown out.'

'You wouldn't know who blew the case would you?'

He does, of course. 'Mark Evans and Ron Bingham were the arresting officers.'

*Christ.*

*Evans was on the leash with Colleen. Dead now.*

*Bingham's the CIB Head and known to be dirty. A big spender in some of Colleen's joints.*

'So, Wally's a perv?'

'I'd say so. Has all the hallmarks of it.'

Amy hangs up.

*Why is a straight cop playing vigilante?*

But she knows the answer. It's why she's been put on Webber from the start.

## THE DREAM

The stolen files.
And because Colleen has something to lose.
It's always the same with her.
It always circles back.

# MIKE
## Fantasyland, Gold Coast

MIKE SNORTS A LINE in his rental car, parked in the gravel carpark off the highway. Fantasyland sits in the distance. What he's about to do is a leap, but his mind is screaming, *make something happen, make anything happen.* He stares into his own eyes via the rear-view mirror and feels a momentary return to form. He dusts his nose and gets going.

The Fantasyland entryway is finished—a pastel Disneyland rip-off—but it cuts a strange visage, too. Like a pink fence line separating the construction site from commuter traffic and the surrounding scrub. Beyond, Mike can see half a roller-coaster in progress and the fibreglass mountain from the other night. There are little clusters of scaffolding and motley powerlines. With night approaching, the place gives off an eerie energy. The workers are gone. It's quiet. Just the echo of galah call and the distant drone of highway traffic and earth-moving equipment.

There's no guard on the gate, so Mike slips through an open piece of the fencing. With no idea where he's headed, he takes an unexpected tour, traversing laneways of poured concrete rendered as cobblestone. Eventually, the cobblestones give way to dirt and mud. Out the back of the site, he spots a lighting rig with two figures standing under the harsh beam. It's Buddy Winters and his female assistant. Mike recognises her from the party the other night. She's incredibly tall. Almost a foot on Buddy, who is built like a country hick.

'Evening,' Mike calls out.

Buddy and the assistant jolt and peer into the shadows.

The assistant immediately puts a hand out. 'Who's that?' she says.

Shielding his eyes, Mike steps out. 'Mike Nichols. We met at the Playroom the other day.'

Buddy whispers to the assistant.

The assistant says, 'You need to make an appointment.'

'The God Minister doesn't do appointments and that's who sent me.'

They both stand there and study him.

Gears crunch somewhere close by. An engine roars into high gear.

Buddy shouts over the noise, 'What do you want?'

'Ten minutes.'

'You can have five.'

Buddy insists on walking and talking. They traipse along an earth wall running the length of the canal. On the other side, under more spotlights, is Noah Winters. The old man is working an excavator back and forth, digging out his canal, as reported. It looks dangerous, like the whole set-up is about to go into the drink.

'As you can see,' says Buddy, 'your political manoeuvring has done absolutely fuck-all to slow my father's DIY project. All you've done is put him on night shift. The engineers are telling me that if he continues at this pace, it'll be three years before the bloody thing is ready.'

Mike struggles to keep pace with Buddy. The man has long farmhand legs. 'How does he have such a stranglehold on this? Don't you have investors?'

'Dad's bigger than the investors. He doesn't have to answer to anyone, not when push comes to shove.'

They come down off the wall and follow a paved line into a maze of palm tree plantings. Mike is sweating, breathing faster than he'd like. 'You know, all over town, everyone's telling me that the real problem is money, not your dad's hole in the ground.'

'Same difference.'

'I don't get it.'

'Dad's the majority stakeholder and while that's in play, the contracts are all in his favour. His lawyer is an evil little prick.'

'I still don't get it.'

The assistant walking ahead of them forces out an angry sigh. She looks at her watch. 'Mister Winters is not legally obligated to open the park until it's completed to his satisfaction,' she says.

'Dad has never been satisfied a day in his life,' says Buddy. 'So, if the minister wants to speed things up, he needs to buy into this in a *big* way, and then swing his weight around.'

'How? I don't figure your dad's selling up anytime soon.'

'There's a piece for sale. And once he's legally outnumbered, which is possible, people can intervene on his behalf. But the way it is, I can't control him.'

They're at the rear of the park now, a long stretch of cleared land. Mike spots a set of lit windows in the distance. Talk is, the Winters family have owned this land for decades and Mike figures the lights are the family pad. Buddy leads him to a long steel gate and stands over it, a foot hooked on the gate's iron rail. 'Jenny?' he says.

The assistant answers.

'Piss off for a sec, will ya?'

The assistant wanders off into the grasslands in heels.

Buddy spits in the mud. 'I need five million up-front and twenty-five points on the back end. That's the sort of buy-in that changes all this. Thing is, Mike, no one has it in this recession. You're here now. You've snuck in, cornered me in this dark field, so that's your straight answer, okay? If the minister really wants this joint to open on time, he needs to cough up five mil and twenty-five points.'

Mike forces himself to pause.

There's something else.

Why send the assistant packing?

*Push him.*

'Buddy, I'm not a business guy. What are we buying and selling here?'

'My stake in it. I want out. You buy me out and the other investors will come across, I guarantee it. They trust me, not Dad. Dad's been cooked for a while now. My father will have to listen if you buy me out, or he'll end up in court, and trust me, once you get that excavator out of his hands, he'll go to pieces. So, you buy me out and wham-o, you can open the park next year.'

'That's a lot of money to fix one old man who can't get his shit together.'

'You'll meet him one day and you'll see what he's like.'

'I reckon I can help.'

Buddy shrugs. 'Even crooked men can't do much when the money runs out.'

Mike looks out at the rising moon.

He feels the fear creeping back in.

It's too dark all of a sudden.

'It has to open,' he says.

Buddy takes a set of keys from his pocket and says, 'If you can walk on water, Mike, now's the time.'

# BRUNO
## Pacific Highway, Ormeau

BRUNO CAN BARELY KEEP his eyes open on the ride home to the coast. Pete Reynolds is back behind the wheel, chain-smoking from his second pack for the day. They're both talked out.

After the airport, the two of them spent the afternoon pushing shit uphill. They worked out of the Brisbane office, checking records up there and following wafer-thin hunches. They called extended O'Grady family and friends in the city. They reached out and kept reaching out, and found nothing, all the way down. To cap it off, the crime scene bloodwork from the O'Grady house came in and, to Bruno's eyes, at least, it was a confirmation: the blood type found at the scene was a suitable match for Phillip, Samson or Marion.

They're dead.

And now Bruno has found himself partnered with crooked Pete Reynolds on a triple homicide with no leads.

'You awake?' grunts Reynolds in the car.

'I don't know.'

'Back at the shed, with Customs, something happened.'

The interior of the car goes stone still.

'Go on,' says Bruno.

'You went to the bathroom after we were done with the videos, and I took them back to that bloke who worked there. He told me to talk to Sorensen.'

'About what?'

'Didn't say. Just, *you need to talk to Sorensen.*'

'And what does that mean?'

'It means what you think it means. The deputy commissioner is watching, meaning there are cops involved in this somewhere. Don't jump to any conclusions. Phillip O'Grady was a magistrate, so we're already in the mix a little. It might be a PR thing. I thought you should know.'

'Thanks. What do we do about it?'

'I've got some people I can talk to, just to make sure we're not about to blow ourselves up.'

'Okay.'

Silence in the car for a minute. The dark highway in the headlights.

'Can I ask you something?' says Bruno.

Reynolds looks over. 'Probably not.'

'How'd you end up in this mess?'

'Come off it.'

'No, I'm serious.'

'What's your worst secret, Bruno?'

'Pass.'

'There you go.' Reynolds pushes the cigarette lighter into the dash. 'You reckon O'Grady's wife knew he was a closet case? I've seen plenty, but those videos were really something.'

'He wouldn't be the first bloke like that who's married with kids.'

'You married?'

Bruno almost laughs. 'No. Not me, mate. You?'

'No. Came close once or twice, but . . .'

The cigarette lighter pops. Reynolds grabs it, dabs the red-hot coil to a fresh smoke. After a few seconds, he notices Bruno waiting for the rest of the story and waves it off. 'It was a long time ago,' he says. 'Before all this.'

AT HOME, Bruno scoops the cat up from his front stair and carries it inside. This is their father's name-less cat. Bruno likes the thing, but the cat isn't too fond of him in return.

'Jeez, what happened to you?' calls a familiar voice. His brother Danny stands across the room in a pair of blue undies. He has a frying pan full of sausages in one hand and a plastic spatula in the other.

It takes Bruno a few seconds to clock it: the bank robbery, his head, the bandages. 'Just some shit at work. I'm fine.'

'You don't look fine. The news said there was another hold-up on the Strip. Was that—'

'I was there.'

'You better sit down.'

Danny fetches him a beer and fixes the rest of dinner.

The kid's a lousy cook, but the food helps. The beer helps more.

After dinner, Bruno lies down and falls asleep within seconds.

HE WAKES in the dark living room, drags himself off the couch and drinks from the kitchen tap. Touching his side, Bruno realises his gun is missing. Panicking, he paces back to the couch, finding it between two cushions. Must've unlatched the holster in his sleep. *What the hell?* He takes the gun to his room and puts it in the safe in the closet. Before he closes the door, he rests a hand on the weapon, reassuring himself it's there.

Reminding and promising himself.

Then Bruno takes off his shirt and looks out the bedroom window. The yard light is on for some reason and it takes a moment to spot Danny out there, sitting on a folding chair with the cat in his lap.

Bruno takes himself down. 'What time is it?'

'Late, I think,' says Danny.

'You all right?'

'Yeah, I'm good.'

There's another camp chair leaning against the Hills hoist. Bruno snaps it open and sits.

Danny says, 'I can't get over your head. You could've died, right?'

'You could've died driving home this afternoon. It's nothing.'

'Jeez, you're a fuckhead sometimes. No offence.'

'None taken, and you should be nicer to me. I almost died today.'

'Why did you sign on for this?'

'For what? The police?' Bruno thinks on it. 'I just wanted a proper job. I worked at the Food Barn, remember?'

'That's right. Jeez, how'd I forget that?'

'It was a long time ago. You thinking about a career change?'

'I am, actually. I don't want to piss away the money Dad left us. We talked a bit about it before he died, you know.'

'What did he say?'

Their father never approved of Bruno's line of work. As a first-generation immigrant, he didn't trust the police.

'Dad told me I should go to uni.'

'To do what?'

'Business.'

'Bloody hell.'

'I know, I know. But it might be okay.'

'You reckon? It doesn't sound like you. You've gotta live your life, mate. I think Dad would've wanted you to be happy, first and foremost.'

'I seem to remember him wanting us to be rich and married, first and foremost.'

'That's true.'

'And now look at us,' Danny says, laughing.

'Could be worse.'

It hits him then. Bruno feels it down in the marrow of his bones. Jokes aside, he *could* be dead right now. Almost was. An inch to the left and whatever grazed his head would have put him in the morgue. *And then what?* He eats the emotion. There's no point sharing it. Instead, Bruno says, 'I'm looking for this missing family at work and I can't stop thinking about it. It's taking me into some shady places.'

'You gonna find them?'

'No. I think they're dead.'

'So, you've gotta catch the people who did it?'

'That's right.'

'I thought you were out of Homicide.'

'I am. But no one seems too fussed that I'm working on this.'

'Sounds pretty shit to me,' says Danny. 'Maybe

you oughta come to business school as well. We can dorm together.'

'Christ, can you imagine?'

'It wouldn't be so bad.'

The cat plops off Danny's lap. The two brothers watch the thing tentatively sniff around the unmown lawn.

Danny says, 'I think our sister is right, mate. I think it's time we started cleaning out Dad's place. I think we need to get on with it.'

'Oh God, not this.'

'Sorry. I promised her I'd say something.' Danny gets up. 'Okay, I'm going back to bed.' He wanders across the yard and places one foot on the rear stair. 'You know . . .'

'What?'

'Nothing.'

'Nah, go on.'

'It wasn't your fault. I don't care what they fucking said.'

'I know,' says Bruno, pushing out a long breath. 'I know.'

Danny waits a few seconds, then starts up the stairs. At the top, he says, 'Come on. It'll be morning soon.'

# PART FIVE
# SATURDAY 2 OCTOBER
## 1982

# VICTOR

*A COUGH TURNS to flu and my descent hastens.
Despite the pills and syrups, some heightened under-
standing of the world remains vivid and clear. I ask
Elda, 'Am I dying?' and she doesn't answer.*

*I'm worried. I can admit that. I'm troubled by the
idea that I will pass with all this business left unfinished. The last project.*

*And where is my blanket?*

*The warmth of the sun?*

*This is the Gold Coast, goddamn it.*

*'Sir?' says Elda, appearing. She has her barrage of
pills and medicine.*

*I'm losing time.*

*If I'm awake, I'm alive.*

*If I'm alive, I have work to do.*

*But ...*

*The pills are the opposite of all that.*

*I look across the room and Elda has vanished.*

*The girl is there instead. The concubine.*

*'Where is he?' I scream and the girl smiles.*

'He's no one's son,' she says, clear as day. 'He's lost to all.'

I blink and she remains.

I blink again and she's gone.

Did I take my meds?

Sounds echo.

Locked doors opening. Unused trajectories. Forgotten passageways.

Familiar footsteps in hallways.

Like the patter of—

Oh no.

For all my power and might, I did not expect this. The one behind the door. Another woman. A daughter.

Not this.

Not now, but . . .

History fights its way to the surface. A signal bright and red, the glimmer of an answer, shining in the dying light.

Heir to the heir.

A way through.

I'm going to stop taking the medication.

# AMY

## Pacific Highway, Ormeau

AMY FOLLOWS BILL WEBBER at a distance. They're out on the highway, heading north, 3.30 am. She picked up his trail two hours back, coming out of the Surfers Paradise police station. Amy was expecting him to head home, but Webber came out of the carpark and walked around the block to a payphone. The moment she saw him in the booth, she knew something was up. The scene had an edge to it.

The rest is a repeat of his last mission.

Webber heads home for a change of clothes.

Grabs his sports bag.

The personal car.

Then back out onto the highway and into the night.

Webber takes the Gaven exit and brings his car into the undulating hill country behind the coast. He drives until he reaches a fancy estate: a two-storey house behind a tall brick fence.

Webber parks but leaves the car running.

He climbs the fence and disappears.

No following him this time. Too risky. Instead,

Amy pulls her car in close, snaps photos with the flash, getting Webber's licence plates and the gate and the postbox all in the same shot. Then she immediately kills her headlights and slowly reverses back down the road to a secluded spot.

She doesn't wait long.

Webber is back out in five minutes.

Running.

The interior lights of his car blink on.

Sports bag thrown in.

The engine fires and he pulls a fast U-turn.

Amy stays with him this time. Back down the Pacific Highway and into the coastal backstreets. She's surprised to see him steer away from his home. *Is it a second stop?* Webber pulls into a late-night servo in Palm Beach and eats a packet of chips. He refuels his car and heads north, past the Strip and up along the Esplanade. In Southport, he turns into the residential streets and snakes his way through to a dark place on Pohlman Drive.

Amy recognises the house.

It's the place she ran surveillance on only a week ago.

The house she photographed.

The photographs she gave to that cop.

*How does this fit together?*

The interior lights of Webber's car show him leaning over into the passenger seat, checking something. He steps out, slips down the side of the house.

Amy watches on, but nothing happens. She winds her window down and listens.

A quiet night on a quiet street.

A few minutes later, Webber reappears, but he's not in a hurry this time. He walks back to his car and drives away, bearing south through the suburbs rather than out onto the main drag.

But these are familiar roads, too.

A familiar vector.

*Don't be crazy*, she thinks.

But Webber keeps moving closer and closer to another place she knows.

The route becomes undeniable.

He turns onto Campbell Street, running down the centre of the Bundall canal estates, and moves along Freyburg Street.

*It's a coincidence.*

Webber indicates right at the next intersection.

Amy breathes out.

But then Webber turns left.

*No.*

Around onto the waterfront and along Marseille Court and from there it's a given, for Amy knows exactly where Webber is heading— knows it in her guts—and there he is, slowly checking street numbers, creeping along until his car pulls up in front of a particular mansion. Webber sits there waiting and watching, his car idling.

Amy is too close to him, but there's very little keeping her together. Her nerves are so fried she's shaking. Hands on the steering wheel, willing him, mentally pushing him to get out.

*Go on, you fuck.*

*Do it.*

*Get out and go inside.*

Webber steps out, walks up the drive of the house and looks around. He fusses with something near the gate.

He looks at the intercom keypad.

Checks the gate.

Then he walks back to his car and drives away.
Amy doesn't follow this time.
It's too much.
She stays in her car and huffs small breaths.
There are tears in her eyes.
A headache washing through.
*Fuck*.
This is the house of her father, Victor Owens.
Her childhood home.

# MIKE

## Mount Gravatt, Brisbane

BY MID-MORNING MIKE'S SO wired he can
barely keep his seatbelt on in the God Minister's limo.
He's in Brisbane. The minister's absent—resting his
broken leg, down on the border—and Mike is filling
in. The timing is fortuitous.

Up front, the driver pumps the brakes and curses.

'Steady on,' says Mike.

The car continues up the hill towards QEII
Stadium. Mike is counting down the minutes. He
needs some fresh air. Last night is a blur. After his
meeting with Buddy in Fantasyland, Mike followed
the highway to the city, figuring if money was the
problem, then money was the solution. Brisbane was
as good a place to look as any. He spent the night
touring the city's high-roller rooms, settling into a
late-late-night crawl of private members' clubs. Mike
kept to the elite spaces on purpose, staying within his
zone of influence, always within the shadow of the
minister. If Sorensen and the Joke boys caught up
with him, they wouldn't be able to do much in those

joints. Thankfully, they didn't find him. His presence would have been noted and circulated back, but for at least one night, Mike was ahead. He did his rounds, bought the drinks, pitched his offer, and then lost consciousness for a few hours in one of the Queensland Club's upstairs guestrooms.

Unfortunately, while Mike got away with it all, none of it worked. The city was bone-dry. Broke. The recession and the Games have everyone's money on lock. The best he could do was two million in promises.

Three million short.

AN HOUR LATER, Mike steps out into the bright hot midday sun. Around him, the Games stadium is packed full like a Roman colosseum. *The bogan version*. It's wall-to-wall families. Pissed-up dads and fly-bitten mums. A legion of shorts and ringer tees. Down on the field, some sort of foot race is underway and everyone's yelling like it's a league match.

'Get me out of here,' Mike says to the government aide beside him.

The aide leads him through to a private air-conditioned box full of pollies and businessmen. Mike takes one look around and thinks: *Here we go*. He cracks a tin of Games-edition XXXX Bitter and gets to work.

Small talk.

Slapped backs.

More of the same.

Horse-trading party gossip.

He hears a lot of stories about tightening the purse strings.

A lot of fuss over the cost of living.

Recession, recession, recession.

Christmas is cancelled.

But luckily, there's cattle money in the room. A group of young fuckheads from the west, spruced up in clean shirts and wide-brimmed hats. They're flush, thirsty and horny—Mike's speciality. He makes a few calls from the bar phone and that's all it takes. By lunchtime, he has another half-million for his Fantasyland kitty.

Thinking through his next victim, he takes a smoke break outside on a little balcony area adjacent to the private box. It's another lucky break, because out there he spots Constable Chris in the stadium below. Chris from the party. Mr *Steady-on-I'm-a-policeman*. The creep is making his way up to the private area, stopping only for autographs and handshakes. The kids love him.

*Time to go.*

Mike moves across the crowded members' box and into the corridor beyond. He pushes through the throng, putting distance in. The fear has him jazzed. He looks back.

Constable Chris is further down the crowded stadium walkway, catching up.

They lock eyes.

There's fifty people between them.

Chris smiles, pure scorn.

The crowd in the stadium roars. The sound of it echoes around the concrete, surging and reverberating.

*Australia wins gold!*

Mike backs away, shoves his way to the fire exit. He takes the stairs three at a time, hits the ground running and stays that way until he's out of the grounds and onto the street. He's still running when he passes a circle of police wagons on the road in front of the stadium. None of the cops give him any trouble. None of them even notice him.

# BRUNO

## Stationhouse, Surfers Paradise

BRUNO AND REYNOLDS GRIND through a morning of dead ends. No bodies, no murder weapon. Phillip O'Grady is a magistrate, a bloke with a thousand enemies. But no one jumps out. No family grievances (they call around), and no busted business deals. No money owed. Samson O'Grady—the sole child—is a private school kid. He teaches tennis for a living. An hour ago, Reynolds posted an APB for the family's missing car: a dark blue Holden Commodore. It's a Hail Mary because everyone is focused elsewhere. The bank heists have all the juice.

Out of ideas, Bruno and Reynolds sit in silence at Bruno's desk, reheating the paperwork.

They trawl through bank records.

They look at recent parolees that Phillip locked up.

Not much is said.

The detective branch secretary sidles up. 'Reynolds, you've got a call.'

He takes it over at his desk.

Reynolds comes back smiling. He pulls his chair

close. 'You're not going to believe this. The print work came in on the bloke you beheaded in the bank. There's a match.'

'You're fucking joking?'

'Nope. His name is Seth Blackwell. Ring any bells?'

It doesn't. The two detectives take the name to the records room. Blackwell has a file. Reynolds opens it up and scans the pages. 'There you go. Look.'

Seth Blackwell has an outstanding warrant and an aggravated assault charge dating back to '79. He beat a man unconscious in the carpark of the Beenleigh rum distillery.

'It's a start,' says Bruno.

SETH BLACKWELL LIVED with his grandmother in a timber-board house behind Miami Beach. The place looks safe enough from the outside. Just the one car in the carport. The windows and blinds are wide open. If the other two robbers are inside, they're taking a relaxed approach to lying low.

Bruno watches the place through the windscreen of their unmarked. 'Should we call it in?'

'Let's have a look,' says Reynolds.

Blackwell's grandmother is home and she's a salty old bint. 'What do you two want?' she says, peering down at them from a window. She lets them in, and it turns out she's not aiding and abetting anyone. Nor are there any tears for her wayward grandson. Could be the shock, but when she hears about Seth's passing, her response is, 'I bloody well said he'd wind up dead if he didn't quit being such a dickhead.'

They search Seth's room and find evidence.

A bag of smack.

An illegal firearm.

A black wig and a pair of blue trackpants worn to a previous robbery.

'This is good,' says Reynolds. 'One down, three to go.'

'Three?' says Bruno, thinking of the trio in the building society.

'Someone's driving them.'

Bruno calls it in via the landline in the kitchen while Reynolds makes the old lady a cup of tea. As the water heats, he says, 'How'd this happen, Mrs Blackwell?'

'It's the family business,' says the old woman.

As told, Seth comes from a long line of deadbeats. His grandfather, his father and his brother are all in the joint. The mother's long gone, but not much better. She did time for fraud. 'It's just me left now,' says the old woman. 'He'll be the last of them.'

'Anywhere else he stays when he's not around here?'

'Nah.'

'Girlfriend?'

'He has women come and go. There's one that was around a bit, a while back. Chloe something.' The old woman gets up and checks the nooks of a desk by the phone. She produces a notepad and says, 'Chloe Kennedy. That's it.'

Bruno asks if he can look through the notepad. 'You write everything down, ma'am?'

'Everything I want to remember.'

'Why'd you write her name down?' says Reynolds.

The woman thinks on it, eyes blank. She looks at the pad in Bruno's hands. 'Did I write it down? It could have been Seth.'

Bruno looks at the page. It's just the girl's name

with the word *cunt* pencilled underneath. He turns the page around to show her.

'Oh yeah, that's me. There you go,' she says, by way of explanation.

For a few minutes, Reynolds gently quizzes her about the various dates of the previous robberies. He gets absolutely nowhere. She can't remember any of it.

'Reynolds?' says Bruno quietly.

The detective walks around the table and stands beside him. He looks down at the open page in Bruno's hand. It reads, *O'Grady*.

Bruno turns the page around and shows her.

'That's not my writing. That's Seth's.'

Bruno turns more pages. There's a list in the same handwriting.

A list of names, some of them crossed out.

~~Wally Stewart~~
~~Michael Miller~~
~~Alfie Baker~~
*Jeffrey Chapman*
*Walter Pronzini*

Bruno looks up at Reynolds. 'You recognise any of these?'

'Not off the cuff,' he says, transcribing them into his own notebook.

Sirens announce themselves in the distance, followed by the sound of cars pulling up in the street.

'I'm not in any trouble, am I?' says the old woman.

'No, luv,' says Reynolds. 'You've been a big help, but this place is about to be crawling with police. How about you come down to the station with me for a spot of late lunch? I can help you with the calls, if you need to make any.'

'I could use a shandy.'

'Whatever you need, luv.'

'They're not going to wreck the place, are they?'

'I'll tell them to go easy,' says Reynolds. He helps her up.

Bruno's surprised. Reynolds is unflinchingly gentle with the old woman. It's not an act, either. Absolutely nothing about the man's grim demeanour flickers. He just helps her.

'You got your purse now?'

Bruno clears away a chair so they can pass by.

'Here we go,' says Reynolds.

Halfway along the hall, the woman stops. 'He's dead, right? You told me that, didn't you? My grandson is dead.'

'I'm afraid so,' says Reynolds.

# AMY

## Currumbin Pub, Currumbin

AMY WANDERS THROUGH THE bar area,
barely in control of herself. After last night—the visit
to her father's street—the rest is like a time-lapse
image, a bright swirling vortex of breakfast beers and
mid-morning shots, and whatever Eddie behind the
bar gave her in the bathroom, on top of a hundred
cigarettes and two hundred terrible conversations, all
piled into one body and yet, it's not enough.

Not nearly.

Off the wagon and into the fire.

The pub stands a full storey above the road and
it's like a fish tank in the sun. It's so white and light.
Glare beaming in, illuminating the dust in the air.
The god-awful Commonwealth Games droning on
the TV, broadcasting scrambled voices, creating more
movement.

*More, more, more.*

Amy necks a beer from a stray table.

*Show me everything then.*

*Let the light in.*

All the fast-tracked boozy detail is burying the

rest, pushing it further and further away. She couldn't go inside her father's place after Webber left. All she could do was sit there in the dark and watch the house and think.

*Think and remember.*

Amy stumbles and capsizes a table. A cacophony of male laughter follows.

'The fuck, Amy!'

'What?' she screams, spinning and dazed, her clothes wet now.

'Have a counter meal or I'm cutting you off,' says the barman.

'Cut this off, fuckhead,' she screams, lobbing a beer jug across the room. It lands with a splash on the top-shelf liquor behind the bar, spraying glass and booze across the punters.

Hands are on her then.

World rolling.

Stairs slap the soles of her shoes as she's dragged out.

'The hell?' she screams. 'What the hell?' But they don't listen.

'This crazy bitch,' someone says.

It's about right.

SHE's a block away when she remembers how she ended up in Currumbin. Bill Webber's house is a short walk, and Amy's coming off an all-nighter in the car, parked in his street, waiting for him to leave. It was the waiting that did her in. All the willpower and good intentions couldn't tamp down the eerie visions of Webber winding his way through the streets of her childhood. It couldn't blot out the destination. The memories located there. Even now, she can see her father's house every time she closes her eyes. 'And now here we are,' she says to herself. Turfed out in the suburbs without a drink.

It takes half an hour, but she finds her way back to the car. She manages to get in and wind the windows down. On the back seat, she shakes in the heat haze and passes out.


AMY SNAPS AWAKE SOMETIME AROUND three o'clock in the afternoon.

Sits up. Scans the outside world, convinced she's been made, somehow lucid enough to be scared.

But the surrounding street is empty.

A lawnmower in the distance.

Smoke in the air.

Amy looks down the street.

*His car is missing.*

Webber's out.

She weaves across his lawn and into the alcove of his front door. Knocks. The booze helps this time: no fear, no hesitation. No answer at the door so she takes her fake bible lock kit with her around back where the lock will be easier to work on. She makes a hash of it but it eventually turns. She steps inside thinking, *Either I'm a genius or this thing has been unlocked the whole time.*

The first thing she does is check the fridge for booze.

No dice.

The second is a piss in his toilet.

Back downstairs to the garage and Webber's safe. She has the combination.

She turns the mechanism.

Twenty.

Fifteen.

Eighteen.

Fourteen.

Five.

Twenty-five.

The door opens.

Empty.

'Who are you?'

The voice startles her. But she knows it, knows before she sees.

Amy slowly takes a look.

Bill Webber stands in the doorway with a rifle aimed at her.

'I'm . . . I'm a private investigator.'

He takes a step closer. 'Name.'

'Amy Owens.'

For a nanosecond, his eyes lose their focus, a fleeting thought. 'What do you want?'

'The police files. Whatever you took that you weren't supposed to take.'

Webber tightens his hands around the rifle. The man is breathing heavy. *Stressed.*

'Easy now. I have photos of what you've been doing. I know who Wally Stewart is. I watched you beat him to death.' Amy squeezes her eyes shut, flinching uncontrollably. 'Anything happens to me and all my boss needs to do is develop the film I've already given her and then you're in a world of hurt.'

'Who do you work for?'

'Colleen Vinton.'

She waits for what comes next. The click. The big nothing.

She's scared, but not as scared as she should be.

He says, 'What the fuck does Colleen want with all this?'

'I don't know.'

He moves a little.

The sound of footsteps on exposed concrete. The barrel of the gun announces itself on her chest.

*Fuck, fuck, fuck.*

'Hey, hey,' whispers Amy, eyes still closed. 'It's your lot, the cops. Colleen has me on loan to Ray Blintiff up in Brisbane.'

The barrel comes away.

Amy forces herself to look. Bill is still there, still holding the gun, but he nods and takes another step back.

Then another.

Then another.

Then he's gone.

Amy stands there for a whole minute, listening to him leave the house.

A strange tear rolls across her cheek.

*It was nearly over.*

# MIKE

## The Esplanade, Surfers Paradise

BACK ON THE COAST, Mike takes the elevator up to the seventh floor and makes his way down a carpeted hall to Colleen's apartment above the Silver Fish. He knocks gently on the door and there she is in a blood-red dress. Colleen notices him noticing and says, 'What do you think?'

'I love it.'

'That's the right answer.'

Mike has a brown Samsonite suitcase with him and places it on the bench of the kitchenette. 'This might be a bit forward, but do you have somewhere I can crash tonight?'

'I'm sure I can think of something.'

Colleen draws the blinds, enclosing the space in a muted afternoon glow. 'Is that what you wanted to ask me?'

'No, uh . . .'

Colleen sits on a large footstool. She slips her shoes off. 'Don't be shy.'

'When you were taking photos the other night, what's the play there?'

'You never know when you'll need someone's attention.'

Mike looks at her legs.

'It got *your* attention, didn't it?' she adds.

'That's what I thought.'

'What are you looking for?'

'Two and a half million dollars,' he says. 'It's an investment, not a—'

'Shakedown.'

'That's right.'

'Honey, it never is.' Colleen gently runs her hands over the soft skin of her inner thighs. 'You want me to work my magic, Mike? I know a few things, a few . . . magic tricks. I'm ready when you are.'

'That's why I'm here. I followed those cops from the other night to the wrong party, and I've stumbled into something a bit bigger than what I was after.' Mike lays the rest on her: Sorensen's estate, Sorensen's underground cinema and the vault. 'I have no idea how it all fits together, and it didn't get me any answers. In the meantime, the minister has given me the go-ahead to buy into the park, but I need capital. He wants to keep his hands clean.'

'So a piece *is* for sale?'

'To the right bidder. It's a big piece, too.'

'How big?' Colleen slips her earrings off and places them on the coffee table.

'Buddy Winters is selling his stake, out from under his own father.'

She smiles at that.

Mike continues. 'But to close the deal, I need to skirt around the Queensland Police, and I need a gigantic pile of money. And I'm going to need a serious backer who can protect me.'

'And you think that's little old me?'

'I keep hearing that. If we can get that money, I can get us the keys to the kingdom.'

'What's my end?' Colleen's eyes stay on him, but she slowly hikes her skirt up.

Mike watches her white panties creep out of the rising hem. He can see the texture of her red bush pressing against the fabric.

'Everything. We'd be in control,' he says.

'I think I'm falling in love.'

# BRUNO

## Stationhouse, Surfers Paradise

INSPECTOR RON BINGHAM LOOKS TORN. He stands behind his desk, arms folded, gently rocking on his heels. Across the room, Bruno Karras and Pete Reynolds wait in silence.

'This is good work, Pete,' Bingham says. 'You should have briefed me sooner, but . . .'

Reynolds shifts in his chair. 'I kept my people in the loop.'

Bruno and Reynolds have spent the afternoon assembling a dossier on Seth Blackwell. Right now, the Robbery Squad is out on the street, knocking on doors and following leads. The case is breaking. An hour ago, two detectives—one of them Lana Cohen—located a known associate of Blackwell's who claims Blackwell was running with a crew of local guys. No imports. But details beyond that are scarce.

Reynolds ashes his cigarette in the guest ashtray on Bingham's desk. 'We've also been running the paperwork back and forth. A maroon panel van was stolen off a street only a few blocks from Blackwell's grandmother's house, back in August. The van was later found in a local quarry. It was burned out. My lot is pretty sure it was used as a getaway vehicle for the third robbery, last month.'

'Does Blackwell have any form for auto theft?' says Bingham.

'No. But it must be the only caper his family isn't into. I got some of the girls to search for recent parolees and known crims with those skills. That's in the mix, too. It might turn up someone we haven't thought of.'

'Good,' says Bingham. 'Okay, stay on it.'

That's it.

There are no further congratulations coming.

Bruno feels a distant fury rising. They're going to fuck him over on this. He can feel it. His contribution will be downplayed and diminished. No doubt.

*It doesn't matter.*

'You coming?' says Reynolds.

Bruno, still deep in thought, lingers in his chair.

Ron Bingham stares at him with those rat fucker eyes.

They both wait for him.

'Anything else, sir?' says Bruno.

'No. Nothing,' says Bingham.

Bruno walks out without another word.

THE TWO DETECTIVES eat pizza off the bonnet of their car at the back end of Burleigh Heads. It's Reynolds's regular spot, and it makes sense: they're headed to a late-night briefing with the Robbery Squad down in Tugun.

Reynolds wipes oil on his pant leg. 'Can I ask you a question? Why do you make it so hard on yourself?'

'Practice, I guess.'

'I'll say.'

'That's a bit rich coming from you.'

'I'm not talking about being chummy with everyone. You just don't have to be so . . .'

'What?'

'You have to roll with the punches sometimes. Everyone does.'

'Is that what you do, Pete?'

'Yeah, look, you *are* in the bad books, but it'll pass, if you fucking let it.' Reynolds slings a half-eaten slice back into the box and slides off the car bonnet. He lights a smoke and takes a long drag; the ciggie pinched hard between his fingers. 'I used to have this doctor once, when I was younger, and he was always on me about giving up these bloody things. Doctor Hussein. He'd tell me, *You have to stop it with these cigarettes, Peter. You have to give them up.* And he'd be telling me this with a pack of Winnie Reds sitting right there beside him. One day he's really getting stuck into me and I say to him, *What about you, mate? When are you giving up the durries, huh?* And you know what he said?'

'I don't, actually.' Bruno closes his eyes.

'He said, *I'm not telling you all this because I'm better than you. I'm telling you all this because I know how bad it can get.*'

'And yet here you are, still smoking.'

Reynolds nods, takes another drag. 'Doctor Hussein died a few years back. Lung cancer.'

'Right. So, what's the point of this?'

'You should listen to me. That's the point of all my fucking stories.'

'So I should kiss Bingham's arse even though he's hell-bent on fucking me over?'

'Suicide's a sin, you know.'

*The fuck.*

Bruno has to take a few steps away from him. Out of the corner of his eye, he sees Reynolds's cigarette butt land in the dirt.

'Sorry, mate, I didn't mean that the way it came out. I wasn't talking about your dad. I'm just . . . I dunno. You need to find a way to fit in. You don't need to come across or take the money or be everyone's best mate. But you can't keep going on like this, or you'll end up in real trouble. You keep walking around like you're better than the rest of us and sooner or later someone is going to go out of their way to prove to you that you're not.'

'I don't think I'm better.'

'Maybe not, but . . .'

The radio chirps inside the car: the call sign for a potential homicide. The two detectives move around to their respective windows. They hang their heads inside. Dispatch describes a body in a motel down in Currumbin. Caucasian single male. *Jameson Leaver, twenty-two years of age. Multiple stab wounds to the face, neck and torso.*

Reynolds straightens up fast, recoiling.

'What is it? You know him?'

'That's Jamie. Local kid. He's been in and out of the station a few times.'

'You want to take a look?'

The man is deep in thought. 'Yeah, we should.'

'What is it?'

'I don't know. Something's happening.'


THE STREET IS CORDONED OFF. Bruno and Reynolds come up the avenue on foot, finding an SIB investigation team photographing a car parked in a bay beside the motel.

It's a dark blue Holden Commodore.

Camera flashes strobe the dark street.

'Hang on a sec,' says Bruno.

He checks his notes.

The plate numbers match.

'That's one of the missing O'Grady cars,' he says to Reynolds.

One scientist has a flashlight. 'Look.' There are squares of black duct tape on the chassis. Bruno squats under the light and peels one of the tape squares back, revealing a bullet hole.

They count four more on the car.

The back windscreen is brand new. A fresh install.

Bruno asks Reynolds, 'Any of your guys ever fire on a getaway car?'

'Nope. Did you shoot at them?'

'No, not at their car.'

From there, they move up to the apartment. Two homicide men are inside, working the scene. Bruno takes a quick look. The description broadcast on the police radio is the polite version. The body of Jamie Leaver is almost completely separated from the head. There's a lot of blood. Pools of it. The bedsheets are drenched and black. On the wall above the bed, there's a word written in gore.

*STOP*

'The fuck?' Bruno hears himself mumble.

'What is it?' Reynolds comes forward and looks.

The man stops breathing.

They take the stairs back down and follow the footpath to the end of the street, back to the car. 'I need to take a break,' says Reynolds as they pull away from the kerb. 'This is getting a bit much.'

'You okay?'

'We've gotta . . . we've . . .'

He hits the car's indicator and turns. 'Let's talk about this tomorrow.'

# BRUNO

## Stationhouse, Surfers Paradise

BRUNO MILLS AROUND THE STATION, double-checking paperwork and treading water. The Jamie Leaver crime scene plays on his mind but none of it coheres. Directionless, he pushes back out into the city, driving the late-night streets. He swings by Pohlman Drive and lets himself into the O'Gradys' house. In the dark, he sits on their leather couch and waits for something to happen.

Car headlights sweep across the ceiling.

*Why did they cut that kid's head off?*

*Who are they warning?*

Bruno sees the blood-stained eyes of the corpse.

The red opening.

The word *STOP.*

Bruno shudders. He gets up and wanders around the house, revisiting the now familiar rooms.

The study. The giant downstairs bathroom. The rumpus with the pool table and TV.

He takes the stairs down into the basement storeroom. Looks at the plain white walls and concrete floor down there. Absolutely empty. He stands in the

Iain Ryan

centre of the room and feels like a sculpture in a gallery. To break the quiet, Bruno claps his hands and hears the sharp ping of reverberation.

Back upstairs, he checks the garage and finds it completely empty, then moves up to the second-storey bedrooms. Samson's room. Then another study. Another split bathroom, the size of a regular room.

He tentatively steps into the dim master bedroom, the crime scene. Someone has dumped the mattress back on the carpet, ignoring the taped-off sections of the flooring.

*Sloppy. But...*

A voice behind him says, 'Put your hands out where I can see them.'

'Easy now. Easy.'

Bruno comes around slowly. He finds a pump-action shotgun pointed at him, the barrel at eye level. The man holding the gun is in the darkness of the walk-in robe. Only the gun barrel protrudes from the void, barely visible in the gloom.

'What are you doing in here?' says the voice.

'The O'Gradys are missing. Can you point that thing away from me?'

The gun stays steady. 'Why are you here?' says the voice.

'I'm working. I'm a cop. Who are you?'

No answer.

'I'll go,' says Bruno. 'I'll walk and that will be that.' He edges towards the door.

'I don't think so.'

Bruno stops moving.

'I'm in trouble,' says the voice. 'I know that. But I'm not a monster. They didn't make me into one. I'm just... I'm caught up in something.'

Bruno's heart pounds inside him. He knows this

224

voice. Can't place it, but he has heard this man speak before.

The gun remains in place.

'I'm caught up in it too,' says Bruno. 'Maybe we can help each other?'

The man laughs. 'Jesus. You idiots are no help to anyone.'

'You don't have to do this. I can leave. I can go.'

Bruno's body is screaming. *Move now or die standing here.*

Bruno backs up. 'I'm going to walk out, get in my car and go home.'

The gun barrel follows him across the room. 'Stop.'

Bruno waits. He has one foot on the bedroom threshold. 'What?'

There's a long pause, until: 'The O'Gradys are dead.'

'Did you kill them?'

'No. I wish.'

'Can I go, please?'

'It's not your case anymore.'

'Okay.'

Bruno steps into the hall, waiting for the explosion of lead pellets to tear the flesh from his bones.

*Don't think or speak.*

*Give up.*

*Run.*

Bruno leaves and no one follows.

# AMY

## Marseille Court, Bundall

THE SUMMER WIND WASHES through her hair as the cab moves along. The driver takes them out of the Strip and onto the empty Esplanade, and out there, the world is split. On one side is a charcoal ocean under a cloudy sky. On the other, all the city lights in their soft sheen. A binary. The vast unknown versus tight construction. Competing nightmares. But none of it reaches Amy tonight. It passes through, coaxed along by the day's chaos and a dozen more drinks. It's all a dream, and nothing matters in a dream.

The car floats on the bitumen.

The familiar vector, one more time.

Into Campbell Street, down into the canal estates. Along Freyburg. Left and around into Marseille Court.

It's like the closure of a loop between the very start of the day and this weird end.

The cab stops and disappears, leaving Amy standing on the footpath in front of her old family home. She uses a loose key from her handbag to unlock the gate, then stumbles up the drive. There's a path along the side of the house and Amy takes it down past the outdoor shower, the garage windows, and the bathroom downpipes she climbed as a kid. The same key unlocks the sliding door to the laundry.

The interior of the house is unlit and unmoving. Another familiar vector takes shape. Amy walks through the quiet living spaces and across the tiled kitchen to the foyer, to the stair, and up along the white marble bannisters onto the soft carpet and through to the place where her father always is at this time of night: in the study, the man in his room.

There's no lamp on tonight, and he's not at his desk. Victor Owens is by the window. A silhouette—a crumpled-up old man in a wheelchair— waiting in the night; a long, warped grid of white moonlight stretching across the floor behind him.

'Dad?'

He doesn't move.

'Dad?'

Amy slumps against the doorframe.

Victor stirs, moving his head slowly.

'Dad, what have you done?'

Half of Victor's face catches a beam, lighting him up.

Stubble, ragged, unshaven.

Victor smiles and it's like a dog gnashing its teeth.

# PART SIX
# SUNDAY 3 OCTOBER
## 1982

# VICTOR

THE CURTAINS *of the viewing room open and close,*
*and I experience strange visitations: children returning,*
*images out of order, glimpses caught in reality and on*
*super 8, transformed, contaminated, and lost.*

*I touch my neck and it's cold.*

*Visions swimming.*

*'Elda,' I yell. 'Elda!'*

*It takes the woman minutes to reach me. Minutes*
*or hours. She stands over me, blocking the sun. 'Yes?'*

*'I'm not taking any more of these. They're making*
*it worse.'*

*'Doctor Best said they'll quell the pain.'*

*'They bloody well quell everything.'*

*'Should I call him?'*

*She walks away before I can answer.*

*'Tell him no more. It's only pain for Chrissake.'*

OUT OF THE *soup and daydream murk and into a*
*vivid stretch.*

*Minutes or hours.*

*But an answer in the noise:* Use the interloper.

*Amy.*

*Yes, Amy will do. She fits.*

*It's fated. She delivered herself unto me. And . . .*

*She has a weakness, a soft spot for lost brothers.*


DOCTOR BEST IS ANYTHING BUT. *His father—the original Doctor Best—was a good man. A lifelong friend of the family. Trust me, you feel your age when you outlive your doctor.*

*Today, in the stark midday light, Doctor Best Junior takes my heart rate.*

*He checks my eyes.*

*Blood pressure.*

*Looks in my mouth.*

*'And?' I ask.*

*'No better and no worse. We can change the medication, though.'*

*'I just need a couple of clear days. I need to get my affairs in order.'*

*'I can make you comfortable.'*

*'Fuck comfortable. Can you make me young?'*

*He laughs.*

*So do I, but if I could, I would kill the little bastard with my own hands.*


HOURS OR DAYS *or weeks later, I'm lucid.*

*I have dizzy spells, hot sweats and cold chills.*

*I vomit up my tea.*

*I cough until there's blood.*

*But I'm clear.*

*Very, very clear.*

*Now we're talking.*

*The last push. Elda brings my tablets and I dissolve them in my tea then send it back.*

# MIKE
## The Esplanade, Surfers Paradise

THE FIRST THING MIKE sees on waking is white dust falling from the ceiling. The floor is shaking, sloshing the waterbed around.

Colleen murmurs beside him.

'Can you feel that?' he says, but she doesn't stir.

Half-convinced it's a dream, he wipes his forearm and looks at the tips of his fingers: powdered residue from the stipple ceiling.

It's an earthquake.

The clock reads 5.15 am.

*Up before the enemy.*

But already under attack.

OVER THE ESPLANADE and down across the deserted beach, Mike wades into the ocean. He almost has the place to himself, just one surfer further down. Mike floats in the water and thinks, *I'm so close.* Close, but in real trouble too. On the wrong side of bad policemen, under the employ of a powerful minister, in bed with a gangster. It's all ominous, but it's all politics in the end. That's the job. A hundred uneasy negotiations. Mike looks back at the Strip and thinks, *That's how this was built.* And even though he knows he should be terrified this morning—fearing the dark assemblage forming, the impossible stakes—he feels a seasick elation too. The finish line is in sight and Mike is running towards it.

BREAKFAST DOUBLES as an emergency pitch meeting with Colleen's frontman, the real estate developer Robert Emmery. Emmery has been dropped right in. No appointment, no consultation. 'Just go see him,' says Colleen. 'He'll sort you out.' She knows where he eats.

Emmery now sits across the table of a hotel bistro down on Hanlan Street. He's imperially neat from the slick haircut down. The *Financial Times* spread open on his lap. 'So you're a friend of Colleen's?' he says.

'It's not what you know.'

'What do you want?'

'Colleen is buying into Fantasyland and I hear you're the man to talk to about moving her money around.'

Emmery is listening, but he keeps his eyes on the newspaper. 'Interesting. She's a bit overextended at the moment. We're building a casino, if you hadn't heard.'

'I heard,' Mike says.

'How well do you know her?'

'Intimately.'

Emmery almost smiles. 'Word of advice?'

'I'll listen to anyone once.'

Emmery leans across the table. 'You can both go fuck yourselves.'

And there it is. At the core, Emmery is just another brawler.

Mike signals the waiter. 'I might grab a bite, actually. We should talk terms.'

'Go on then.' He folds up his paper. 'How much are we apparently investing?'

'For you? Four million.'

'Forget it. Tell her she can't have it. Bloody have a look around. The city is dead on its feet.'

'Fantasyland is recession-proof, Robert. One hundred per cent recession-proof. No one gives a fuck about the economy when they're with their kids at a theme park. You've got kids, right?'

'I'm well aware of the project's merits.'

'Then you know why it's a smart play.'

Emmery takes a sip of his tea. Mike spots a small red dot on his shirt cuff. *Is that blood?*

'How are you planning on doing all this?' says Emmery.

'Charm and good looks.'

'No, really.'

'Someone is cashing out.'

'Who?'

It's Mike's turn to lean across the table. 'Your mum.'

'They'll never let Colleen anywhere near it. You know that, right? Noah Winters won't even sit down with me. So, either you're full of shit, or you're into something very dicey, and I don't like either of those options.'

'It's the second one. And I think we're a bit turned around here. I'm trying to be polite, but Colleen's already in. So, I figure *you're* in. I'm not here to ask a favour, Robert. I'm here to find out how quickly you can get me my money?'

'I can't do it. It'll delay the casino.'

'Then delay the fucking casino.'

He's rattled now. 'Four million, you said?'

'Four.'

'I could do three, maybe three point two. But this better be real.'

'It's better than real, mate.'

'Do you know what Colleen will do to you if this doesn't pan out?

She'll cut your balls off and feed them to you.'

'Who doesn't like a good time?'

They shake on it.

Then Robert asks him to leave.

DOWN THE STREET, Mike runs into Allan Watts. Allan scratches his ear. 'I didn't realise you were still down here, mate. Come and have a cuppa.' They duck into a nearby restaurant, and almost immediately Allan excuses himself for a slash. The place is empty. Mike sits there and waits as a dark feeling arrives, dragged into focus by the quiet. He got to Sorensen's afterparty via those cops at the Silver Fish. That's Allan's place. Mike flashes back to Allan making the introductions. He flashes further back to that first night at Fantasyland, to what Allan said about Mike's predecessor.

*He's having a long spell from walking around.*

Mike gets up and leaves.

On the way out, he spots Allan at the bar, hunched over the phone. Ten minutes later Mike steps through the door of the crash-pad above the Silver Fish where Colleen is awake and dressed. She's standing in the living room, smoking. 'We have to move you,' she says.

'What is it?'

'There's an APB out. Every cop on the Strip is looking for you.'

'Why?'

'Wanted for questioning. Something to do with a murder down on the Tweed. They found a friend of mine dead in your motel room. They cut his head off.'

'That's . . . I was here with you all night.'

'I know.'

'What do I do?'

'Lie low. Keep working on the deal. I'll handle the rest.'

# BRUNO
## The Esplanade, Surfers Paradise

BRUNO REPORTED THE MAN with the gun the moment he left the O'Grady house. It took an hour for the Emergency Squad to muster, but by midnight, it was all over with nothing to show. The man had slipped away, leaving just enough proof (a window ajar, boot prints) to keep Bingham from talking a blue streak. Unfortunately, it wasn't enough to keep Bruno's colleagues happy. *You've got us out here for what, exactly?* It's bright morning by the time Bruno's done with the paperwork. He enters the day on three hours of broken sleep, snatched from the back seat of his police car.

THE MID-MORNING SEA rolls gently out past the breakers. Just one other bloke further up. Some young blond guy floating in the glimmer and looking at the Strip. Bruno catches three choppy waves and spends the rest of the time sitting there, desperately praying his body will catch up to his mind. A short respite.

· · ·

241

BACK AT THE STATION, Bruno leads Chloe Kennedy, aka Seth Blackwell's girlfriend, to an upstairs interview room. There's no sign of Reynolds, so Bruno goes ahead without him. It's not ideal, considering Bruno killed Blackwell, but Chloe doesn't know that and, besides, oversight on this case is already at an all-time low.

Turns out Chloe's no good Samaritan. The girl is tight-lipped and pissed off. Rail thin, greasy black hair. She has the complexion of a junkie, and she's only here because of an outstanding warrant: seems young Chloe got into a drunken spat in a Kmart last year. Unfortunately, Chloe knows very little about Seth Blackwell's criminal enterprises. 'We hung out. He's just some guy,' she says. 'I didn't know he was robbing banks. He told me he was a plasterer's apprentice.'

'You don't seem too upset about his passing, Chloe?'

'Nah, it's not like that. We haven't seen each other in a while, that's all.'

'His grandmother seems to think you were his girlfriend.'

'That old biddy doesn't know what day it is.'

'So, you two were broken up?'

'I guess, if you want to call it that.'

'Did something happen?'

Chloe picks at her fingers. No answer.

Bruno says, 'I can talk to someone about that warrant as soon as we're done here.'

'Cool.'

'But, come on. There's more, right?'

Chloe pushes her tongue against the inside of her lower lip. 'Okay, fuck it. I quit hanging around with him because he was a bloody poofter, wasn't he?'

'And what gave you that idea?'

'He brought another bloke to bed one night. I was okay with it at the start. I mean, fuck it, right? I can handle two. That used to be a quiet weekend for me once. But these bloody two . . . they started in on each other, like. I thought it was gross, so I told Seth to rack off. And he did. End of story. Like I said, it's not like we were engaged or anything.'

'Tell me about this other bloke.'

'No thanks.'

'I can arrest you. Tell me.'

'You're a piece of shit, you know that?'

'Chloe.'

'His name is Samson. That's all I know.'

'Samson O'Grady?'

'Maybe.'

'What did he look like?'

Chloe gives a rote description of every second man on the coast. 'Look, I don't know the guy. I know nothing about him. I'm not exactly gonna be best mates with some poof who's sleeping with my boyfriend, am I?'

'I guess not.' Bruno lets her go.

But he doesn't talk to anyone about her warrant.

AFTER THE INTERVIEW and an attempt at running some deskwork, Bruno locks himself in a toilet cubicle in the station and waits. There's a torrent flowing through him—fatigue, worry, some other torment—and it's pulling at every corner.

*What am I doing?*

Too many grim details circle this case. There's a lot of blood and bad energy. The chain of events are fucking disastrous: a dead family, dead bank tellers, dirty cops, illicit porn, a motel room beheading. *What is this?* Bruno closes his eyes and sees a stream of abuse screening in his head, a blurred VHS vision of German men sucking each other off and black-blood lettering smeared on a motel room wall, all soundtracked by Chloe's bogan whine—and Reynolds talking about his doctor—and a hundred forgotten leads in an unravelling case.

Coming back to the world, Bruno hears two detectives outside the toilet cubicle talking about shot-put and the Games while piss sprays the stainless-steel urinal. It's all haunting and present. Harsh and close.

*Where is Reynolds?*

And how is any of this making any sense to anyone?

Bruno gets up and flushes, watching the water withdraw.

He opens the cubicle door and the detectives take one look at him and share a smile between them.

Bruno ignores it.

Washes his hands.

Thinks about his gun.

# AMY
## Marseille Court, Bundall

ON THE EAST WING of the family home is Amy's childhood bedroom. Her posters are gone and the desk is new—the bed used to be over there, but now it's here—and yet, it's the same four walls and windows. It *feels* the same: a mix of safety and dread.

Amy walks downstairs barefoot. The staff are around—waiting out of sight, as always. The place feels deserted. All the canal-side curtains are open. Bright light and a cool breeze through the high doors. She wanders and inspects and remembers. Eventually she finds her father out on the ground-floor patio, his wheelchair beside a small table and a pot of tea. Amy plants herself in a chair a few feet away, cups her hand around a cigarette to guard it from the wind. 'Morning.'

There's a loud toad-like croak as Victor clears his throat. The voice that follows is quieter, rendered raspy from all the medication he's on. 'What do you want, Amy?'

'I like what you've done with the place. It's very . . . end of life.'

'Your ranting and raving upset Elda last night. She had to put you to bed.'

'Who's that?'

'The nurse.'

Amy stands up and takes in the sun, feet on the lawn. She looks out into the yard and at the water and the yacht moored on the landing. 'New boat looks good. What are you going to do with this place when it's all over, Victor?'

'What sort of question is that? Come here.'

Amy approaches. It's been years, many, many unkind years, and Victor doesn't look good at all. He's in his late eighties by her count, and his hair is almost gone. Skin as thin as cellophane. This is the skeleton of the man, drawn down to his essence.

'Give me one of those,' he says, pointing at her cigarette pack. 'Quick, before she comes to check on me.'

Amy sorts him out.

The old man wheezes and coughs on it. 'Have you seen your sister?' he says.

'Angela's around.'

That seems to be enough of an answer for him. 'I hear you're working for Colleen Vinton these days.'

'So, you've still got some pull, huh?'

'Isn't that why you're here?'

'No, I came to make sure you're still alive. I don't know why.'

'You never were much of a liar. The other two were more practised with it. What do you want, Amy?'

'What can you tell me about Allan Watts?'

'Nothing,' he says, but even just hearing the question seems to satisfy him. 'You go and tell Colleen that if she goes anywhere near Allan, I'll cut her fucking legs off.'

'I don't think so, Victor.'

He looks up at her. 'Whatever you think I did to you, I should have done so much more. Working for that cunt . . . it's a disgrace. No daughter of mine should be so stupid.'

'I don't know, I feel like Angela's giving me a run for my money.' Amy can feel the hangover surging, loosening that grip on herself. 'You still feel like the big man, don't you? You don't seem so big anymore, you busted-up old fuck.'

He waves it off, disgusted. 'You're a mess.'

Amy laughs. 'Okay. Is this just dawning on you?'

'You can go.'

'You know, Victor, you *did* kill my brother, and one day, you're going to burn in hell for it.'

'Is that right?'

Amy loses all control. She grabs him by the face, his slack, loose skin is cold. 'You, you—'

It's a mistake. Her rage turned against her. Victor's hand comes up steady, the sun glinting off the blade. He has the knifepoint pressed into her throat before she fully realises what's happening. 'Don't you ever presume to know what will happen to me,' he says in a horrible rasp. 'You don't know. No one knows. *I* am the one who decides what happens to me.'

Amy lets go, backs away unsteadily.

Victor resettles himself, hides the knife away then brushes the pant legs of his pyjamas. 'And to answer your earlier question, when I die all this will go to your brother. That's right, your brother.'

Against her every desire, Amy is crying. 'Wh-*what* are you saying?'

Victor backs up his wheelchair.

'Why?' she screams. 'Why are you like this?'

But he doesn't answer.

The help come running like bats fleeing a cave.

AMY GOES straight to her local and orders a drink.

Taps the bar in anticipation. Fantasising about it seconds ahead of tasting it.

*Fuck the cases.*

The barman puts a pot of beer down and says, 'The boss is looking for you.'

'Here?'

'Everywhere.'

*Shit.*

She puts her hand around the beer and almost flinches. It's her bad hand. The one that serves as a cold reminder: *you're owned, do as you're told.*

'Fucking pour it out,' she says.

The barman grabs the drink back, and he's already got the phone for her.

Amy calls Colleen and cops it.

'Where have you been?'

She feels small, lost, afraid.

It's too much.

Father and mother in one day.

# MIKE
## The Esplanade, Surfers Paradise

MIKE PACES BACK AND forth on the shag pile, alone in Colleen's apartment above the Silver Fish.

He's waiting on a callback from the minister.

Whispering to himself.

He kneels and takes a bump off the coffee table. Needs it to stay alert. He's still down there, holding the rolled-up note to his nose when he sees flickering movement under the apartment door.

Someone knocks lightly.

'Hello?' A female voice.

He waits.

To his horror, a key slots into the lock.

Mike starts frantically wiping up the powder but gives up as the door swings open. A woman in black jeans and a black long-sleeve shirt steps inside. She has a small leather handbag at her side.

'Who the fuck are you?' he says.

The woman closes the door behind her and takes stock of the room, the pulled blinds, the coffee table, Mike's ruffled state. 'Colleen sent me. I'm Amy.'

'She didn't mention sending someone.'

'She's busy. Take a seat on the couch for me.'

'Are you sure this is—'

'Sit down.'

He does it. 'So, ah, what's the plan?'

'Getting you the fuck out of here.' Amy comes over and sits beside him. 'May I?'

Mike hands her the note.

Amy snorts up a line. 'I try to stay away from this shit, but . . .'

Mike forces out a breath. 'Colleen definitely sent you?'

'She definitely did. I know what I'm doing.' Amy does another line and wipes her nose. 'Now let's get this show on the road. Go pack your stuff.'


As THEY'RE LEAVING, the phone rings.

Mike picks it up. 'It's me.'

'Hello, Mike.'

He's expecting the God Minister, but that's not who this is.

'You remember me, Mike? It's Arthur Sorensen. You came to my party the other night. How are you?'

'I'm, I'm fine.'

'That's good to hear. I just wanted to ring and give you my number.

You got a pen there, Mike? Where are you?'

Mike doesn't answer, but Sorensen doesn't care. He rattles off his digits as Mike just stands there, barely comprehending it.

'Now, Mike, now that you have my number, I figure we should have a little chat. You're in a lot of trouble, son. Wanted for murder, I hear. Tsk, tsk. There might be a way we can salvage things, you know? I . . . are you there, Mike?'

Amy asks, 'Who is it?'

Mike stammers, 'It's, it's the deputy commissioner.'

Sorensen is talking into the receiver. They can both hear his voice. 'The police?' says Amy. 'No.' She snatches the phone off him and slams it down. 'We're leaving.'

It's not an elaborate escape. There's a fire exit staircase at the southern end of the building. They take it, floor after floor, all the way to the basement, only to find that the door is locked.

'Is it usually locked?' asks Mike.

'I don't know,' Amy says.

They go back up four storeys, checking each door and cursing until they find one that opens. Both of them are sweating, panting for breath.

Amy checks the hallway. 'It's clear.'

They move out into the open, across the carpet, to the lift.

Amy hits the down button.

Minutes elapse. Minutes of standing there where everyone can see them.

The elevator arrives.

They ride down two storeys before the elevator stops and the doors slide open. Two uniformed cops are standing there. The cops look at Mike and Amy for an awkward second, perspiration dripping from their faces, then the cops step into the lift and turn back towards the closing doors. As they descend again, Mike steals a glance at Amy. She has her hand inside her handbag. She silently motions to the gun on the man's hip in front.

Mike shakes his head. *No fucking way.*

Amy's eyes intensify: *Yes fucking way.*

The cop in front of Amy scratches his shoulder and says, 'I could murder a beer.'

'Same,' says his partner.

The lift comes to a halt.

The doors open.

The cops disembark.

The lift moves again.

'What the hell?' hisses Mike.

'You should buy a lottery ticket,' Amy says, slipping a pair of brass knuckles off her fingers and dropping them back into her bag. Her eyes lose their focus momentarily. 'Goddamn, Mike, that's really good coke. My heart is racing. Christ almighty. Thank god we're not driving.'

# BRUNO

## Heron Avenue, Mermaid Beach

BRUNO GOES OFF SHIFT and returns home to find a note from his brother.

*At Dad's. Cleaning up.*

He showers and tries to nap.

It's no good.

He knows why. He needs to do his part.

Needs to, whether he likes it or not.

Forever and ever.

THE KARRAS FAMILY home is a low-set brown-brick building, well back from the water in Labrador. It's the sort of place that will never be a holiday rental. Too ugly, too lived-in. Bruno loves the house, but he knows that its sunny aura is just the overlay of memory. It's all the Christmases and birthdays that happened inside. The bunk beds with Thunderbirds sheets. Home-cooking and board games. It's where he grew up.

It's still dusk when he arrives, and yet his siblings

have every light on. As Bruno steps in, he finds Danny standing knee-deep in brown cardboard boxes, holding two identical glass vases. 'I don't even remember these,' he says, grinning. 'Do *you* remember them?'

Bruno shakes his head.

'Remember what?' says a voice. It's his sister, Gracie. She comes to the mouth of the hallway, her hair pushed back under a blue bandana. 'Look what the cat dragged in.'

Gracie's daughter Megan appears by her side. She's five years old and shy.

'Hey, Megan. What are you doing back there?' says Bruno.

'Grandpa has a lot of old stuff,' the little girl says.

Gracie pats the kid's hair.

'We're really doing this, huh?' says Bruno.

'It seems like it,' says Danny.

Gracie rolls her eyes. 'It's not that bad.'

OVER THE COURSE of a few hours, the siblings declutter and pack. There are three piles forming: one for the dump, one for the op shop and one to keep. Bruno works in the study. He disposes of paperweights, a desk lamp and his father's collection of small business periodicals—the sort of thing Bruno couldn't imagine anyone reading once, let alone archiving. He sorts through a decade of his father's taxes, dumping the majority of it. For what it's worth, their father's death wasn't legally complicated. He had a will. His affairs were in order. Which is worse, in the scheme of things.

· · ·

It all started with their mother. Bernadette. She died when Bruno was sixteen years old. Cancer, caught late, meaning the entire ordeal was mercifully swift. She was gone inside of five months, but her death was no quiet journey into the afterlife. Bernadette died miserable, with a hundred unsaid things left inside of her. For the rest of them, the loss lingered, turning up all sorts of damage later on. They were never quite the same.

Fifteen years later, it's Dad's turn. Lung disease.

It's almost as if Bruno's life has neat cycles.

His birth to his mother's death.

Her death to his father's death.

Except this is Dad. He's the fucking sun. The tireless career man. The single parent. The church-goer and dutiful ALP man. When the world slowly destroys this man, it rots the footings, and under the footings, there's only sand, all the way down.

That's not even the worst of it. The worst part is that the old man feels the dread too. Can't fight it off for his children. There's been too much trouble in his life and now it's caught up with him. He can't cope. Desperate, dying, mad, he does a terrible thing. He waits until Bruno and Danny are up the shops, then he visits the kitchen pantry and reaches into the place where Bruno keeps his service revolver during after-work visits. With the gun in hand, he goes to the garage, takes two puffs on one last illicit cigarette before putting the gun in his mouth.

It takes them an hour to find the body.

It's agony when they do.

Then the aftermath causes further heartbreak for Bruno at work.

A Queensland policeman is in command of his firearm at all times.

He's responsible.

BRUNO SQUATS in the garage and looks at the spot where his father's blood used to be. He touches it and has instant recall; not to his father's body, but to something else: the blood under the carpet of the O'Grady's master bedroom.

*Is this progress?*

Could be.

'There you are,' says Gracie.

His sister stands in the doorway, the yard light illuminating her figure. 'Danny said you were struggling. I'm sorry I've been pushy of late. I've got—'

Bruno stands. 'Nah, it's okay. We had to do it.'

'We're behind on the mortgage,' Gracie says. 'Gareth's work is slow.'

'It's fine,' says Bruno. 'Really.'

'I should have said this a while back, but I can't believe that Dad did this to you. Some days I hate him for it.'

'Yeah, me too. He knew I put the gun in the pantry because I was scared Megan would touch it. It just got to be a habit. I wanted to be here with him so much that I got sloppy.'

'He was out of his mind. I keep telling myself that.' His sister looks around the shed. 'It's a shit place to die, isn't it? I had visions of holding his hand in some hospital bed or something.'

Gracie comes closer and hugs him.

There's a pause.

She lets go. 'Okay, I better get home. I've had enough for one day. What are you doing?'

'I'm going out. I'm gonna have a couple of drinks and decompress.'

'Sounds like a good idea.'

Bruno smiles. 'Ask me tomorrow.'

'You taking Danny?'

'No. He's too pretty.'

# AMY

## The Strip, Surfers Paradise

AMY STASHES MIKE IN a half-finished skyscraper on the Surfers Paradise foreshore. The guy is some sort of political operative, but all Amy knows is that Colleen wants him kept alive and away from the police. 'He didn't kill Jamie,' the boss says. 'He was with me all night.' And it must be true, because Jamie Leaver was a decent earner for Colleen. People are dispensable. Money-makers, less so.

The way Mike tells it, he's into something bad with the cops. Claims he went to the wrong party and that the Deputy Commissioner of Police has a secret file room in a bunker under his tennis court. Mike says he bribed Jamie into letting him into the bunker. To cap it off, Mike has a piece of paper—a one-page ledger he's lifted—that has dates, names and figures. 'It's got all sorts of people listed. *Everyone's* on it.' It sounds insane, and it *is,* but there are dark overlaps forming.

Bill Webber has stolen police files too. He's hospitalising pedos. He's got his own list.

He's lurking outside her father's house.

On the loose.

Has she been working for this same group of crooked cops chasing Mike? Ray Blintiff works up in the city with Arthur Sorensen. Blintiff is paying her to find these files Webber lifted.

*Are they the same files?*

*Am I going to get beheaded like Jamie?*

*Am I next?*

Amy helps Mike settle in, then leaves him be.

Back down on the street, she calls Colleen from a payphone. Colleen knows the details. She's thinking the same way, except it's not fear with Colleen. It's fury. 'These fucking dickheads are making a mess. Here's what you're going to do,' and then she lays it out.

JAMIE LEAVER LIVED in a six-pack apartment building in Mermaid Beach. It's one of Colleen's investments, so it isn't in Jamie's name and the police haven't arrived yet. They haven't worked it out or someone is pulling on the reins. Either way, Amy has the head start.

She rolls on a pair of surgical gloves and cases the place by torch-light. Jamie wasn't big on decorating. He's got roadside furniture and zero kitchenware. He has a thing for clothes, but that's it. Casing the place takes fifteen minutes flat.

She rolls the mattress.

She pulls out drawers and turns them out.

She searches the back of his closet.

Amy drags out shirts and jackets until she finds something.

A set of keys on a hook, at the back of the closet.

She shines the beam on them and lights them up. They're freshly cut.

Amy exits, takes the stair to the building's open carports. Jamie's spot is empty, but there's a bag of trash propped in the corner. Amy grabs it, drives to a deserted park a few streets over and sorts through the garbage on a picnic table.

A flattened shoebox.

Empty shampoo bottles.

A couple of spent condoms.

Finally, a bank statement smeared in dry coffee. It's old, but there's a transaction Amy knows well. *Hamilton Storage.* It's an industrial park out by Coolangatta Airport. She has the key *and* the lock now.

HAMILTON STORAGE IS CLOSED. The night guard is a pain in the arse, but he looks like an ex-crim so Amy drops Colleen's name on him and he's all ears after that. Amy slips him a fifty to get in the gate. Another fifty buys her Jamie Leaver's shed number. It's number thirty-six, one of the bigger units, a small warehouse rather than the usual single-car garage.

Amy rolls the door and hits the lights. There are two cars parked inside, both under tarpaulin covers. Nothing fancy: a silver Ford Falcon and a white Sigma. Amy writes down the plate numbers. She tries Jamie's keys and they take. Clean inside, but the cars have been worked on. Mechanic's tools line one side of the shed. On a hunch, Amy pops the bonnet of the Sigma. It has a new V8 engine installed. Definitely a custom job.

Amy gives the rest of the shed the once-over. There are two beds in a room partitioned off in the corner, something more like an office than a bedroom. One bed has clean sheets, the other looks slept in. There's a few personal items—toothbrush and a glass of water on a paint-tin for a bedside table.

Amy returns to the main room. She studies the bench, the cabinets, a steel-frame shelving unit. It all looks pretty unremarkable except for a long timber box under a workbench. Amy drags it out. There's a padlock and the last of Jamie's keys snaps it open. Inside, she finds four pump-action shotguns.

She lifts one out and takes a long whiff.

*Recently fired.*

AMY CALLS it in to Colleen. 'I've got a bad feeling.'

'How bad?'

'So bad I don't want to say it on the phone. I think we're into something even worse than the other stuff.'

'What about Mike?'

'Cut him loose. I don't know how it all fits together, but the whole thing is going to rain down on us like a tonne of bricks if we keep going.'

Colleen thinks on it. 'I don't want to,' she says. 'I'm too close.'

'Close to what?'

'Just . . . stay on it.'

'*Stay on it?* I should be leaving town.'

'No, Amy. You're going to do what I tell you to do.'

The line goes dead.

# MIKE
## The Strip, Surfers Paradise

THE ONLY SOUND MIKE can hear is construction Visqueen flapping in the breeze. The Strip looks different from up here—better, a romantic sprawl of high-rises and homes and glowing light. They have him stashed on the fifteenth floor of a half-finished apartment building by the beach. His spot is sealed-off, the start of a holiday suite already partitioned into rooms with the first layers of plasterboard. But, like a film set, there's scaffolding just beyond. Mike stands out on the open lip of the building, a beer in hand, nothing separating him from an easy suicide. Not that he's thinking that way.

With a few drinks in him, with the fear pushed down a little, he's thinking in the opposite direction, actually. His mind is alive with scenarios and strategy. He's thinking through the angles. There will be a way out of this. There always is. But he needs to move fast.

Mike returns to his makeshift office. It's two milk crates: a table and chair.

He scans his diary and planner with a flashlight.
*I have leverage.*

*A major stake in Fantasyland within spitting distance.*

*A list of names, dates and transactions.*

*The God Minister's blessing.*

*Colleen Vinton's network.*

*God* and *the devil on my side.*

Mike figures he just needs to stay alive for the next couple of days and everything will be fine.

THIS LINE of reasoning carries Mike through the rest of his six-pack and into the late hours of the evening. In those darker hours—with the booze in recline—he finds himself visited by other thoughts, things located further from ambition. He thinks about his family. He thinks about his wife. His children.

FIFTEEN MINUTES LATER, still sitting there in the dark, Mike feels an urgent sickness bloom in his stomach. He stands up, pats his pockets for the car keys.

Down the steel stair. All fifteen flights.

Over the construction fencing and into the street.

His car is back at Colleen's. It's a twenty-minute walk.

A ten-minute jog.

He runs.

He's half a block from his hiding spot when he sees a phone booth and goes in.

The call connects.

His son answers. Mike almost cries just at the sound of it. He can hear the TV on in the background.

'Mate, what are you doing up this late?'

'Dad!'

Mike laughs, the relief softening every muscle.

'You won't believe what happened, Dad!'

'What's that? Is it movie night up there?'

'No, Dad, Constable Chris is here.'

'What?'

'Constable Chris from the TV is here. He's talking to Mum in the kitchen. He's been here for ages.'

'Oh, uh . . . can you go get him for me?'

His son yells out.

The phone moves around.

'Mike?' says a familiar voice. It's him.

'You listen to me, you—'

'Real nice family you have here, Mike. Sorry to intrude, but there was no other way to get hold of you. I've been sitting here for hours.'

'If you fucking touch them, I'll . . .'

'I'm listening,' says Chris. 'Oh, are you done? That's good because I think you might know how serious this is now. You want some advice, Mike? You better call Sorensen back and make it right. You can still get out of this alive. You all can.'

'I don't even know what I've . . .' Mike forces himself to breathe. 'I don't even really know what this is. Just don't hurt them, okay? If you leave right now, I'll do whatever you say.'

'I like the sound of that,' says Chris.

Mike's wife is in the background. He can't make out what she's saying.

'It's okay,' says Chris. 'We've found him.'

'Leave,' says Mike. 'Please leave.'

'No problem,' says Chris, and then he lowers his voice. 'Where are you?'

Mike slams down the receiver.

He runs halfway up the block. 'Think,' he shouts

at himself, crouching on the footpath. His hands shake. '*Think.*' Mike races back to the phone box.

He calls the only number he has for Colleen.

No answer.

'Fuck.'

He calls the house again.

'Where are you?' says Chris. 'One chance.'

Mike tells him. 'Put Sonya on.'

He gets his wife. She mumbles something to Chris, her hand over the receiver, and then she says, 'What is happening, Mike? What—'

'You need to get him out of the house.'

'What?'

'Get . . .'

Pain spikes up Mike's arm. He's going to keel over.

'Are you there?' says Sonya. 'They're leaving. I'm watching them walk out now. Mike, what is—'

'When they're gone, you need to get in the car and get out of there.

Find somewhere to hide.'

'No, I . . . I—'

Mike spots a police car rounding the corner up the street.

'Sonya, they're going to fucking kill us. Please. *Please.*'

'Okay, okay, shit.'

'I love you,' he says, and hangs up.

The car pulls in by the phone box.

Mike hammers in another number.

Two cops get out of the car, both have their hands on their holsters.

By some miracle, the God Minister answers Mike's call.

Mike goes straight in. 'I'm about to get arrested. The cops have threatened my family. I'm fucked.'

One of the cops smashes his fist against the phone box glass. 'Out!'

'I see,' says the Minister. 'What's this I hear about a dead body in your motel?'

'It's—'

The cop yanks the door open.

'Wait, wait,' screams Mike.

They have his arm.

Mike struggles to keep his ear to the phone. 'You have to do something! WHY HAVE YOU—'

# PART SEVEN
# MONDAY, 4 OCTOBER
## 1982

# VICTOR

*Yes, yes, lucid now.*

*Full of pain and life once again. Emerging as if from sleep.*

*I don't let on. I play possum. Eyes closed, slurring and swaying. It's the last tool I have.*

*As expected, all this emboldens the liars and thieves around me. The staff are slipping. I hear them with the radio on down the other end of the house. Phone calls come in without messages. They are readying themselves for my departure.*

*But I'm back.*


*AFTERNOON and the house is empty, bar for the echoing of my voice. I'm shouting for Elda. 'Bring the phone! Elda! Bring the phone to me.'*

*She does it slowly, convinced it's a deranged whim. 'Who are you calling, Victor?'*

*'Everyone.'*

*I make a big show of placing several mundane calls: my accountant, the yacht club manager, my insurer. I pretend to ring my children and pretend they don't pick up.*

*'I'm . . . I must put my affairs in order,' I tell her.*

*Elda says, 'Sure, sure.'*

*It makes sense.*

*An old man finally accepting his fate.*

*But in reality, it's all about getting an extension lead on the phone. It's all about having the phone available to me in my new bed in the living room. A lifeline.*

DEEP *in the darkness and deep in the pain, it takes every ounce of strength I have to force myself awake. I can hear a distant murmur. I can feel movement and tension.*

*I reach over with tremendous ache and slowness, and gently pick up the white plastic receiver.*

*Elda is speaking with someone.*

*A voice on the other end says, 'He always was a wily old fuck.'*

*I know her.*

*Colleen Vinton.*

*Queen of the Damned.*

# BRUNO

## Fortitude Valley, Brisbane

BRUNO STANDS IN THE corner of the nightclub, a ghost-like figure in the strobe lights. He's up in Brisbane city, in the Valley, deep in the red-light district. It's not safe, exactly—nothing is completely safe—but the city offers a type of cover. He's not from there. People don't know his face on the streets. No one has seen him in uniform.

He takes a sip of his drink.

Watches the dance floor heave to Ultravox.

Guys come past and keep going.

Some girl asks him for a light.

It's the tail end of a late night, the witching hour where a hundred lonely souls like Bruno pray for relief and get this instead: a crowded mess, sweat condensation dripping from a basement ceiling.

Bruno orders another gin and tonic and pays the barman. Turning back to the crowd, he finds a man waiting. Early twenties. Thin toned arms. A rolled cigarette slipped behind his ear. The guy is looking at the liquor shelf behind the bar, but his eyes pass over Bruno and he smiles.

'You want something?' says Bruno.

'What are you drinking?'

He orders another.

The two of them find a table and there's an attempt at conversation. Bruno doesn't dance, so he watches the man go out. He orders another round.

Later, the guy kisses him lightly and says, 'Come with me.'

They hit the bathrooms and find a cubicle. The guy's hands are on him immediately, in his hair, pulling him close. Bruno slides a hand over the guy's crotch, finding a thick, tight bulge. He rubs at it with his palm.

'Get out of it,' the guy says, taking Bruno's hand and pinning it to the cubicle wall. He kisses Bruno's neck as he unzips him, sits on the closed pedestal and works on Bruno with his mouth. Bruno closes his eyes and tries to block out the bathroom and the overhead lighting and the music.

It doesn't take long. 'I'm gonna come,' he whispers.

'Show me,' he says, and they both watch as Bruno ejaculates. Then the man gives him a rough kiss on the cheek and says, 'That was fun.' With that, he's gone.

Bruno takes toilet paper and wipes up after himself, mentally preparing to step out of the cubicle. He sets his eyes dead ahead, opens the door, makes his way to the sink and slowly washes his hands under the tap.

Behind him, another cubicle door opens.

A man steps out, just a shape in Bruno's peripheral vision.

The tap runs in the sink beside Bruno, water pouring out.

Pouring and pouring.

The water keeps coming.

Annoyed, Bruno looks over.

Pete Reynolds is standing there in a blue silk dress shirt.

'Fuck,' says Bruno. He moves, almost runs.

'Wait,' says Reynolds. 'Stop.'

Bruno is already at the bathroom door. 'We never—'

'Hold on.' Reynolds finally slips his hands under the running water. 'We better have a chat.'


REYNOLDS KNOWS a late-night bistro on Ann Street. They get a table up the back. Reynolds slumps sideways in his chair, his back against the wall. They order coffee and sit there waiting, ashing their cigarettes in the same ashtray.

'You serve up here?' asks Bruno.

'My posting before the coast.'

Bruno leans in. 'Look, we both could have been down there for all sorts of reasons.'

Reynolds shakes his head. 'I'm sure you've got a lot of shit going through your head right now, but . . .'

'I could have been down there with anyone.'

'No, don't do that.'

The coffee arrives. They wait it out as the waitress sets the cups down.

Bruno says, 'So what do you want to talk about?'

'Give me a minute.' Reynolds looks around the bistro, a sullen glare.

'I guess I don't need to worry about you dobbing me in.'

'No. But . . .' Reynolds swallows deep. 'There is something I need to tell you, and it's not entirely unrelated to all this. That kid from the other night, the—' Reynolds draws his thumb across his neck. *Jamie.* 'I knew him. You asked me the other day how I ended up in the shitter at work. Well, Jamie is how it happened. He does a bit of side-work for Colleen Vinton and . . . there's pictures of us together. So now I work for Vinton as well. Her and the boys up here. It's all much of a muchness. Once you're tarred with the brush, you've got to clock on for whoever wants you.'

*Photos.*

Bruno's stomach clenches. 'You could leave?' he says.

'You mean, quit the Force?' Reynolds fiddles with his lighter. 'I'm not fucking quitting. The job is virtually all I have. It took me a long time to work out what was going on with me. I'll be forty fucking years old next year, and let me tell you, you don't end up at The Terminus at my age if you've got someone waiting for you at home. My life is a mess. I take it you don't go out much at home?'

'No.'

'Your family know?'

'No. Maybe. I've never said anything.'

'It's not easy.'

'I was going to tell my dad before he went, every day for weeks on end, but you know . . .' Bruno lays his palms gently down against the tabletop. 'Ran out of weeks.'

'I never told my old man. Or my mum. I don't even know if I regret it. I guess I do.'

'It's late,' says Bruno. 'I'm driving back tonight. What are you doing?'

'Can I get a lift?'

'Really?'

'Yeah.' Reynolds gently rubs his forehead. 'I want to show you something.'

BACK IN THE CAR, back on the highway, two detectives driving into the night, smoking with the windows down and the radio off.

'Take the next exit,' says Reynolds.

They weave their way through a thin strip of suburbia lining the Pacific Highway, out into the cane country of Alberton. A few minutes later, Reynolds directs Bruno onto a dirt road. No streetlights.

'Where are we going?'

'You'll see.'

Bruno slowly takes a hand off the wheel and drops it down by his side. He touches the place where his gun normally is, before remembering that he's not at work.

'Okay, this'll do,' says Reynolds.

They stop and Reynolds gets out of the car. He stands on the shoulder of the road and Bruno follows suit, staying on his side of the vehicle.

'What am I looking at, Pete?'

'See that back there?'

Bruno can just make out a house in the distance.

'That's where I grew up,' says Reynolds.

'Your family still own it?'

'Nope. The farming life wasn't for me. I had bigger plans than all this.'

'Yeah?'

'Oh yeah. I had big dreams, mate. I was going to be a policeman.'

# AMY
## Hamilton Storage, Coolangatta

AMY SNAPS AWAKE. SHE'S in the car, parked across the street from the storage complex. She wipes crust from her eyes and curses. There's a car parked in front of Jamie Leaver's unit, a black BMW. Can't have been there long. Amy remembers the start of dawn and it's only eight thirty now. She takes down the plate numbers and walks them up the street to a busted phone booth where she calls Dirty Doug.

It seems like it might be a bit early for Dirty Doug and his nefarious dealings, but the man picks up.

'It's Amy Owens. Can you run me a quick plate check?'

'How quick?'

'Can you do it now?'

'For a fee.'

She reads off the digits and says, 'I'll be waiting.'

'Hang on. I have the other thing for you.'

'What other thing?'

'From the other night here. That house out back of Gaven belongs to Walter Pronzini.'

279

It's the house she followed Bill Webber to two nights back. His quick visit.

'Okay. Thanks, Doug. Call me back.'

Amy racks the phone and pain surges in her bad hand. She's slept on it.

A wave of nausea blooms.

*Old history.*

Standing in some street across from a shed full of guns.

Trading one headache for another.


IN AMY'S ESTIMATION, it was about five years ago that the wheels came off.

The dark old days.

After her brother died, and after her academic career collapsed, there was a long stretch of slower, less spectacular decline. Amy took her family-money and moved out. She lived on the Strip and partied every night. She didn't even pretend to work or to have a job. There were no board seats or community service for her. No galas or fundraisers. No husband or family, either. Just an endless state of distraction. The Gold Coast in the seventies.

Mid '75, she cocked up one of her father's business soirees. Knocked over the champagne fountain at the launch of some shopping centre. That was enough for Victor.

He cut her off.

It didn't stop her.

She still had the rep. A party girl, she knew how to bring people to a place and keep them there. A hundred wannabe socialites, a thousand lonely strangers. She slipped into club promotion like a hand into a silk glove. All the clubs she worked for were owned by Colleen.

At first, the grifts were small-time.

Free drinks went top shelf. Pinching play money from the till. She passed around a bit of blow. Acid if you wanted it. Pills on the down low.

She connected people.

Then Harry Harvey entered the picture. Harry was a scumbag Colleen had running the clubs. He mentioned to Amy that he had his own line on powders. It was double your money for the same risk. Amy figured she was already doing the bit, so why not. Maths was never her strong suit. It didn't take Colleen long to work out why sales were dropping off.

One August night, Amy is asleep in her bed, having just got in.

The front door flies in.

Footfall in the hall.

Three men and no words.

They drag her out of the apartment screaming, and absolutely no one in the building says a word. They ram her in the back of a car alongside Harry.

The drive takes forever, but it's no more than thirty minutes, out of the coast and into the hinterland, off the bitumen into the gravel.

It's pitch-black.

Amy's adrenaline is pumping.

She's going to die.

They turn off into some no-name part of the bush.

Headlights wash over a figure in the trees.

*Oh fuck*.

It's Tommy Lomax.

Everyone knows Tommy. He's the last person

anyone on the coast wants to see, because he's the last person a lot of people see. Everyone in the trade is completely terrified of him.

The rest of what happens is a lurid, blurry nightmare.

They both cop a beating.

Tommy uses a leather belt.

He spits on them, presses his dirty fingers into their wounds. He's relentless. Demon eyes blazing in the headlights. He has a roll of electrical tape and he wraps Harry's dying head in it, then tapes Amy's hand to Harry's face, her palm covering his eyes, because *I don't want that dog looking at me*, and then Tommy takes a handgun and presses it into Amy's hand and pulls the trigger, killing Harry and exploding Amy's whole life up to that point, spraying her face in pink mist.

A sound comes out of Amy like she's never heard before. She tries to escape, to pull away, but she's still taped to Harry's wet, heavy skull. She's caught like a wild animal.

Tommy grabs her by the hair. 'Colleen wants you in her office on Monday.'

And then they're gone.

Men disappearing into cars.

Cars backing out.

Cars driving away.

Amy sitting there in the absolute darkness of the scrub, still attached to the dead body of her former boss. Dazed and in shock, it feels like she's falling, like Harry's body is dragging her down like an anchor.

She starts to sink.

And it never stops.

. . .

# THE DREAM

THE PHONE in the booth rings, bringing Amy out of the haze.

'Doug?'

'The car is registered to Marion O'Grady. Fifteen Pohlman Drive, Southport.'

She hangs up.

*Goddamn.*

That's the fucking house again, the one she photographed for Colleen a week ago.

She calls Colleen and lays it out.

Colleen barely listens.

She isn't putting together the pieces.

Bill Webber drove past that house the other night as well. Now the O'Gradys' car is here, one degree of separation from a dead Jamie Leaver down in Coolangatta.

'Mike's in the lock-up,' Colleen says. 'I just got word from a guy in the station house. They brought him in last night.'

'How did they get to him?'

'I don't know, Amy. How did they find him?' screams Colleen. 'You have to fucking fix this. Call in everyone. Everything. Just . . . whatever it takes. *Fuck.* I was so close. Goddamn it. And *you*, you had one fucking job. I better not . . . you better not be involved.'

'He was safe and sound when I left.'

'I hope that's true, for your sake. In the meantime, you fucking fix this. *Fix it.*'

The phone goes dead.

Amy stands in the booth. She thinks and thinks.

No answer arrives.

Amy sits in a patch of dry grass by the phone box. She puts her head between her knees and tries to breathe. What she wants, above all else, is a drink. But that's the problem. The start and the middle and the end of every problem.

The sun illuminates everything around her.

Sweat running from her pits.

She can't move.

*Fix it.*

# BRUNO
## The Esplanade, Surfers Paradise

BRUNO CAN'T SLEEP. HE gets enough to operate, but nothing more. By nine o'clock he's out in the water, attempting to surf, but quickly finds he can't do that either. He settles for sitting in the dunes, thinking about Pete Reynolds and his depressing story. There are implications. *Connections.* He's still there ruminating on it when a woman in black comes ambling down through the beach grass.

'You got a minute?' she says.

'I don't think so,' says Bruno, taking her in.

'You know who I am?'

He does, after a moment. Her name is Amy Owens. She's one of Colleen's minions. Amy has spent a few nights in the lock-up for public intoxication. Could be that she's headed back there this morning.

'What do you want?' he says.

'I'm the one who put the photos under your windscreen wipers.'

Bruno doesn't know whether to laugh or cry.

*Working for Colleen Vinton all along.*

*Same as Pete.*

'What does that mean?' is all he can muster.

'I think we're both into something here,' the woman says. 'Don't suppose I can buy you breakfast?'

'Can we do it down at the station house?'

'It's a bit early for that.'

Bruno looks out at the surf. 'Okay. Let me get changed.'


TO HER CREDIT, Amy comes through with breakfast. She disappears for fifteen minutes and returns with takeaway teas and two rounds of toasted cheese sandwiches. They stand across the street from the Cavill Avenue Mall and eat without saying much to each other. The shrieking of children echoes out of the Grundy's water slides.

'I hate that thing,' says Amy, nodding at the slides.

'It looks like the plumbing under my sink,' says Bruno. 'So, what are we doing here?'

Amy shakes her hand like she's trying to sling water from it. It's a nervous tic of some sort. 'I think we can help each other.'

'You mean, I can help Colleen?'

'I have some information to share.'

'Oh yeah?' Bruno folds up the white paper bag his sandwich came in.

'I need a straight copper.'

'And yet here you are, trying to turn me out? I *was* a straight copper until those photos turned up.'

'I'm not the one jerking off guys behind a shopping centre.'

And there it is.

*The other photo.*

# THE DREAM

The bottom of the deck. The one in his bedroom safe.

'No names.'

That was one of the first things Bruno said to him.

He was beautiful, though. Had a face like a cigarette model—a cowboy—but maybe a foot too short, and a touch too blond, to pull it off. Bruno met him in the Pacific Fair Shopping Centre about a week after his dad's cancer diagnosis. He was out with Danny at the time. It didn't matter. The attraction was immediate and obvious. They hooked up a half-hour later. They exchanged numbers when it was done.

Bruno would call.

The man would answer.

It was good. The whole thing was primarily about fucking, but the clarity of it made it easy. In a lot of ways, the relationship ran counter to all of Bruno's impulses, but it never felt sullen and it always felt tender. He looked forward to their time together. His breath on Bruno's neck. The man's hands. It all worked.

Until it didn't.

Turned out the guy wasn't quite so taken.

He cut it off fast.

Bruno now knows why.

# AMY

## Cavill Avenue, Surfers Paradise

THE COP LOOKS LIKE he's about to puke up his toasted cheese sandwich. 'You really are a piece of shit,' he says.

'I hear you, but—'

'I could arrest you right now. I don't know why I'm not.'

She lets him simmer down a little. Then, 'I thought I was going to be an artist.'

He can barely look at her. *He looks inches away from pulling the whole thing down and taking her in.*

Amy goes for it. 'I thought the worst thing that could happen to me was I'd end up a wedding photographer. And then Colleen got her hooks in me.'

'Who gives a fuck?'

'You can still be a straight cop,' she says. 'You haven't wrecked yourself yet, trust me. If you think this is dirty, you're living in a dream world.'

'For the last time, what do you want?'

'I want the same thing you want. I want all of this to go away. You have a bloke in custody called Mike

Nichols. It's related to the murder of Jamie Leaver. From what I hear, the Joke is hot for him. He's some political lackey who works for the minister.'

'What minister?'

'*Your* minister. Anyway, he didn't kill Jamie. They're fitting him up.'

'Why would they do that?'

'He was snooping around and got in over his head. It's something to do with the deputy commissioner.'

Some part of it lands, because Bruno takes a second. 'You need to tell me everything you know, from the start. And I'm not agreeing to anything. I don't work for Colleen. That's finished. I'm not having a bar of it. Do what you like with the photo.'

'I don't care how we get it done.'

He studies her. 'If there's more, we should find a place to hole up. I've already been talking to you for too long out in the open.'

'There's more,' she says.

AMY POINTS him to her building. The flat is as it always is—a wreck—but seeing him take it in makes Amy hyperaware of the carnage. Bottles and empties on the floor. Junk, books, mail. Half a poster hung on the wall. A poisonous kitchen. Summer rot and mildew.

'What?' she says, looking right at him.

'Can we open a window?'

It takes her five whole minutes to unjam the sliding door. It's been that long.

Bruno plants himself out on the apartment's small patio, facing in.

'You want something to drink?'

'I'll stick to these,' he says, lighting a smoke.

'Don't suppose I can bum one?'

He hands one over. 'Let's get on with it.'

'What did you find at fifteen Pohlman Drive?'

'Nothing much. Why did you send me there?'

Amy tells him the truth: she doesn't know. 'Colleen keeps her cards close to her chest, even with the help.' The initial instructions were simple. Go to an address and run surveillance. Colleen didn't need photos. They were a bonus. 'I was testing out a new camera. After a week of sitting on the house and watching absolutely nothing happen, Colleen told me to deposit the photographs under the windscreen wipers of your car. That was the end of my part. I left town for a couple of days after that.'

'Why me?'

'Pete Reynolds told us you were in Missing Persons and that you were the sort of cop who'd follow it up. Colleen doesn't trust anyone so she had me include the other photo. You've been on her radar for a minute.'

He nods. *And?*

'I showed you mine,' says Amy.

'Remind me again, what am I going to come away with here?'

'Your job.'

Bruno gives in. He describes how the O'Grady family is missing, presumed dead. Two parents and one son. He tells her there's something going on with the family finances—emptied bank accounts, something shady about the bank. He says he's witnessed the bank crew in action and that they're wild dogs, killing and shooting without hesitation, but that there's some sort of targeted planning as well. 'I killed one of them. A local crim called Seth Blackwell. He was involved with the O'Grady kid, Samson, romantically, I think. It looks like Samson got himself mixed up with Blackwell and it might have gotten him and his parents killed. Your turn.'

'Do you know a cop called Bill Webber?'

'Sure. He's all right. He's in Robbers at the moment.'

'He's up to something. The talk is, he has internal police files he's not supposed to have access to. I've been following him, and he's been past Pohlman Drive a few times. He stops and looks at the place. I don't know what he's up to, but I think he's someone you should look into.'

Bruno's mouth drops open a little.

'What is it?' says Amy.

'Maybe later. What else has Webber been doing? You said you followed him.'

'There's more, but . . . I can't share it at the moment. I reckon you don't want to know.'

'Is he connected to the O'Gradys?'

'I don't know. At first, I thought he was working off those stolen files, but now I have no idea what he's up to. Colleen has me on loan to some of the Licensing boys up in Brisbane. They're circling Webber because of the files. There's a pattern with the people he's keeping an eye on.'

'And what's that?'

'They're all scumbags.'

'I see,' says Bruno. 'Come in and talk to me on tape. I'll look after you.'

'That's kind of you to say, but fuck no. What I need you to do is go check on Mike Nichols, then we can talk some more.'

'Yeah, I don't know about that. I'm not sure we're entirely past the going down to the station part.'

'Hang on a sec.' Amy walks into the tiny second bedroom, the space she uses as an office. There's a padlocked closet in there. She opens it, takes an envelope from a shelf, and gives it to Bruno. 'That's half of them. Consider it a down-payment.'

'What is it?' he says, but looks at the images of himself inside. He takes the negatives and holds them to the light. 'Okay, deal. I want the rest when I'm done.'

'I'm helping you. You're helping me. That's how it works.'

He folds the envelope in two. 'Can I make an ask? If we're going to scratch each other's back, I want your photos of Pete Reynolds as well. The photos and the negatives. I think you probably know the ones I'm talking about.'

'Well, there you go,' Amy says. 'Look at you. We could work up to that.'

'Maybe I won't go in today? Maybe this Mike Nichols guy doesn't need checking on.'

'Nah, I think you will, Bruno. I think you're the sort of guy that might worry about an innocent bloke getting topped by Queensland police officers. I reckon you'd have trouble sleeping at night if that happened.'

'I already have trouble sleeping at night. How do you sleep?'

'I don't. I just pass out intermittently.'

Bruno gets up to leave.

'Believe it or not, I'm trying to do the right thing here,' she says as he walks past.

He stops at the door. 'Why?'

'I've had enough,' she says.

'And you can see a way out of all this?'

'No. There's no way out of where I am. Not with this stuff.'

He waits.

'There's just through, Bruno. Just through.'

# BRUNO
## The Strip, Surfers Paradise

BRUNO REELS, HEART RACING in the car.

A web of leads forming. Amy Owens, as the source, giving him:

The man at the O'Grady house.

The man with the rifle in the closet.

The familiar sound of his voice.

Bill Webber.

'*It's not your case anymore.*'

He's a policeman. A rogue cop running his own show, camped out in the crime scene.

Bruno parks on the street, hits the front desk of the Surfers Paradise station house. 'Is Webber on duty?'

The uniformed kid at the desk scans his book and says, 'Nah. He's off sick.'

Bruno takes the stairs two at a time up to CIB, along the corridor of interview rooms, checking the windows. Right down the end, there's a man inside. He's alone.

Blond hair.

Blue eyes.

Looks halfway between a car salesman and a rugby forward.

A National Party stooge, all the way.

Bruno knocks on the glass and the man startles.

*Looks pretty alive to me.*


BRUNO ROLLS into the Robbery Squad section. It's a non-starter. His old partner Lana Cohen is alone, holding the fort, seated not five feet from Bill Webber's empty desk.

'You looking for work?' Lana says, swivelling in her chair.

'No, thanks. I was chasing Bill, actually.'

'Does he still work here?'

It's a joke, but there's an edge to it.

'Any news?' asks Bruno.

'Not really. Your mate Seth Blackwell may have been a knucklehead, but the crew he was running with is a tight ship. Everyone on my team is out interviewing anyone who has ever met the bloke, and we're *still* getting nowhere. How about you? I saw the transcript of your chat with the missus.'

'The gay stuff?'

'Yeah, what do you reckon happened with the O'Grady kid?'

'I don't know. The O'Gradys have money. Blackwell's a crook. I can't see them turning up alive.'

'Two plus two generally equals four,' says Lana.

'Okay, I'm gonna push on.'

Bruno scans the bullpen. The office secretary, Anne-Marie, is at her station—and she'd have access to Bill Webber's personnel file—but there's no way she's handing it over. No chance.

Bruno visits the records archive himself. He asks after missing files and knows it's grasping.

The clerk on duty laughs. 'Mate, who fucking knows? None of you dickheads ever sign anything out.'

BACK DOWN THE corridor and down the stairs, Bruno spots a familiar figure through the stairwell window: Pete Reynolds smoking a durrie, arse planted on the back of his car in the station carpark. Two minutes later, Bruno joins him, the two of them shielding their eyes to see one another in the glare. Bruno has every intention of tearing strips off the man, but Pete looks like death warmed up. Bruno suddenly feels his own misplaced culpability. He got *himself* caught, got *himself* photographed, just like Pete before him. While Pete may have put him forward for the O'Grady thing, Bruno feels the same pinch now.

'How's the head?'

'Not great,' Pete says.

'A friend of yours visited me this morning. Amy Owens.'

Pete goes still.

'It's okay,' says Bruno. 'You and I have more in common than I thought.'

Pete looks at his shoes, grinds one of them into the bitumen. 'I'm sorry to hear that. I thought you said you were careful.'

'I was. Can I talk to you about something and not have it reach Colleen?'

He nods.

'Something's going on. I need the file on one of your guys,' says Bruno.

Iain Ryan

'Which one?'

'Bill.'

'Bill Webber?'

'I'm pretty sure he's the guy who pulled the gun on me at the O'Grady house a couple of nights back.'

'Can't be. What would he be doing there?'

'Not sure yet. Has he ever stepped out of line?'

'Never. Bill's as straight as they come. He's been off sick a bit lately, but even then, he's been coming in where he can. He was at the scene the other day. What are you looking for in his file?'

'Home address. Whatever else I can get.'

'He didn't top the O'Gradys. There's just no way.'

'Whatever he did, he's out of line and we need to take a look at him.'

'Okay.' Reynolds starts off across the lot. At the door to the station house he turns and says, 'Wait here.'

# BRUNO
## San Michelle Street, Tugun

BRUNO PARKS IN THE driveway of Bill Webber's house as if this is a social visit. It's the way Pete Reynolds wants to play it. 'We're not going to mess him about,' Reynolds says.

Webber's file is sparse: an exemplary policing record and nothing wayward around the edges. He was born and bred on the coast. No family or significant other. His emergency contact is a woman called Ruby Fisher, which might be a girlfriend, but Reynolds isn't sure. 'I can't say he's ever mentioned one.'

Today, Webber's place looks shut up tight.

To be sure, Reynolds pounds on the door. 'Knock-knock,' he yells.

After a minute, he heads back to the car. 'No dice.'

'Come on,' says Bruno. 'I've got an errand to run. Let's come back.'

The errand is a call to Amy Owens from a phone box around the corner.

She doesn't pick up.

Bruno talks to her answering machine instead. 'Mike Nichols is sitting in an interview room upstairs at Surfers Paradise Station House. He's fine, but he's alone. Maybe you want to send a lawyer down. Call me back.'

He can't say what he wants to say. He can't make that recording. *I did your bidding, now turn over the information you're sitting on.* Just the call itself—plain and simple—is a violation of the code. There's nothing hazy about it. Colleen Vinton asked and he answered. It's the first properly crooked thing Bruno has ever done on the job, and by Bruno's way of thinking, a little is the same as a lot.

*I'm corrupt now.*

BACK IN THE CAR, Reynolds tells him they're going for a drive.

'Whereabouts?'

'Southport. You're going to like this.' Reynolds turns out onto the highway and heads north. 'While you were on the phone, I radioed in Bill's emergency contact, this Ruby Fisher. She lives on Falconer Street.'

'I don't know it.'

'Have a look,' Reynolds says, tapping the street directory on the bench between them.

The directory is open. The map looks familiar.

'Oh shit,' says Bruno.

Falconer is two streets south of Pohlman, five minutes' walk from the O'Grady crime scene.

'It's not looking good for Bill,' says Bruno.

. . .

# THE DREAM

Ruby Fisher yells at the two of them through the screen door of her house. 'What do you want?'

They can't see her. She's just a voice echoing out.

'We're police. We work with Bill,' says Reynolds.

A woman shuffles into view. She's a white lady in her late forties, dressed in baggy cream capri pants and a blue striped shirt. 'Sorry, sorry. I thought you were the Mormons. Is Bill all right?'

'He's fine,' says Reynolds. 'We're just doing the rounds looking for him.'

Ruby invites them in. As Reynolds quizzes her on Bill and his whereabouts, Bruno scans the living room and kitchen. There's a framed picture of Bill on the wall by the back patio doors. He looks young in the shot, Ruby with her arm around him. Across the room, Bruno can hear the woman explaining, 'That's right. He came to live here when he was six. Ronnie and I couldn't have kids of our own and we figured adopting him would be near enough. His parents were killed in a robbery. Some nutjob broke in and tried to rob them and ended up killing them both. They found Bill hiding in a closet. That's all I know about it. All I want to know.'

'Is Ronnie your husband, ma'am?'

'That's right. He's at temple. What's this about?'

Reynolds spins her some yarn about Webber being off-duty and needing him back at the office. 'If you see Bill, can you get him to call me? I'll give you my card.'

'He hasn't done anything wrong, has he?'

'No, ma'am. We're just trying to track him down.'

Bruno searches other photos nearby.

Ruby and Ronnie on holidays.

Ruby, Ronnie and Bill at a rollerskating rink.

On the kitchen wall, taped beside a calendar is a

faded polaroid of Bill and another kid. 'Who's this?' says Bruno.

Ruby peers over. 'Oh, that.' She comes round the kitchen bench. 'Let me see. That's Bill and Sunny.'

'Who's he?'

'A kid from the neighbourhood.'

'Can I keep this?'

'I love that photo of Bill. He never smiles like that. Will you bring it back?'

'I think we can handle that,' says Reynolds. 'You can report it stolen if we don't.'

The woman isn't sold.

'I'm from the Robbery Squad,' says Reynolds. 'I'll be the guy who picks up the phone.'

She lets them take it.

# AMY

## Stationhouse, Surfers Paradise

BRUNO KARRAS'S ANSWERING MACHINE
message comes in after lunch, but it's five o'clock in
the afternoon before Amy finds herself at the police
station following up. In the time in between, there's a
lot of confusion: Colleen Vinton's usual channels
don't work. None of the Gold Coast boys will walk
Mike Nichols out of the station. On top of that,
Robert Emmery starts acting up. Emmery is Colleen's
pet straight man and the go-to for legal help. But as
soon as Emmery hears the name Mike Nichols, he
ums and ahs, talking about a busy calendar and sched-
uling conflicts. Emmery says he needs a day or so to
sort things out. Amy circulates that news back to
Colleen and Colleen goes right off the handle,
screaming down the line so loud Amy can practically
feel the spit landing on her face. Two hours later,
Emmery's lead solicitor calls and suddenly she's available to work. They go to the station house together.

But the whole thing is to no avail.

None of it washes with the cops. The front desk
guys stonewall them from the get-go. The uniformed

teenager they have working reception calls in the sergeant on duty, wherein the sergeant denies everything: 'We don't seem to have a Mike Nichols in custody. If he was here, he's not now.'

'You must have a record?' says the solicitor.

The sergeant stares at them, a little for each. 'Yes,' he says.

Amy leans in. 'I want to talk to Ron Bingham.'

The sergeant phones Bingham, nods, then puts the phone down. 'He's unavailable.'

'*Unavailable?*'

The solicitor places a hand on Amy's arm. 'What can we do here, fellas? Just tell us how we sort this out.'

'I don't know,' says the sergeant. 'We didn't charge him.'

The solicitor takes it in her stride. She turns and walks out.

On the footpath, Amy clenches and unclenches her hand. 'What are we going to do? You reckon he's still in there somewhere?'

'I wouldn't say so. Might've just missed him.'

'We're fucked then.'

'That would be my professional assessment, yes.'

'Do you have any other advice you want to offer up?'

'I'd counsel you to proceed with caution, Amy. In my experience, there's only one thing that scares the cops more than Colleen.'

'Oh yeah, what's that?'

'Other cops.'

AMY MEETS Colleen at The White Light and repeats the story of Mike's disappearance. The woman is on her feet immediately, knocking Amy offside with a slap and snaking her fingers through Amy's hair as soon as her knees hit the ground. 'Say that again, bitch.'

Amy freezes, terrified. 'I don't . . . I don't know what to do.'

'None of you do,' Colleen says, twisting her hand. Amy's scalp pulls away from her skull. 'You're all fucking hopeless. Are you fucking listening to me?'

Amy stares up at her.

'I said *are you listening*?' Colleen nods Amy's head for her, like a ventriloquist with a puppet. 'Good. Here's what you're going to do, or I'm going to fucking cut your head off. I've heard from another little birdie that your geriatric father is up to no good. Him and Allan Watts. You'd think someone's own daughter might have some idea what's going on, but not Victor Owen's deadshit garbage, no. His . . . what was that? Speak up.'

'I . . . I promise, there's—'

'*Enough*. You were supposed to find out what was going on and you didn't. You were supposed to take care of Mike, and you didn't. So here are your options: go out there and find out whatever happened to Mike, or, so help me god, what Tommy did to you will feel like a loving caress. You hear me? How'd you like to have holes in both hands?'

Colleen drops her.

It takes Amy a few seconds to compose herself. She touches her hair and comes back with blood spots.

Overhead, Colleen smooths out her dress. 'Amy, listen to me. No bullshit this time. If this thing with Mike disappears, you disappear. It's two strikes and you're out. You understand?'

Amy breathes.

'Nod your head, darl.'

Amy nods.

But what she's agreeing to is an end to all this.

*So help me god.*

*I want to disappear.*


AMY IS a roving orb of bad energy now. A slow bottle in her lap. Drinking and driving, barely under control. She's cruising from location to location. It's pure desperation. She's floundering, looking for anything that might unravel this situation with Colleen.

She calls Dirty Doug and tells him to put his feelers out for Mike Nichols.

She hits up favours from Brisbane to the Tweed.

*Nothing.*

She hits the storage shed out by the airport. The black BMW is still parked out front. It's got nothing to do with Mike but it's as good a place as any to sit and think.

Amy cops the dying light and feels a sick sense of closure looming.

Any way you run it, things are fucked up.

Out of nowhere, she thinks about the crazy girl, the one she drove to Adelaide.

Her missing baby.

*'Start what over?'*

It's nothing.

More guilt.

Not even a blip on Amy's mental tally. There's so much more. Things so much worse than a baby taken from her mother. Only the re-emergence of the memory is interesting. Only that it's *this* and not a hundred other things. It doesn't compute.

*Fuck it.*

Amy takes her gun out of the glove box and puts it under her chin.

Closes her eyes.

*Go on, then.*

But behind her eyelids, she sees even more horror.

She sees Victor.

Then a dozen men like him and their angry mores.

All the drugs and thieving.

Dealing, seeking out . . .

Tommy Lomax in the black scrub. Her hand covered in electrical tape and gore.

The rest of her sad little life ever since.

The jobs that followed.

Photographing naked men and women, men in their houses, women in their cars, inhaling powders, smoking weed, sucking and fucking and jerking each other off, then men in brothels through two-way mirrors, men in harnesses and leather, props and toys and the raw sewerage of unrestrained desire, the will of cops and politicians and TV presenters and disc jockeys and businessmen and businesswomen and models and housewives and all sorts. A guy who fucks farm animals. A guy who chokes himself with a belt. A guy who let people extinguish cigarettes on him. Sordid shit. Peeper material. A guy who lived in a penthouse who cleans women with a toothbrush beforehand. A guy Colleen fancied, a priest's kid who took it up the arse with a strap-on, but only from Colleen, and only when she was dressed like a nun. And a woman—some famous musician—who liked to piss in a cup and force other people to drink it. There were a thousand sins, a thousand more. Sins giving way to deals, giving way to other deals, all nested within even bigger crimes. No one could see the whole thing. It was a train wreck of minor transgressions that must have destroyed a thousand lives by now. And there was no cure for it outside work and the bottle and pushing on.

Because you can get so dirty, you stop wanting to be clean.

All because you—

Amy pulls the trigger.

Nothing happens.

The safety is on.

'Goddamn it.'

She checks the gun, finds the latch.

Puts it back under her chin.

Pushes this sad final vista out of her vision: the airless macabre vibe of the car's interior, the place she's parked, out by industrial sheds near the airport.

*No, you deserve this.*

Amy opens her eyes.

She forces the scenery in.

*Look at it.*

*Godspeed to bad rubbish.*

But . . .

A sound draws her eye. A man steps out of the door across the way, out of the shed and around to the driver's side of the BMW.

Amy doesn't recognise him.

The car pulls out.

The timing is such that Amy can't help but wonder if it's preordained.

# AMY

## Albion Avenue, Miami

RUNNING ON PURE INSTINCT, Amy follows the BMW for twenty minutes, from the storage shed in Coolangatta to a house in an average neighbourhood street in Miami. It's dark now. The house isn't much: a modest two-storey structure, its weathered timber facade adorned with gaudy brown-glass window features that glint under the streetlights. Amy parks around the corner and watches from a distance.

The black BMW idles by the kerb.

Connections cohere.

The storage shed ties into the bank jobs.

Dead Jamie Leaver had the keys.

Jamie's body, found in Mike Nichols's motel room.

Amy gets a bad feeling.

The man from the storage shed gets out of his vehicle. Amy cranes her head to get a look at the driver across the way. He's a black shadow. No discernible features. Could be anyone. He takes a large object from the boot of his car and puts it in the boot of another car parked in the driveway of the house.

It's a drop.

The man gets back in his car and pulls away.

Amy watches the house.

Gives it five minutes, then collects her lock kit and creeps over, staying low to the ground. The other car is an old Ford Falcon. The boot pops with minimal effort.

Her hands reach inside and pad around.

There's a large canvas duffle bag.

Amy grabs the bag and closes the boot.

A spotlight comes on, a bright bulb attached to the house. There's a man standing under it.

'Might want to put that back,' he says.

Amy's eyes focus. He has a gun aimed her way, but the car is between them. 'Okay, hold on,' she says.

'Do it now.'

She recognises him, then. It's Allan Watts. He stands by the garage door wearing white slacks and a baby blue polo shirt.

'I know who you are,' he says. 'You're that cunt who works for Colleen. Go and tell Colleen that—'

Amy drops the bag and brings her gun up.

Allan doesn't shoot, but his entire body tenses up.

'Don't do it,' she says.

'Do you know what's in the bag?' His hands waver, the gun shaking a little.

'Where's Mike Nichols? We can trade.'

'What?'

Allan's still moving. He won't stop.

'I'm backing up,' says Amy. 'I'm—'

Allan's first shot lands wide, sparking the paint-work of the car's roof. It's the last thing Amy senses before her own gun goes off, fingers gripped around the trigger, pulling. When it's over, Allan's gone.

Amy looks under the car.

Allan's lying on the ground. There's blood everywhere—on his face and neck, spreading across his baby blue polo—but he's still alive. His eyes locked onto her.

She runs.

Down the drive and into the street.

*Fuck.*

Back for the duffle bag, then back across the street with it. The bag weighs a tonne. She ambles around the corner to her car.

Amy cranks the key in the ignition, panicking, oblivious.

The engine stutters.

She hears neighbours in their houses.

Yelling.

Calling out.

She hears sirens.

The engine takes, roaring to life and shunting the car forward so fast it mounts the kerb before fishtailing out onto the street, leaving a cloud of burning rubber to float across the way to the body at the front of the house.

# BRUNO
## Palmer Drive, Labrador

BY SEVEN O'CLOCK, BRUNO and Pete
Reynolds are done. They started the day in the bathroom of a nightclub, now both are bone-tired and
silent. Bill Webber remains at large. Reynolds has officially filed his disappearance, to no avail: it's a busy
night on the coast. A shooting in Miami. A drunken
brawl in Cavill Avenue. Nevertheless, the night-shift
guys promise to call through if there's news.

'He'll pop up,' says Reynolds as they sit in the car
out front of Bruno's family home. 'I thought you
lived in Mermaid Beach?'

'It's my father's place. My brother and sister are
cleaning it out. I promised to put my head in.'

'Try to get some sleep.'

'You too. See you tomorrow.'

The yard light is on, some of the interior lamps as
well, but the place is empty. A handful of boxes
stacked in quiet piles. A vacant living room. A few
pieces of bedroom furniture wrapped in bedsheets.
Danny and Gracie are long gone.

Bruno takes a shower and uses an old towel

313

hanging in there. The only bed left intact is his father's. Even stripped bare and dusty, the thing smells like the old man, like his hair wax and deodorant. Bruno feels a huge swell of emotion building in his chest as he lies there, a sickly feeling heating his neck and face.

*No.*

*You can't afford it.*

*Not after the day you've had.*

Bruno steadies himself. He gives himself the seconds he needs.

Within a minute, he's asleep.

But Bruno remains close to the surface of consciousness, prodded and poked by the trouble he's in. At ten thirty, he comes all the way awake and uses the bathroom. As soon as he ventures out into the house, barefoot on the plastic hallway runners, a part of him knows that's all the rest he's getting.

But the night has barely begun.

Bruno calls home and his brother answers. 'Sorry I missed you two today,' he says.

'You didn't miss much. Where are you?' When Danny hears the answer, he laughs. 'You're really turned around, aren't you, brother?'

'It's been a weird couple of days.'

'I'll say. Are you on the phone in the kitchen?'

He is.

Danny says, 'Look out the window.'

Bruno checks the yard. There's a rectangular blue box sitting on the lawn. 'What is it?'

'A coffin.'

'Pretty small coffin.'

'It's Dad's old fishing esky. We cleaned out the shed today and guess what we found in the esky?'

'What?'

'The skeleton of a possum.'

'How'd that get in there?'

'No idea. It was up on top of the drawers in the shed. Nothing on top of the lid or anything. I figure Dad had it open and the poor bugger took a nap in there and something went wrong.'

'Bloody hell. That's dark.'

'Yeah, it's not cool. Gracie was beside herself.'

'The possum's not still in there, is it?'

'Nah. She made me bury it. You picked a good day to stay away.'

'Sounds like it.'

They move on to slightly cheerier topics, but not by much. Realtors are booked to come through in the morning, sizing the place up. Gracie's keen on a fast sale, still talking a blue streak about needing the cash. Her marriage is shaky.

Danny yawns. 'Can you let the agents in tomorrow?'

'I've gotta go in.'

Danny doesn't have much to say about that.

'Sorry,' says Bruno.

'It is what it is. But, you know . . .'

'What do I know?'

'This is actually happening, mate. You can face it now or you can face it later.'

'It's going to have to be later.'

Danny sighs. 'With you, it always is.'

Bruno puts the phone back on the hook and stands by the glass sliding doors, looking out at the esky. He feels compelled to look inside it, so he walks out and stands over the thing. He's surprised to find that he remembers it. This is the esky they dragged out every Christmas for the prawns and beer. Bruno's fairly certain it came on camping trips and school excursions. It was where they put the meat and milk during power blackouts.

After a few seconds, he reaches down and lifts the lid.

Empty.

Scrubbed clean and smelling of bleach.

Bruno runs his hands along the hard plastic lining. It's still wet inside. It's strange to think of a dead body in here, touching what he's touching now. A mass of death and decay nestled within this anti-septic interior. To the eye, it's clean enough to eat off. A sparkling white rectangle. Almost new.

Bruno stands up.

Something clicks.

# BRUNO
## Pohlman Drive, Soutport

BRUNO KILLS THE ENGINE out front of the O'Grady house. The dashboard clock reads 11.35 pm. Not a light on in the entire street. He drags his father's sledgehammer out of the passenger seat footwell and takes it through the front door and across the foyer to the stairs, then down the stairs to the basement storage area.

A plain white empty room with a concrete floor.

Like the plain white empty esky.

The walls are almost glowing. Freshly painted and re-rendered in Bruno's mind by one simple match: the dead bank robber, Seth Blackwell, he had a job.

'*He told me he was a plasterer's apprentice.*'

Bruno knocks on the walls.

Solid.

Solid.

Solid.

Hollow.

Bruno takes the sledgehammer and marks the spot and swings.

Dust fills the air.

He braces for the stench, but as the hole appears, nothing like that floats out. He keeps working, smashing a hole large enough to crawl through. When it's done, he shines a torch inside and finds a secret room. A rug on the floor. The legs of furniture.

Bruno goes through on hands and knees, half-terrified of the dark as he shuffles through with the flashlight. He stands up on the other side and puts the wall firmly against his back.

Something isn't right.

He waves the light around, the beam flashing over indistinguishable shapes. He's scanning for horror. He's scanning for a demon squatting in the corner. Another man with a shotgun. Bruno's cop instincts run rampant, screaming at him to leave and call for back-up.

But he did that last time and it was for naught.

So, he slows himself down.

The torchlight finds a desk.

There's a lamp and a switch.

Moving very carefully, Bruno walks across the space and hits the lights.

It's an office.

A workspace: a chair, stationery, paper on the walls, a screen for a projector, electrical equipment and bookshelves. There's a small single bed and a shelf packed with what looks like linen and towels. Just as Bruno is about to breathe out, he sees something else, something out of the corner of his eye.

Three squat objects.

Three waist-high plastic barrels.

Chemical hazard stickers on the side.

A funeral wreath on the floor beside them.

He knows immediately.

Phillip O'Grady.

# THE DREAM

Marion O'Grady.

Samson O'Grady.

Dead bodies in barrels.

Buried in the basement of the house in which they were killed.

# PART EIGHT
# TUESDAY, 5 OCTOBER
## 1982

# VICTOR

*In ANOTHER ERA, I might have lashed out quickly. There can be advantages to it—to sudden and extreme violence, delivered or implied—but I learned long ago about the disadvantages as well. A sudden move can make work, you see. And while this house is partially built on fast moves, I see now that it's also built on the detritus created. The body in the slab. Her children running free and wild and making their own mess of things. Poor Allan. He didn't even get to die in the driveway of his nice house.*

# AMY

## The Strip, Surfers Paradise

AMY HOLES UP IN the same place she took Mike, the half-finished skyscraper on the Esplanade. No light on the horizon. Ocean wind sailing through. She stands on the lip of the building, watching and drinking. The streets of the Strip are near on empty. No screaming squad cars. It's just another day for a hundred thousand people.

But for Amy, there's a strange future rolling out.

Dead Allan Watts's duffle bag is full of money.

A lot of money.

Three hundred thousand, give or take.

Bank robbery money.

*Has to be.*

But it's also *disappear-and-never-come-back* money.

Amy looks over the edge of the building. She grips a piece of steel scaffolding and leans out, dropping her empty beer bottle.

It takes seconds to land.

A dull pop.

She walks back through the half-built floor.

There's an enclosed area—a collection of walls in the centre, the first apartment on this level. There are still traces of Mike here: the milk crate he was sitting on, a plastic six-pack ring. Amy lies down on a paint-flecked leather couch and closes her eyes.

THE WORKERS WAKE her as they trundle up the steel-frame stairs outside.

Amy sits up. Bright daylight coming in through the unfinished seams of the walls.

A grizzly old bloke steps into the apartment. Hard hat and beer gut. 'Who are you?'

'No one,' Amy says.

'Fair enough. You better get out of here, though.' A

my grabs the duffle bag and walks.

The man whistles, high-pitched.

'What?' she says.

'Jesus, luv. Are you okay?' The man is holding out a Samsonite suitcase. 'Found this the other day.'

Amy recognises it. She grabs it, tries to smile.

'Have a good one,' says the bloke.

THE BUILDING IS FINISHED from the ground floor down, giving the basement carpark an eerie, empty air. Without a soul in sight, Amy places Mike's Samsonite suitcase on the bonnet of her car and rifles through. It's the usual: clothes, toiletries, paperwork from his job. Amy pats down the lid and finds a slot. Inside the slot there's a notebook. It's his work diary. There's all sorts of stuff in there.

The phone numbers of famous people.

Big figures in lists.

A meeting schedule.

Jotted notes.

Amy turns to the last page.

His last day.

Nichols met with Robert Emmery in the morning. *Fantasyland bid.*

Then bumped into Allan Watts afterwards.

Amy flashes back to Allan's fading eyes. Blood pumping from a hole in his throat.

She turns the page.

A polaroid of Mike with his dick out.

Then there's a folded piece of foolscap paper stuffed into a random page towards the back. It's a rough handwritten ledger. All pencil. Names and dates and numbers. Big players. Legal people, judges and lawyers. Entertainment celebs. Bankers and brokers. Several names have been crossed out. She recognises three.

*Wally Stewart.*

*Walter Pronzini.*

*Phillip O'Grady.*

Amy recognises them because she followed Bill Webber to their houses.

The scrubland of Cedar Creek.

The outskirts of Gaven.

Pohlman Drive, Southport.

*But how does Mike Nichols fit into Webber's mess?*

*More to the point, how does Colleen?*

*And her father?*

Victor isn't on the ledger, but he's on Bill Webber's route.

*It doesn't matter.*

It's time to cash out, blow town, and let these people destroy each other.

·  ·  ·

AMY DRIVES past her apartment twice, checking for cops.

She parks and walks up.

*Ten minutes tops.*

Amy has returned for two things: her negatives, and a photograph. Of all the images she's taken, *this* is the one she keeps for herself: a faded holiday snap of Will, Angela and Amy on a beach in Cairns as children. Just three little people without a hint of regret on them. Some strange, vivid snapshot of what could have been. Amy keeps the photo in an old encyclopaedia under the coffee table. Can't have it on display. Can't be reminded of *all that* every day. And yet she can't leave the coast without it.

On the way out, she leaves the door unlocked. The place can be raided or firebombed for all she cares. Nothing lost. *Fuck the landlord.*

She takes the internal stairs back down, footfall echoing around the brickwork. Along the ground-floor landing. Out into the front yard and over the hot grass to the driveway.

She's rounding the back of her car when it happens.

'Stop!'

A man in the middle of the street. Tracksuit pants. T-shirt. Black balaclava. A rifle pointed at her. 'Don't,' he says, the moment she thinks of running. 'Don't move.'

Another man appears further down the street, moving out from between two parked cars. Same get-up. Except there's something different about him, something that registers despite the adrenaline and shock.

'Keys,' screams the first man. 'Where are the fucking keys?'

The other one is on her immediately, hands patting her down.

Amy's handgun is yanked loose.

A fist yanks her shirt collar. 'Where's the bag?' says the man behind her.

'Okay, okay. It's in the boot.'

'Open it.'

A police siren squawks.

The man over in the street spins the gun away. 'Argh, here we go.'

Amy fumbles with the lock.

'Move your arse.'

The boot swings open.

The man behind her pushes her with one hand and grabs the bag with the other. 'Go.'

The other man fires his gun, the blast echoing out over the quiet suburbs.

Brakes squeal.

Amy struggles. 'You don't need me. That's everything.'

'Go.'

The men run, taking Amy with them. The black BMW is waiting, doors open, engine running. Amy is shoved into the rear seat, followed by the duffle bag and one of the men. The other one jumps behind the wheel and peels out, momentarily collecting the side of a parked station wagon, sparks thrashing Amy's face and shoulder through the open window.

# AMY

## The Strip, Surfers Paradise

THE CAR ROARS ALONG suburban streets with the police in tow. Amy finds herself curled up in the rear seat—compacted by fear—while the two masked men remain quiet, seemingly unbothered by the chorus of sirens.

'Helicopter,' says the one in the back.

'Yeah,' says the driver.

They come out onto the highway and the speed ramps up, pinning Amy in her seat as they cross the canals before darting into the suburban sprawl. In the tighter streets, there's a minor collision of some sort, a dread-inducing shudder spinning the car momentarily. The driver curses, turns in his seat as he reverses up.

'Oh fuck,' yells one of them as the rear windscreen shatters.

The rear seat is awash with glass.

'Those fucking—'

The driver is out, running.

Amy pushes down on the door release and falls onto the road in one fluid movement. Heart racing, rippling through her whole body, erasing the present. Glass grinds into her palms as she connects with the bitumen.

A hand grips her ankle.

Kicking loose, scrambling free. Crawling across the street now. She gets to her feet and runs a few steps before a solid mass crashes into her back. Someone is on her, dragging her. Amy screams and a rough hand covers her face. 'Look! Look!' Her head is locked, and she's forced to watch the driver in the distance. The man walks around the front of a stationary police car in the street. There's a dead cop behind the wheel. In the passenger seat, another cop is fumbling with his seatbelt, struggling and hollering until the driver puts the shotgun in against the man's body and pulls the trigger. Blood sprays the interior of the windscreen.

'He'll kill you,' says the man holding Amy. 'He will. He'll kill anyone.' And then he's pulling her back to the car.

They careen along at high speed through the back-streets of Broadbeach. The driver pulls a handbrake turn into a quiet road and slows, somehow loose of the chase.

'There,' says the man beside Amy.

'I see it.'

The car hooks around into the open garage of a house.

As soon as they're parked, the man beside Amy jumps out and lowers the garage door. 'House,' he says.

The driver gets out and disappears through a connecting door into the dwelling. A couple of seconds later, there's a loud shriek, followed by the crashing of furniture.

'I'm okay,' yells the driver from inside.

'Out,' says the other one. He marches Amy into the house where a terrified teenaged girl and her little brother are on the living room floor. They're huddled together—the girl's arms around her brother as he trembles—while the masked driver stands over them with a shotgun. 'You two, follow me,' says the one with Amy. He takes the children into the other room.

Amy stands in silence with the driver.

There's a low murmuring through the wall. A TV comes on.

The other man reappears. His balaclava is rolled up, revealing his face.

It's Bill Webber.

'What are you doing?' hisses the driver.

'It's hard to calm children down when you're dressed like a fucking rapist,' says Bill.

'What are we going to do with them?'

'Nothing.'

'But, they've fucking—'

'We're past that.'

The other man shakes his head. 'Fuck. My face feels like it's on fire.' He pulls his mask up, revealing a young white guy in his early twenties, blond hair and blue eyes. He looks like the last guy on earth you'd expect to be under there, if not for the violent intensity radiating off him. Amy knows him, recognises him at least. He's the man who met Allan Watts in the workman's pub down in Miami.

The man notices Amy watching. 'Don't look at me,' he says.

Amy shifts her gaze.

Bill says, 'I better call the boss and let him know.' He walks into the hallway, leaving the two of them alone again.

Amy takes a few steps towards the kitchen and stops. 'Can I get a drink of water?'

The blond man nods, and follows her to the kitchen counter, watching.

'Do you want one?' she says.

'Yeah.' He knocks his drink back. 'Go sit down.'

When she's on the couch—presumably away from the knives and heavy objects—the man carefully lays his gun on the counter and takes a bag of powder from his shirt pocket. He chops out a quick line and snorts it back, rolling his head around as the drug hits.

Amy lowers her voice to a near-whisper. 'Who are you?'

'Keep talking to me, bitch, and you'll find out,' he says.

# MIKE

## Unknown

I'M NOT DEAD.

Mike Nichols holds an army canteen above his head, shaking the last drops of water out. He's in the back of a white van, one hand cuffed to a steel bar attached to the driver's-side compartment. It's been dark for a long time, suggesting the van is parked inside of something. He's not underground. That would be a blessing. No, the interior of the van is as hot as hell—all the windows are wound tight. Mike stopped sweating hours ago. He knows it's a bad sign.

The last bad sign of many.

Back at the police station, he was interviewed by a lanky detective with a cowboy's name. *Lloyd? Landon? Lowell.* Lowell swanned around asking questions about Jamie Leaver. Hearing Mike's answers, Lowell took notes as one might jot down a takeaway order. 'You went to a party at Deputy Commissioner Sorensen's house?' Lowell said, brow lifted. 'I didn't even know he had a place down this way. You sure it was his joint?'

Mike told him about the men in his house, about his family.

'I can look into that,' said Lowell.

Then he left him in the interview room for hours.

No one followed up.

No word on Mike's family.

Mike started wailing at the interview room door and got told to, *Settle down, mate, we've got a mobile patrol looking into it.*

Three hours later, Mike started up again and this time no one told him anything. Instead, three policemen braced him against a wall, bundled him up, and took him to a holding cell out back. After he simmered down, Mike called out and asked for a phone call, to which a uniformed cop told him that if he made any more trouble, he'd regret it. 'He's right,' said the bloke in the adjoining cell. 'If you keep yelling out, all that'll happen is you'll cop a flogging. They do whatever they like back here.'

Hours passed.

Then Lowell returned. 'Come with me.' The guy marched him out of the cell, down a corridor to the rear carpark where a van was waiting. Three men in overalls stepped out.

'What's this?' Mike said.

'I'm saving your life, dickhead,' said one of them.

It sure didn't feel like it when they cuffed him to the van's interior.

They put a hessian sack over his head.

They drove.

No one said a word.

About an hour later, they parked.

They took the sack off and gave him the canteen.

'Stay here.'

That was a day ago.

# THE DREAM

. . .

THE FEAR and dread and time alone in the hot van is clarifying for Mike. He's thinking about his life, which is what he assumes people do when they're thinking they're going to die. After they've cycled through thirst and headaches and delirium, after they've vomited on their clothes from heatstroke, and pissed in their pants and shit themselves from fright. If this is the end, Mike figures, it's a lowly one, and to compensate he tries to make good in his mind.

It doesn't work.

All he gets in return for his mental penance is more blame and guilt, like a compounding loop.

*You fucked up.*

*You fixated on money.*

*You strived for nonsense.*

*You ruined your family. You hurt them. You may have even—*

Mike screams and yanks on the cuffs for the thousandth time.

He's caught.

And he can't turn off the rest of it.

WHEN HE WAS A KID, they didn't have a pot to piss in. Four brothers and not enough house to go round. Mike was the youngest, the one taking scraps and getting endlessly hazed. He was quiet back then, like his own son is now. The world isn't built for quiet people.

While his father and brothers and his mother lived week to week, slowly fading out on hard work, beer by the carton, and a clip round the ear, Mike churned away, full of desire. He watched his brothers become versions of the old man, like some sort of fucked-up assembly line, marrying motherly women and producing more of the same, over and over. All the men in his family worked with their hands and backs. All the women stayed at home, hair pinned, sweating through the laundry and dishes and Christ knows what else. Everyone voted Labor. Everyone watched football. Everyone was the same, and then the same, and then the same. Fucking years of the same, not a day different. Households cluttered together and conjoined. Lots of talking, but no one saying anything.

Except Mike. He wasn't born with whatever defect held his family in place. He didn't watch the TV and say, *All right for some.* He didn't lie in his bed in the corner of his brother's room and sleep tight. He lay there and resented the snoring. He dreamed of more. He wanted out.

He quit school at sixteen.

Got a job.

Got another job.

Saved enough to live for six months in the city, then told them all to get fucked and moved to West End where he put it together, piece by piece.

A job in the Boundary Street fruit shop.

A second job in the bottle shop.

A stint tending bar.

Then a big break: moonlighting at a public service function, a late-night after-hours catering gig. Mike gives free pours to the right bloke and gets the inside word. *Son, you know how to read a room. How'd you get here?* The night unfolds like answered prayers.

It leads to a shit job working hospo for the National Party.

Then a better one working for the boys as a party driver.

It's more than moving people around. It's about keeping powerful men happy, keeping them entertained, on track, on time, with a side gig in information trafficking and backroom networking. Eventually, Mike gets into a car with the man who brings him *right* inside. This bloke has Mike pinned from the jump. 'Keep doing what you're doing, but bloody hell, go to night school and then call me.'

Mike did it.

He destroyed school on the second go. Crushed it.

He took his diploma back.

The party obliged. It was the ground floor, but the fast track too, knowing what Mike knew.

In no time at all, he worked his way up through the underworld of Queensland politics.

Through naked ambition.

Through Sonya.

And now here he is, on the job and handcuffed to the driver's seat of this van, while the only thing he can think about, *the only thing*, is that Sonya and his children are in trouble. Real trouble. It *kills* him. Because right now, Mike's old family, they're probably out there, living their sad-sack fucking lives, nestled together where it's safe, all because they never really wanted anything.

# BRUNO
## Pohlman Drive, Southport

BRUNO AND REYNOLDS ARE in the backyard
of the O'Grady house, on a ciggie break by the in-
ground pool. They have their notebooks out. Inside,
the SIB team are picking over basement debris.
Dusting surfaces and cataloguing evidence. An hour
ago, they called in extra hands to remove the barrels,
loading them on to the back of a truck. No official
word yet on what everyone knows: it's the O'Grady
family, dissolved in chemicals. Bruno and Reynolds
are more interested in the rest of the basement. The
details. The paperwork and records kept down there.
There's a collection. Some of it opens up whole new
avenues of enquiry. Some of it makes wild associations
clear.

Without a single word between them, the two
detectives stub out their smokes and get back to work.
In the living room, the furniture has been cleared
away and a sheet of clear plastic laid on the carpet.
They're sorting items. Some of it is hard to look at.
Violent, perverted pornography from downstairs.
Weird stuff, gay and straight. Paedophilic material.

Slide carousels, magazines and prints, and rolls of eight-millimetre film. There's documentation too. Careful, handwritten records. Ledgers. Diaries. Catalogues and parcel packaging. Bruno and Reynolds know the truth now: Phillip O'Grady was a Gold Coast magistrate and a straight-up sex offender. For it's not just a collection: Phillip O'Grady is *in* the collection, and it runs deep and dark. He abused his wife and son. He abused other victims. He was a monster.

'If I knew all this, I would have put him in a bloody barrel too,' says Reynolds.

Bruno squats down and scans polaroids from a shoebox. 'Same here.'

The entire day has been like this.

A nightmare.

The sort of police work that haunts you.

An hour later, they're still in the living room going through it, when one of the scientists comes in with a fresh box. 'We missed one,' she says. 'This was pushed into a cavity behind the desk.'

'Fuck me,' says Reynolds. He immediately starts fussing with his cigarettes.

'What's in it?' says Bruno.

The scientist says, 'More files.' She waits a beat and adds, 'But, our sort of stuff.'

'What?'

'See for yourself.'

They kneel and the scientist opens the box. The first thing out is a bound pile of court documents bearing the Commonwealth insignia. On the cover of the first file, someone has scrawled the word *Torney* in blue marker. Reynolds snips open the ribbon and they take a look. It's a pre-trial dossier of some sort, notes on a serial offender up in Brisbane.

'I remember this guy,' says Reynolds. 'It was a big case. The guy disappeared.'

'What do you mean?' says Bruno.

Reynolds glances at the scientist. 'Dunno what happened. They never got him, though. He slipped away on bail.'

The scientist has her hands back in the box. 'Some of the stuff at the bottom is . . . delicate. You two might need to talk to Internal Investigations.' She fishes out a crime scene photo. 'This looks like it's been through our evidence log. See, it's marked here, and on the back.'

They look. Bruno feels the rush of the floor dropping out beneath them. There will be records of this stuff back at the station—a paper trail—and the thought of *this* nightmare threading itself through the Queensland Police is too much to handle.

It's sickening.

And dangerous.

'We'll . . . I guess . . .'

'Leave it with us,' snaps Reynolds, turning away.

The scientist is only too happy to oblige. She *knows*. She stands up and takes one last look at the box and the monstrous collage of evidence on the floor and her eyes soften. 'Fuck,' she says, quietly. 'You two . . . ah, good luck.'

The two detectives wait for her to leave.

Reynolds rubs his neck. 'What do you think?'

Bruno picks up the last box. 'I think whatever a guy like Phillip hides from *himself* is the sort of thing that gets your whole family killed. What do you reckon?'

'Let's do another hour and call it a day. I need to eat.'

'I actually need to clock off for a few hours, too,'

says Bruno, thinking of his siblings back at the house. 'Sorry.'

'Don't be. One more pass?'

'Yeah, let's just take another look at it then take a break.'

ONE MORE PASS turns into two and three and four until they lose count. Hours disappear as the shadows extend across the O'Grady living room. The mysterious file box from the bunker begs a lot of new questions.

They find names and dates.

Figures and tallies.

Memos and notes scratched in the margins.

Paperwork with official insignias.

Bank account statements on familiar letterheads.

Addresses and facilities.

'Holy fucking shit,' says Reynolds.

There are a hundred suspects now. A hundred people who would want this man dead. And woven through it all are a thousand sinister and soft connections: officials, police officers, lawyers and so on. There's a system at work. O'Grady was tied into powerful circles. The whole thing screams *cover-up*.

Bruno and Reynolds try to stay calm. They package up the extra-sensitive parts of the evidence and place it in a cardboard box and put that box in the boot of their car where they can keep an eye on it.

'Let's go to mine,' says Bruno.

# BRUNO

## Heron Avenue, Mermaid Beach

THERE'S AN UNFAMILIAR CAR in the driveway of Bruno's place, but Reynolds recognises it. 'Ah shit,' he says.

Up in the living room, Bruno finds a bad scene unfolding: his brother Danny sits at the kitchen table, looking like he's seen a ghost. Across the table from Danny is a young, wiry bloke. Mid-twenties. Wearing a muscle-tee and covered in jailhouse tatts. The bloke has a retractable Stanley knife in his hand and the cat on his lap.

Bruno looks directly at the man and says, 'You okay, Danny?'

Danny says, 'I'm all right,' his voice slow and steady.

Colleen steps into view. 'Oh, finally. I just put the jug on, fellas. Take a seat.' With that, she disappears back into the kitchen.

'Colleen?' calls Bruno.

'Yeah?'

'Tell this fuckhead to put my cat down or I'm gonna shoot him.'

345

'What have I done?' says the bloke.

Colleen reappears, holding a carton of milk this time. 'You can't shoot Sando. He's new. And what then? Are you going to shoot me too?'

'That depends,' says Bruno.

Reynolds takes a step forward. 'Come on. Calm down. No one's getting shot.'

'Okay, Sando,' says Colleen. 'Leave the adults to chat.'

*Schlick.*

Sando's knife retracts. He dumps the cat and walks.

'He seems nice,' says Reynolds, taking Sando's seat at the table. 'Where'd you find him?'

'Where I find all of you,' Colleen says. She puts a cup of tea on the table for Reynolds. 'It's white with one, yeah?'

He nods.

'Danny, you can take off too,' says Bruno. 'Don't talk to anyone about this.'

'I think he should stay,' says Colleen.

'The threat's enough, Colleen,' Bruno says. 'Go on.'

Danny doesn't get up immediately, but after weighing it up, he pushes gently back from the table and leaves. Two minutes later, Bruno hears his motorbike engine roar to life.

'He seems like a good egg,' says Colleen, standing back by the kitchen bench, sipping her tea. 'But you'll need to have a chat with him when he gets back.'

Bruno bites. 'Yeah, why's that?'

'Because his brother's a poof, that's why. It seems he didn't know.'

'Christ,' curses Reynolds.

Bruno bolts across the room, pulling up inches from Colleen's face.

Colleen doesn't show a lick of fear. 'I love that you two are working together,' she says. 'What a world, aye?'

'What do you want?' hisses Bruno.

Colleen puts a hand on his shoulder. 'Son, I will burn your whole fucking life to the ground if you don't go and sit at the table like a good boy.'

Eye to eye.

*She means it.*

Bruno goes back to the table.

Stares into space.

His ears are ringing.

'Good choice. Now, both of you, where is Mike Nichols?'

Reynolds shrugs.

Bruno's eyes remain empty. 'He was at the station yesterday. I told Amy this.'

'Amy has disappeared too, and I don't like what I'm hearing. Talk around town is that she's a suspect in the shooting of Allan Watts. A neighbour of Allan's described her and her car. I believe many of your brethren are out there looking for her as we speak.'

'This is the first we're hearing about it,' says Reynolds. 'We've got our own problems, Col. We just took three bodies out of that house you had him looking at.'

'The O'Gradys?'

'That's right. I don't suppose you'd like to share how this all came to be?' says Reynolds.

'That's a long story,' says Colleen.

'He was a pedo,' says Bruno. 'There are piles of evidence. Photos of him doing it.'

Colleen takes this in. 'I knew he was a perv, but I didn't know about the rest. That shit doesn't fly with me. I put Amy on the house because O'Grady has money in my casino project. He's also a client of one of my boys, Seth Blackwell, who's dead as of a couple of nights back. Seth was feeding me info. Phillip had financial trouble. Someone was putting the hard word on him, so I started looking into it.'

It makes sense. The *casino project* she's talking about is the giant hotel complex being built on reclaimed land in Broadbeach. It's the first legal gambling establishment in Queensland. A big win for Colleen.

Reynolds fires up a smoke. 'What did Seth Blackwell tell you exactly?'

'Seth was a deadshit. I liked the kid, but he'd sell his own mother

if there was a dollar in it. For what it's worth, he reckoned Phillip's kid Samson had a line into Fantasyland.'

'Sounds a bit rich,' says Reynolds.

'It was some backdoor deal via his boss at the Silver Fish.'

'That's the recently departed Allan Watts, right?' says Reynolds.

'Yep, the one and only. My guy, Mike, was also trying to get in on Fantasyland. As sworn police officers, it might be time to have a look at the Winters family and their theme park. Everyone I know who goes anywhere near that thing winds up dead or missing.'

Reynolds scratches at his face. 'Is that really in their repertoire? From what I hear, Noah Winters is a bit of a straight shooter.'

348

'I want you two to find Mike. I'm worried about him.'

'Why's that, Col?'

She looks into her tea mug. 'That's my business.'

It's minuscule, but Bruno and Reynolds are seasoned detectives and they both spot the tell: a moment of weakness in Colleen.

They exchange a glance.

Bruno says, 'Tit for tat, Colleen.'

'That's not how this works.'

Reynolds comes in. 'How about we find Mike and then keep your name out of the O'Grady thing. It could easily go the other way.'

Colleen looks at Reynolds. 'How about I let you off the hook and keep him?'

'No dice,' says Reynolds.

'Well fuck you both, then,' she says, placing her mug carefully on the bench.

Reynolds runs a hand through his hair. 'He's not going to be much good to you. He's too bloody honest. And I've done my time.'

'Okay, okay. *Jesus*. You're both off the books if you can find Mike. But no Mike, no deal. I swear to god, if you two don't deliver, a few homo pics will be the least of your troubles.'

With that, Colleen leaves.

The two men watch her, making sure she's all the way out.

# AMY

## Somewhere in the Back Streets of Broadbeach

BILL WEBBER AND HIS blond accomplice wait until dark. It's not an easy time. The blond one is so coked-up he can barely sit straight in a chair. He paces the room with his gun, keeping Amy's heart rate up. Around five o'clock, they feed the kids in the other room a frozen pizza. There are a few slices left for Amy, but she finds she can't take a bite.

'Let's get some fresh air,' says Webber. 'I mean you,' he adds, looking at her.

He stands with her in the backyard.

'You're not going to hurt those kids, are you?' says Amy.

'No,' says Webber. 'He's fucking crazy, but he won't do that. Might be the only thing he won't do, in his current state.'

'Why would you two do any of this?'

'You'll see.'

AT SEVEN O'CLOCK, the owners of the house return from work and it's bedlam. A mother and a father, both jumped in the garage. The two of them soft around the middle and completely helpless. Both comply immediately, bursting into tears as soon as they realise what's happening and that the kids are in peril. Thankfully, no one gets hurt. The blond one makes his threats and puts the barrel of his gun under the husband's chin. That's all it takes.

Webber bundles them into the room with their kids.

Closes the door behind him.

Amy hears the sharp rip of electrical tape.

When Webber reappears, the first thing he does is yank the phone from the wall. 'Let's go.'

They take the family car, a green Falcon station wagon. Amy is handcuffed to the door handle, while the men ride in front. As they're backing out, the blond one turns in the passenger seat and lays the gun through the centre console, the barrel pointed her way. 'She better be bloody worth it,' he says.

Webber drives steady. 'It's his daughter, mate.'

AND SO, it repeats.

Bad men leading her back to the source.

Bill Webber driving the familiar vector.

Campbell Street, where her brother fell off his bike in fourth grade.

Down along the shark-infested residential canals.

Along Freyburg.

Left and around into Marseille Court.

*Home*.

*To Victor*.

. . .

HER FATHER'S condition has worsened since her last visit. The moment she sees him, she knows it's his final days. The nurse has him propped up in a makeshift bed in the downstairs lounge room. The lights are out. There's a flickering film screen against the wall. Victor's watching old home movies from his deathbed, or would be if he were conscious.

The nurse, Elda, touches his hand.

The old man stirs, squints into the darkness. 'Amy, is that you?'

'Yeah.'

The blond man steps around her. 'We did our part.'

Victor winces. 'You two need to give me a few minutes alone with my daughter. You too, Elda.'

'Call if you need me,' says the nurse.

'Go,' says Victor. 'Do the rest of it.'

Then they're alone.

On the screen, the image shifts to a beach scene. Amy watches her younger self run terrified from the surf while her sister, Angela, stands knee-deep in the water and laughs.

Amy looks away. 'You getting sentimental at the end?'

'Look at how open the foreshore is,' says Victor. 'There's barely anything there. It was just wide-open space back then.'

'Yeah, I know. Why did you drag me here?'

'You shouldn't have shot Allan. It's caused me a lot of trouble, Amy.'

'He tried to shoot me first.'

'I'm sure he did, but . . . it's a mess now and I don't have time to sort it out. I want you to sort it out.'

'Me? No thanks.'

'You need to clean up after yourself.'

'No, I don't. Why would I help you?'

'I'm your father.'

'What's that supposed to mean?'

'You know I'll win, even . . . even like this. You know I will. There's no . . .' He starts coughing. He reaches for a plastic cup and spits in it. The fit subsides. 'I'm not going to change, Amy. Your choice is to go with those men and help me finish what I started, or you can go with them and get buried in the scrub somewhere.'

Amy believes him. 'I don't want to hurt anyone else,' she says. 'I'm tired. I just want to leave town.'

'It's too late for that. You're my daughter, and like it or not, deep, deep down, there's a bit of me in you. So, I need you to go with those men and do what Allan was supposed to do. You can represent the family.'

'Or they'll kill me.'

'Like everything in life, you're either part of the problem or you're part of the solution.'

Amy moves closer. She places a hand around the old man's bony throat. She doesn't close his windpipe. She just rests her hand there and looks at him. 'Here's my counteroffer.'

Victor smiles.

'Good,' he says. 'That's good.'

'Any last words, dickhead?'

'Open the drawer.'

'I don't think so.'

'Go on. Open it.'

Amy pauses, fights back revulsion and tears.

She lets him go.

She opens the drawer.

There's a bag of money inside.

A lot of money.

On top of the stacks, there's an envelope.

'It's a million,' says Victor.

'Bit late in the game to be buying me off.'

'I'm not buying you off. I'm hiring you. If you decide you want to live through the night, that money is yours, and it's just the down-payment.'

Amy picks up the envelope. 'What's this?'

'That's the job. Tonight's just the audition.'

There's a knock at the window, a thud of some sort, like a bird hitting the glass.

Amy's gut lurches, forcing her across the tiles to the back patio. She slides open the door just in time to see Bill Webber and the blond man drag Elda's limp body onto a square of black plastic sheeting. Webber has her feet. A blood-soaked hammer on the pavers.

'Come on, lift,' Webber says. 'Watch what you're fucking doing, Sunny.'

# MIKE

## Unknown

THE VAN SHUDDERS.

*Bang.*

*Bang.*

*Bang.*

Mike struggles against the handcuffs, half asleep.

The side door rolls open.

The harsh spray of a flashlight finds his face.

'Fucking hell,' says a voice. 'This guy needs a shower.'

Another voice commands the others, 'Pull him out.' It's a woman.

Mike's delirious. He fights them off, kicking and scratching. Amid the tussle, someone grabs him by the face and screams at him to stop.

'Calm down,' says the woman. 'Just breathe, you idiot.'

He knows her.

It's Buddy Winters's personal assistant. The tall woman.

They pull him outside into open air. More flashlights in his eyes. Darkness everywhere else.

'Where am I?'

The assistant towers over him. 'You're at the end of the canal.'

'What's . . . what's happening?'

'Calm down. You've been invited to dinner. The big man would like a word.'

Mike turns and looks back at the van. It's parked in a shed in some sort of industrial area. There's service works in fenced cages all around.

Gear stores. Tractors and machinery. As they trundle along a gravel path, Mike's eyes adjust, and he sees familiar scaffolding in the night sky. An in-progress roller-coaster.

Fantasyland.

They pass through thick scrub out into a field.

The lights of a house in the distance.

They're taking him to the Winters family compound.

MIKE GETS OUT of the shower and shakily stands on the white bathmat. He's in the pool house bathroom. That's what they called it. The pool house is lavish—about the size of the home Mike grew up in. The bathroom is like something out of a magazine: seamless white surfaces, gold trimmings, a wall of mirrors.

They have a suit picked out for him, hanging from a rack.

He puts it on, and it fits.

He combs his hair.

There's a small window above the toilet pedestal and Mike figures that, at a stretch, he could squeeze through. He carefully slides it open.

Takes a look.

Buddy Winters's tall assistant is standing out there under a house-light, looking at a clipboard.

'Bad idea,' she says.

Mike shuts the window.

He brushes his lapels.

There's a knock at the door. 'Dinner's ready.'


THE WINTERS' mansion looks like the White House. It's a long rectangle, broken up in the centre by a broad, protruding column. On either side of the column are rows of pale two-storey pillars, holding up the eaves. Every light in the place is on, but Mike can't see anyone moving inside. They lead him in through a rear door, and only the assistant follows. 'That way,' she says. 'And don't do anything stupid.' They walk through a service kitchen and into a long dining room where a small party is silently seated for dinner. The guests watch him settle into his spot.

Mike notes familiar faces.

Amy Owens, dressed up for a change.

Fantasyland owner Noah Winters, in a tux.

Buddy Winters, the son, also in a tux.

And across the room is God himself: the minister.

'You're late, Mister Nichols,' bellows Noah.

Mike spreads his napkin across his lap. 'Sorry about that. I was tied up.'

A waiter steps in and offers Mike a pour of wine. He takes the red. 'Hold on,' Mike says, and slugs back the entire glass. 'Yeah, that's good.' He holds his glass out for another and receives it.

'Mike,' says the God Minister.

'Yes, sir?'

'Steady on.'

'Can we eat, please?' says Buddy. 'I'm starving.'

The entrée is French onion soup. Mike isn't sure he can stomach it, but as soon as he forces down the first mouthful, he remembers he hasn't eaten in days. He finishes first and wipes out the plate with table bread. He requests another glass of wine and waits for something to happen, but no one speaks. They all sit there listening to the ticking of an ornate clock in the adjacent room. Mike ducks his head and whispers to the assistant beside him. 'Am I supposed to do something here?'

The assistant shakes her head.

The main course is steak. It's a little undercooked for Mike's taste, but he demolishes it.

Then Noah Winters swallows a mouthful and says, 'Do you know how my family came to this country?'

Mike assumes the question is for all of them, but when the assistant nudges him, he responds. 'Uh, no, no sir. I don't.'

'We came here as thieves and whores. That's who I'm descended from. That's my genetic stock. But within one generation, we owned the place. We had the beginnings of a respectable life, after just *one* generation. That's all it took. But do you know who ran the show once we had it?'

'No.'

'No one ran the show. The men sent to colonise this place were lunatics. Religious fools, deranged monarchists, you name it. God and Queen types. Zealots, every last one of them. In the end, they were no better than the convicts they lorded over. The people who sent my family over here couldn't even manage their own jails, and yet they presumed to make this whole country into a prison. Doesn't make sense, does it? Then, within a few years, half the colonial police force were ex-convicts of one form or another. In short, *my people* took over. And it's been the same ever since, from then to now, because a convict—'

'Dad,' says Buddy.

'—because a convict is a convict is a convict. They became us and we became them. The police are just . . . they're nothing. Uniforms and badges. A veneer. And say what you like about this arsehole of a place, but it really strips everything away in the end. It reveals everything sooner or later.'

The old man takes another bite.

'That's a bit much, Noah,' says the God Minister.

Noah's eyes darken. 'Oh, that's right, Russell, I forgot that you're the Minister of Police. Case in point,' he says. 'Fat lot of good *you* are. Another leader of men who can't keep himself or the rabble in line.'

The God Minister slowly clenches his fists on the tablecloth. 'Let's not squabble with one another, Noah. I'm not sure you're one to talk, either.'

'Are you talking about my son? Are you sitting at my table, talking about my son?'

Buddy Winters—who, up until this point, seems to have been barely listening—looks around. 'What? What's this about?'

'I'm just teasing, Russell,' Noah says. 'And yes, Buddy, we're talking about you, you little shithead. We may as well get on with it. You nearly ruined everything.'

'Dad, I—'

'Shut up. You think I didn't know about your little deal? Your stupid little venture is why we're all here. It's also why I'm out there pretending to dig out the canal every night, or did you think I was failing, son? Did you underestimate your father? I should cut your throat right here. It'd be the best thing for you.'

The assistant beside Mike bolts upright, knocking her chair back.

No one else moves.

'Dad?' says Buddy.

'I should cut your throat,' he mutters. 'We should be eating *you* for dinner.'

# BRUNO

Stationhouse, Surfers Paradise

REYNOLDS AND BRUNO LOOK for Mike Nichols at the station. Reynolds throws his weight around and gets the sort of cooperation Bruno rarely enjoys. They check with Bookings, then move to the cells out back—*Nah, he's not here*—then back to CIB where even Lowell Sennett kowtows to orders, telling them that Nichols was sent home.

'Who did that?'

'I don't know,' says Lowell.

They check the CCTV footage, and it seems Lowell probably does know, because they watch someone just like him—someone tall and careful enough to keep his face from the cameras—take Mike Nichols out back and deliver him to a waiting van.

And yet, they catch a break: the van's licence plate is visible.

'I'll deal with Lowell later,' says Reynolds. 'Run the plate.'

Bruno checks his watch. 'At this time of night?'

Reynolds knows a number to call.

Within half an hour, they have it locked down.

The van is registered to Dick Arnolds. They look him up and call, getting the answering machine of Arnolds Cross Construction.

A call to a union bloke confirms it.

'They're contractors for Fantasyland.'


IN THE CAR, on the highway, Bruno checks his gun.

'Good idea,' says Reynolds.

'I don't know if this is worth it.'

'We'll take a look. If anything's out of place, we'll call it in.'

'Deal.'

The road tracks under their tyres.

Bruno says, 'I've got a feeling that we're headed right into it.'

'What gives you that impression?'

They both laugh.

Bruno takes out his smokes. 'You up?'

'Fuck yes.'

He lights two and passes one over.

Reynolds rolls his neck. 'Let's run it down. O'Grady is a judge and a pedo, but he's connected to all the right people. He's got official police files stashed in his creepy bunker. On the side, he's fucking Seth Blackwell who is part of the robbery crew we're chasing. Bill Webber is . . .'

'The one who put a gun on me the other night, in the O'Grady house. He also grew up two streets away from the crime scene. You reckon he could be in the robbery crew? It's gonna be something like that.'

'Fuck me, I hope not. He's working the bloody case.'

'How does Fantasyland fit into it?'

'Colleen said the O'Grady kid, Samson, had a line into Fantasyland.'

'There it is,' says Bruno.

He rechecks his gun.

The turn-off appears.

They take it.

# AMY
## Fantasyland, Gold Coast

AMY WATCHES THE TALL assistant steady herself before collecting her chair and sitting back down. Beside her, Mike Nichols looks frazzled. His eyes dart around, fixed on whoever is talking. *Is he drunk already?* Across the table from Nichols is the minister. Amy recognises him from the paper. He seems completely unfazed, shovelling food into his mouth despite the unfolding melee.

'You tried to sell me out, you dirty dog,' Noah Winters hollers at his son.

Buddy shakes his head. 'Dad, Dad—'

'Judas. Shut your mouth.'

'Dad, can I—'

Noah throws his wine at Buddy Winters. Not the wine on its own but the glass and all. It collects Buddy square in the face. The man yelps, hands waving around, completely under attack.

The minister dabs his mouth. 'Noah,' he says, gently.

Noah wheels around. 'Yes? What is it, Russell? Eat your fucking dinner.'

The minister grumbles, turns back to his plate.

Amy signals to the waiter. 'Can I have another glass of that wine?'

'Certainly.'

As the wine is poured, Amy feels eyes on her.

They're all watching.

Noah Winters leans forward, lowers his head. 'Enjoying your dinner, Miss Owens?'

'It's fine,' she says. 'Are we done with the family drama?'

Noah doesn't answer. He just watches her.

'Do you have something to say?' asks the minister.

The front doorbell chimes.

*Right on cue.*

Noah motions for the butler to answer it.

Amy lays down her fork.

As they wait, Buddy stands up, making to leave.

'You might want to stay for this,' says Amy.

The butler is thrown into the room, landing on the timber floor and sliding a few feet. Bill Webber and the blond man called Sunny appear. They both have guns.

'These guys work for my father,' says Amy.

If Noah is concerned, he doesn't show it. 'Go on.'

'My father and Allan Watts were hoping to buy Buddy's share of the park. Unfortunately, Allan is dead, and my father isn't too far behind him. It's a long story, but these two are Allan's silent partners. They've been knocking over the banks here on the coast. I'm sure you've seen it on the news.'

'I see,' says Noah. He turns to Buddy. '*This* is who you would leave me with? *This!*'

Buddy is beyond caring. 'I still might sell it to them.'

'Over my dead body.'

Amy clears her throat. 'You say that, Noah, but do you mean it? Because he does,' she says, nodding at the blond one. 'That one is capable of anything.'

'I can deal with men like these,' says Noah. 'Men like these, I understand. It's the rest of you I have trouble with. What do you want?'

'Let Buddy offload his stake, and then open the fucking park as planned, and you'll never see these two again. They need to leave town, so they'll be truly silent partners, all the way.'

'How can we be sure of that?' says the minister.

'My father informs me that his word will be enough. He's heading up all this. It's his show.'

Noah smiles. 'Your show, too?'

'For the time being,' says Amy.

'Get him on the phone,' Noah says to one of the staff. 'I'll take it upstairs.'

They wait in the quiet.

The clock ticking.

Mike Nichols says, 'What about me?'

'Quiet down,' says the minister.

A voice from the other room says, 'We're calling now, sir.'

Noah slowly gets out of his chair. The old man leaves.

The clock ticks over and chimes.

*Midnight.*

# PART NINE
# WEDNESDAY, 6 OCTOBER
## 1982

# VICTOR

THE CALL COMES *in while I'm watching one of my movies. There she is on the screen. The strange girl, sad-eyed, hair dark at the root but white gold everywhere else. A metaphor, I guess. A prize for hire.*

*I told her, 'I'll look after you,' and I had every intention of doing so. But she wouldn't play by the rules. She wanted her own money, was addicted to her own ventures. She had another father for her unborn child. Some dupe in the wings. It was her downfall, obviously. She summoned some other dark entity and disappeared in an instant. I give and I give and—*

*The phone keeps ringing.*

*It takes ten whole seconds, but I manage to answer on my own. 'Victor, you sneaky bastard. I should have known,' says the voice on the line.*

*Noah Winters.*

*I take my time. Breathe deep. 'I take it the deal has been presented to you.'*

*'I could kill her, you know?'*

*'You'd just be killing the messenger.'*

*'It'd feel good.'*

'I'm dying, Noah. I don't have a lot of time. What do you want to say to me?'

'I thought you'd be able to raise the money without these crooks. Have you fallen on tough times, Victor?'

'The banks won't bet on an old man.'

'Don't I know it. If I did take this deal, I'd want your word that this is the last of your meddling.'

I cough. 'It's ending, Noah. It's all ending.'

And then the call is cut short by shouting.


THE FILM ENDS and I want more. Instead, I get a blank white screen. A stern square of whiteness announcing itself in the darkened living room.

'Elda!'

I'm hurting.

The world feels wrong.

'Elda!'

I can't reach the jug I piss in.

'Elda!'

Grasping for it, I come round too fast. My legs slip from the bed and gravity has me. Without really experiencing it, I fall from the bed and my head collects edges and objects. My face and jaw bounce off the tiles.

I murmur one last time for Elda before remembering that she's dead.

That pleases me to no end. I close my eyes.


IN WHAT MIGHT BE HEAVEN, or a dream of heaven, I see my son.

William.

We're on the coast, walking along the tideline of some ancient version of Surfers Paradise. All the build-

*ings are absent. There are no roads or streetlights. It's twin planes: an expanse of land and water.*

*'Dad, where are we going?'*

*'Forward, son. This will all be yours one day.'*

*'Who does it belong to now?'*

*'It belongs to me.'*

*'I can't take what's yours,' says William.*

*He's so soft. Not the youngest, but the littlest, always. The kid hugs me there on the beach for no reason. Thin arms gripping my leg, half a game and half just wanting to be close. He brings me over into the sand.*

*We're both laughing.*

*A golden day. A real day, too. An actual event.*

*I remember it because it's the day I know I have to change him, lest he change me.*

*The rest of it is morose detail. The recent past. The events. It's all a bunch of . . .*

*It's not needed.*

*I turn to my son and say, 'We'll remember this day, because today is the day that—'*

# MIKE, BRUNO & AMY
## Fantasyland, Gold Coast

MIKE GETS UP FROM the table.

'Where are you going?' barks one of the gunmen.

'It's all good,' says Mike, hands raised. He walks to where Noah's butler is lying. 'You okay, mate?'

'I'll live.' The man has blood all over him, but it's mostly coming out of a small gash on his scalp.

'Sit down.'

'Fellas, I've got—'

A gun appears in Mike's face. 'Are you testing me?'

'Okay, okay.'

Mike's about halfway back to his seat when the doorbell chimes again.

The gunmen look at each other.

They look at Amy Owens.

Amy shrugs.

'Go and check,' says one of them.

Seconds later: 'Cops!'

Then gunfire.

.  .  .

OUTSIDE THE HOUSE, Bruno dives for cover, his trousers ripping around the ankle as two miracle shotgun pellets pass through the fabric of his pants and around his leg, only scratching the skin. Behind him, Reynolds is firing into the windows, retreating. They both make it behind the car and take cover. Another round of shots sound, spraying the car and blasting up dust from the gravel drive.

Bruno cracks the driver's-side door.

Slides up for the radio.

Calls it in.

Reynolds is reloading. He fumbles bullets. 'What the—'

More shots.

Sharp pings glance off the car.

'We've gotta move or we're gonna get shot,' says Reynolds. He nods at the yard. 'The fountain, then the wall.'

Bruno looks at it.

*Don't think.*

'Go,' Bruno says and starts shooting.

Reynolds makes it to the fountain, returns fire and covers Bruno.

They do it again and both of them make it out.


IT'S FUCKING chaos inside the house. Amy hides by the wall of the dining room, catching glimpses of Webber and Sunny in the long, adjoining living room, firing out of the windows. As soon as the initial gunfire dies down, Sunny yanks his gun out of the window and runs through the house. Amy can feel his footsteps shaking the entire place as he races up the stairs, going for Noah Winters. Seconds later, she hears him screaming, 'Who did you call? Who did you just call?'

No response.

Only the booming retort of a shotgun.

More screaming.

Another blast.

Then nothing for a few seconds.

Sunny comes back down, his face sprayed with gore. 'If anyone moves, they're dead,' he says.

'What have you done?' says Webber.

Sunny ignores him. He stomps around the dining room.

'What have you done?' says Webber, louder now.

Sunny grabs Buddy Winters by the shirt. 'Is there a safe?'

Buddy is almost convulsing with fear. 'Yeah, yeah.'

'Let's go.'

Sunny drags Buddy upstairs.

In their absence, Webber produces a duffle bag of weapons. He sorts through, loading a couple as a warm wind comes in through the broken windows. They can all hear the sirens on the highway.

'Sunny, we've got to go. Sunny!' yells Webber.

From her hiding spot, Amy watches Webber pace back across the house. He checks the rear windows and curses, ripping one open and firing out into the field behind the house.

'Stay back!'

There's no return fire.

Webber looks around the dining room, from frightened face to frightened face. 'Who are the guys outside?' he says.

Buddy's assistant can't look at him, but she mumbles an answer from her spot under the dining table. 'That . . . that, that'll be the park security.'

Webber runs to the stairs, calls up, 'Sunny!'

'What?'

'We're in real trouble down here.'

BRUNO AND REYNOLDS watch the squad cars and equipment roll in. It's a motley collection of uniformed coppers and CIB. The cavalry includes more high-ranking police than you'd expect at this time of night. They set up a perimeter and block the roads. Bruno gives a statement and takes a senior sergeant in closer to show him the lay of the land, then he repeats the process when the Emergency Squad show up half an hour later. Inspector Bingham makes an appearance. He gets on a loud-speaker, demanding the gunmen release their hostages.

'No way, dickhead,' is the response.

Five minutes later, while Bingham is still thinking about the next move, a radio message comes through: they're all to pull back.

*Right back*.

'Word from on high,' says the guy holding the receiver. 'Deputy Commissioner Sorensen has a nego-tiator on the phone to someone in the house.'

They move back, everyone except the Emergency Squad. They begin suiting up: strapping on vests and helmets, double-checking rifles and pistols.

Bruno and Reynolds exchange a look.

Orders are orders.

AMY TRIES TO BREATHE. The gunman called Sunny is on the phone upstairs, shouting obscenities at someone and demanding they send in a helicopter.

He's threatening to kill everyone if he doesn't get his way.

Bill Webber isn't calmly taking this in. He's standing rigid against a wall in the living room, looking like he's ready to vomit. He's pale. *Knows it's the end*, Amy figures. Couldn't feel otherwise, not with his workmates outside. There's no going back now.

'I want to live,' she says to him, calling through.

Amy takes a look into the room, on her hands and knees, just her head around the wall separating the dining room from the living room.

Webber nods, sweating.

'Tell me what needs to happen here,' she says.

Webber squeezes his eyes closed. He comes to some conclusion. 'Where's the lackey?' He comes across, squats down and points at Mike Nichols. 'You. Come with me.'

Mike says, 'Why? What's happening?'

'I need you to talk to them.'

Mike slowly crawls out and Webber takes him to the front door, kicks it open and yells, 'I'm sending someone out. I want to talk to Bruno Karras. I'll only talk to him.' Webber pushes Mike into the open doorway, awash in spotlights. 'Go and find out if they're serious about Sunny's demands. And tell them he's definitely serious about what he's saying. Tell them you've seen what he can do.'

'Okay.'

'Hang on.' Webber stops. 'You too.'

He's looking over at Amy.

'I'm not going out there,' she says.

'Yes, you are,' he says. 'I need someone to go back and forth, and you're it.'

Mike waits for her at the threshold.

Iain Ryan

Webber says to Amy, 'Tell them whatever you need to de-escalate this thing. And if one of you tries to do a runner, I'm going to shoot the other one. Okay?'

'You won't need to do that,' says Amy.

'Please,' says Webber. 'Just do as I ask.'

# BRUNO, MIKE & AMY
## Fantasyland, Gold Coast

BRUNO FINISHES A CIGARETTE on the bumper of a police van. He's heard the demands— they all did—but he doesn't want to go back to the house. Having already been shot at once tonight, he's not feeling particularly heroic. There's other things on his mind. His brother. His sister. A niece. There's already enough death and mayhem to go round. But someone in the house keeps yelling for him.

*Send Bruno Karras up!*

Across the way, Pete Reynolds leans against their unmarked car, watching the house through a pair of binoculars. They both figure Bill Webber is one of the men inside. Reynolds hasn't spotted him yet, but it seems likely.

Reynolds startles. 'Oh shit.'

'What?'

'They just dumped a body out of the upstairs window.'

Bruno walks across, puts his hands out for the binoculars, and looks through just as a second blood-stained corpse is pushed out of an upper-storey window. Its raw weight collides viciously with the ground, head bouncing, a leg landing across the first body. Bruno focuses the lenses. He can't make out a face on either victim.

'I'm going to have to go up,' Bruno says.

'I'm coming with you.'

'There's no point in both of us getting killed.'

Inspector Bingham approaches. He's holding a bulletproof vest. 'Deputy Commissioner Sorensen is on the radio asking if you'd go speak to them. We'll be right behind you.'

Bruno tucks his gun into his waistband at the back.

'Don't do anything stupid,' says Bingham.

'Stupider than this?'

Reynolds and Bruno approach the house alone. At the fence line, Bruno tells him, 'If something goes wrong, tell my family I didn't opt in to this. I don't want them thinking I was reckless.'

'Sure. You'll be fine. Just sing out and I'll come in after you.'

'Sounds good.'

Bruno takes the dark gravel drive.


MIKE STANDS alongside Amy at the end of a concrete pathway, about fifteen metres from the house. Behind them are two dead bodies, one on top of the other, in a pool of blood. It's Noah Winters and some poor lackey—a young guy who got caught up in the crossfire upstairs.

'You want to make a run for it?' Amy says to him.

They're both staring at a bullet-ridden police car not twenty feet away.

'Now would be the time,' says Mike.

Eventually, the cop appears in the distance, making his way in.

'What a fucking night,' says Amy.

'I think I'm in shock or something.'

Up close, the cop is a thin, dark-haired bloke. He stands close and nonchalantly takes a look at the house and the dead people. 'This isn't great,' he says. 'How are you two holding up?'

'I'm okay,' says Mike.

'I've had better nights,' is Amy's reply.

The cop looks at her. 'It wasn't you who landed me in this shit, was it?'

'No,' says Amy. 'Bill Webber's inside. He wants to talk.'

Mike says, 'Do you two know each other?'

'We're acquainted,' says the cop. He holds out his hand to Mike. 'I'm Bruno. What's your name?'

'Mike.'

'Mike Nichols? Jesus, of course. I've been looking for you. So, what's going on inside, Mike?'

'They want us to tell you they're serious and that you should give them what they want.'

'I think we got that message,' says Bruno. 'Who are the bodies?'

'Noah Winters and some aide,' says Mike. 'The guy upstairs did it. The one they're talking to on the phone.'

'He's out of his mind,' says Amy. 'Capable of anything. He could kill all of us and then top himself without a second thought.'

'How many are we dealing with?'

'Just two,' says Amy. 'Bill Webber, and the one upstairs, Sunny.'

'Is anyone injured?'

Mike says, 'The butler needs some stitches, but he's all right.'

A voice announces itself from the house. 'Bruno?'

'Yeah, I'm out here, Bill.'

'Amy, come back in for a minute,' says Webber.

She walks back.

As they wait, Bruno scans the house again and lowers his voice. 'When you turn around to go back in, I'm going to slip a gun into your waistband. You ever fired a gun, Mike?'

'No.'

'That's okay. It's all set to go. All you need to do is get as close to them as possible and pull the trigger. I'm talking me-to-you away, that close. Unless you're virtually touching them, you'll miss, all right? You understand what I'm saying? Nod your head if you understand.'

'Do I have to do it?'

'You might have to, yeah,' says Bruno.

Mike nods.

'Good man.'

Amy returns. 'They're willing to trade all the civilians for you, if you come in now.'

'Uh fuck, really?'

'That's about the size of it,' says Amy.

Bruno takes out his radio and calls it in.


THE HOSTAGES ARE FREED, totalling four house staff, two chefs, the bleeding butler, and a catatonic Buddy Winters, alongside his tall assistant. Amy watches them go and thinks, *That should be me.* Instead, she returns to the house with Mike and Bruno.

In the living room, Bruno freezes as soon as he

sees the God Minister slumped in the corner. The big man is sitting there, pressed into a single lounge chair, his bulk overflowing onto the armrests. He's fine. In fact, the minister maintains the same dead-eyed composure he's carried himself with the whole time, neither angry nor afraid. An impartial observer.

'This wasn't the deal,' says Bruno.

Webber isn't having it. 'He's not a civilian. Neither is she. Now sit over there, all three of you.' He directs them to a long white linen couch.

'Sir,' says Bruno, taking the spot closest to his boss. 'You okay?'

'Fine, I'm fine,' says the minister. 'Don't worry about me.'

Amy can hear the other gunman upstairs pacing around frantically, still talking on the phone. The louder words echo down:

*Better.*

*Helicopter.*

*Kill.*

She watches Bruno slide forward on the couch a little. 'Bill, what are we doing here? This is crazy.'

'It'll be over soon.'

'You better believe it will. They're going to storm this house if you don't get this wrapped up in the next couple of minutes. You know the protocols. The Emergency Squad are a bunch of nutters, and they're gearing up as we speak.'

Webber looks out the window, speaks over his shoulder. 'The protocols are different when you've got the Minister of Police as a hostage.'

'I don't think so, Bill.'

Webber almost laughs. 'Don't kid yourself. There's one rule for them and one rule for the rest of us. That's . . .' Webber turns around. 'That's the whole fucking thing. *That's* why we're all here.'

'I'm here because you asked me in,' says Bruno. 'Can you sit down, Bill? You need to talk to me.'

Amy sighs, fatigue washing in. Beside her, she can feel Mike fidgeting around. The man can't stop moving since they came back inside. *I guess those feelings of his are back in action.*

'Bill?' says a voice from the stairs.

It's Sunny.

'Yeah?'

'Put the minister on the phone.'

Webber grabs the fancy cordless receiver from the wall and walks it to the minister.

He grabs it, listens.

They all watch.

'Oh, no, no. No problem here. I'm fine,' says the minister, phone pressed to his face. 'Yes, I think that will work.' The minister looks at the keypad then turns to Bruno. 'How do I shut this thing off?'

'What's the deal?' says Webber.

The one called Sunny descends the stairs. 'They're sending a chopper. They're saying half an hour.'

Bruno bolts up.

The two gunmen jolt, bring their weapons up.

Bruno ignores them. He points at Sunny and stammers, 'You, you—'

'Sit down!'

'Sunny,' cautions Webber. '*Sunny!*'

'You're not fucking Sunny,' says Bruno. 'You're Samson O'Grady.'

# BRUNO
## Fantasyland, Gold Coast

BRUNO FORCES HIMSELF TO sit.

Mind reeling.

'How?' he says, mostly to himself. 'I don't understand.'

'I'm going to fucking shoot this cunt,' screams Sunny. 'That's the one who killed Seth.'

Webber edges around, gun pointed directly at Bruno. 'Go upstairs, Sunny. Go on. See if there's anything worth stealing up there.'

'Fucking pig cop,' says Sunny. 'This isn't right.'

'We'll take care of him,' says Webber.

Sunny looks at them, but he doesn't move.

'Samson, come on now.'

Sunny lowers his gun. He spits on the carpet. Then he slowly retreats up the stairs.

Webber lets out a long, unsteady breath.

'Sit down a minute, Bill,' says the minister. 'You're going to give yourself a heart attack, if you keep this up.'

Webber takes up residence on the opposing couch. He puts his gun down beside him on the fabric. 'Probably not going to make it through the night anyway. Not with him.'

'We can all just walk out of here,' says Bruno.

Webber smiles sadly.

'You want to tell me how you got into this mess, while we wait?'

He does, it seems.

It's why Bill Webber invited Bruno in.

'Take your notebook out,' he says.

BILL WEBBER GREW up with Samson O'Grady, or Sunny, as he's known in the Webber household. 'Samson means *sun* in Hebrew,' Webber says. 'Dad's Jewish. He never called him Samson, not a day in his life. None of us did. Sunny practically lived at our house. Had that big place of his own, but . . .'

'I know what his father did,' says Bruno.

'How?'

'Found the room downstairs. I figured Sunny was in one of those barrels. I thought he was dead. Was that the idea?'

Webber shakes his head. 'I wish.'

He tells them that Sunny's father, Phillip, was tall. He says he didn't quite fit in one barrel. As he tells the rest of the story, Webber's eyes catch the light, lost in the horror of it.

'You helped him?' says Bruno.

'It was an accident. Well, kind of an accident, in the beginning.'

Sunny had fallen on hard times. Severely addicted to coke, he pissed away his chances at an inheritance, but landed himself back home, nonetheless. He was on a strict regimen of straightening up and repaying broken promises. 'Bit rich, if you ask me,' says

Webber. 'But his dad was a pious old prick, despite everything.'

Phillip got Sunny a job through a family friend.

'Her dad,' says Webber, nodding at Amy. 'He sorted it out.'

Victor knew Allan Watts was looking for help with the Silver Fish. Victor knew the O'Gradys.

'It was some rich-guy thing,' says Webber. 'Hands washing hands, all that, or at least that's how it looked at the start. These days, it looks more like Victor moving everything into place. It didn't help Sunny any. There was plenty of coke to be had at Allan's spot. The Silver Fish was lousy with it.'

Cocaine and untrammelled ambition.

Allan hears about a big score: Fantasyland.

Buddy Winters is looking to cash out and run away from the family business. He has an asking price and all sorts of backroom bullshit sorted out. Buddy is *ready*. His stake is promised to the highest bidder. A neat takeover with compliant co-investors. The whole deal.

'Allan actually heard all about Buddy and Fantasyland from our lot,' says Webber. 'The Joke wants to buy in. They're sizing it up. Sorensen, Lewis, they're all about it. And there's Allan, serving drinks to them in the private room of his restaurant, soaking up the inside skinny. They underestimated him.'

A consortium came together.

Allan Watts with a piece.

Victor Owens with a piece.

Samson O'Grady vying for a piece.

'To his credit,' Webber says, 'Sunny asked his father to invest before he started making demands. And old Phillip was a greedy fucker, bent in every way, so Sunny figured it would work. It did, kinda. The old man agreed at the start, but . . .'

The problem: Phillip O'Grady was owned wholly and solely by the Queensland Police.

Had been for years.

They kept him out of jail.

In turn, Judge O'Grady kept other evil men out of jail, on their behalf. 'They told him he couldn't invest in Fantasyland because he'd be bidding against the boys, and essentially slitting his own throat. Couldn't have Sunny doing it either.'

There's a pause.

'I take it Sunny didn't like that?' says Bruno.

'No,' says Webber. 'He figured his father owed him.'

Another pause.

Webber stares at the carpet. His hand gently touches the gun barrel on the lounge beside him.

Bruno pushes on. 'Bill, we found the bodies in the barrels. We found the room. The whole thing is breaking open. There are pictures and records from that room. I can guess why you were involved.'

'Phillip was a monster.'

'There's not a jury in the country that isn't going to take what he did to Sunny into account. You know that, right?'

'It wasn't just him,' says Webber.

Bruno starts to answer before the full extent of it announces itself. Webber is a victim too. 'We can . . . We can still . . .'

Webber seems to hear it and not hear it. With a completely neutral tone, he says, 'It was a shakedown at the start. We put the hard word on Phillip one night. He either had to cough up the money or we were going to blow the whistle on the whole thing. I was a cop, for crying out loud. I mean, I fucking tried to dob him in years ago. I made submissions, back before all this. God, I probably ended up a cop in the first place just to get back at him one day. When I first signed on, I wanted to stop people like Phillip. But I couldn't, could I?

'For a long time after I signed on, Sunny didn't want to say anything. He had it worse than me. It was a weird situation. But then . . . that night at the house, we demanded the money from Phillip and he didn't do the right thing. He sent us packing. He said Sunny had stolen enough money from him over the years and it'd all gone up his nose. As for what he'd done to us, he told me I could tell anyone I liked. There was nothing we could do about it. He was protected. He just stonewalled us. I got out of there. I went home. Later, I got a call in the middle of the night and knew as soon as I picked up the phone. Sunny had snapped and done them both. I don't know why, but I went over and helped him clean up the mess. It was Seth Blackwell and me. We both helped him.'

'Was Seth another victim?'

Webber nods. 'He went to school with us for a stretch. We all came up together. He wasn't much more stable than Sunny.'

'How do the banks come into it?'

'I knew that disposing of the bodies would only buy us a little bit of time, even though we were smart about it. We had maybe a couple of weeks at best. Maybe a month or two, and then we'd be in the shit. Victor offered to take care of Sunny if we came through with our share for the Fantasyland bid. Victor said he could get Sunny out of the country on his boat. Get us all out, if we wanted.'

Webber blows out a breath.

'We didn't just hit any old bank. I want you to know that. I had a lot of information on these fuckers. Phillip had records, but Arthur Sorensen had them too. The Joke was taking a cut, of course. They were shaking these pests down while they were protecting them. That's part of the system. When this is all over, I've got enough to pull the whole thing down. For Jamie as much as the rest of us.'

Amy frowns. 'Jamie Leaver?' she says.

'Yeah,' says Webber. 'Jamie was my line into the Joke. An informant, off the books. He was a friend of Seth's, actually. Between what he could get me and what I could find out for myself, I had most of it down pat. Just didn't know what to do with it exactly, until all this. We robbed them. They used shared safe deposit boxes to move money around, as drop points and pick-ups. That's the money we got, for the most part. I worked over Phillip's network for keys and codes and box numbers, whatever we needed. Sunny cased out the banks. Seth did the driving. Jamie stayed out of it, mostly. It was pretty clean, in the beginning. No one got hurt at the start. To be honest, it's not that difficult, you know. Most bank robbers are junkies and psychos. Knowing what I know, we got through it without too much hassle.'

'But things got out of hand?' says Bruno.

Webber nods, points upstairs and taps his nose. 'Of course it did. Killing his parents did his head in. But, to be honest, a lot of those bank people deserved what they got. He wasn't totally out of his mind. The manager and his assistant on the last bank job, the one you were at, they knew the sort of money they were handling. And we both knew the sort of people they were.'

'What about his mum?'

'Who?'

'Marion O'Grady,' says Bruno. 'What did she do to deserve all this?'

Webber doesn't like it, but he acts straight. 'She knew what she was married to.'

'What about the cops you shot yesterday and the bank guards and everyone else?'

'I didn't shoot anyone.'

'You didn't stop him from doing it.'

'No,' Webber says slowly. 'I didn't.'

'We can still walk out of here,' says Bruno. 'It's the right thing to do, Bill. Come on.'

Webber looks like he's thinking it through. Tongue moving around in his mouth.

Calm suddenly.

*Relief.*

Until: a droning sound in the distance.

Louder and louder.

'Holy shit,' says Sunny upstairs. 'Holy shit!'

It's a helicopter.

'It's too late for that,' says Webber.

# BRUNO & MIKE
Fantasyland, Gold Coast

SUNNY AND WEBBER BUSTLE them all out of the house, even the minister.

Through the back door.

Around the pool.

Into a field under a dark green sky, with a helicopter circling overhead. As the helicopter lands, the wind from the rotors whips the grass, churning up a cloud of dirt. The sound is immense, a loud mechanical roar, and it's enough to mask the arrival of the Emergency Squad: a half-dozen armed police in fatigues, creeping out of the darkness.

'Halt!'

Sunny and Webber turn and aim.

A fast stand-off in the maelstrom.

Webber puts his shotgun flush with Mike's neck, while Sunny walks forward aiming at one particular policeman.

Everyone's screaming at each other in the din.

No one can hear a thing.

Bruno slowly crouches down.

·   ·   ·

Iain Ryan

MIKE THINKS ABOUT RUNNING.

Held in place by Webber, he sees a policeman with Sunny in the darkened distance, the two of them face to face. The policeman points his pistol in the air—a gesture, a brief surrender.

Behind Mike and Webber, the helicopter pilot hits a spotlight, and the field turns white.

Mike can see the policeman's face now.

It's Constable Chris.

The man who invaded his house.

Threatened his kids.

'No,' Mike says to himself. He takes two steps forward, but Webber's arm grips his bicep, holding him back.

'What are you doing?' Webber shouts in the wind.

Then Sunny jolts.

Gunfire, he's hit.

Sunny staggers momentarily. His shotgun erupts and Constable Chris's arm detaches at the elbow, flying back in the gale like a snapped tree branch.

More shots in the night.

The helicopter starts moving, preparing to lift off. Webber drags Mike towards the light and pushes him into the cabin. Webber gets in beside him and they both watch as Sunny staggers through the grass towards them.

Webber jumps out.

The pilot panics and the helicopter shudders.

Sunny is pushed into the cabin. He grabs hold of a stray seatbelt and pulls himself upright with one arm as they rise into the air. No sign of Webber. Within seconds, they're high above the ground, banking right.

A hand grasps hold of the lip of the cabin from the outside.

Sunny reaches out, grabs his friend's hand.

Mike pulls the gun in his waistband and pushes it into the back of Sunny's skull.

A second of recognition.

Mike pulls the trigger, blasting the interior of the cabin.

Sunny slackens, falls forward and tumbles out, collecting Webber on the way down, his hand ripped from the cabin edge in an instant.

Mike grabs a door handle, checks the exterior to be sure.

He's gone.

They're both gone.

Down below is Fantasyland. The bright lights of make-believe shining up, the fake mountain, the cosy colonial houses, the paving and gardens around the man-made canal that Noah Winters dug out with his own excavator. From this vantage, Mike can even see the mock version of the *Endeavour* floating in its dock, waiting for the first day of the invasion re-enactment.

Up the front of the helicopter, the pilot is yelling something, but Mike can't hear him in the wind.

It doesn't matter.

*It's over*, he thinks.

The elation is profound.

Profound and short-lived as a blast of light explodes through the cabin, shredding it into a thousand metallic fragments that rip through Mike's body as it falls back to earth.

# PART TEN
# TWO WEEKS LATER,
## OCTOBER
### 1982

# AMY

## Southport Funerals.

VICTOR OWENS, DEAD AT last. A big turnout
for the funeral. Four hundred mourners who haven't
seen Victor in years and never saw the real man, either
way. *He would have been happy with this*, Amy thinks,
glumly.

His career outlined in a glowing eulogy.

His legacy praised by all of its rich inheritors.

The daughters dragged to the church by
expectation.

Victor, immortalised and unreal.

The perfect crime.

COLLEEN VINTON SIDLES up during the wake, a
drink in hand and her little cigarette camera at the
ready. The woman looks like hell. Word is, she's struggling with the death of Mike Nichols, despite everything else. She's been wiping away tears in brothel
backrooms, her temper running permanently foul. As
such, Amy's kept a low profile.

'My condolences,' says Colleen.

'You too,' says Amy.

'I was hoping to run into Elda.'

Victor's nurse. Officially missing, presumed dead. Unofficially, rotting somewhere in the canal water behind Victor's mansion.

Amy makes a show of surveying the room. 'How did you and Elda know each other?'

'Everyone knows Elda. I have some work for you when you're ready to come back in.'

'About that . . .'

'Yes?'

'I'm stepping aside.'

'Are you now?'

'See that guy over there, the one by the door? That's Ronnie. He used to work for Buddy Winters out at Fantasyland. Ronnie works for me now. Sort of my personal assistant. Today he's here to get rid of anyone who acts up. Figured a few undesirables might show, but it's been okay so far.'

'Well, look at you,' says Colleen, forcing out a fake little laugh. 'If Tommy were here, he'd have loved this.'

Amy leans over, keeping her voice to a whisper. 'My debt to you is done with. Anyone who says otherwise, or *does* otherwise, is going to end up buried under something in Fantasyland. You understand? This is my father's funeral.'

'Oh well, we'll see,' says Colleen, like she's just heard an amusing anecdote. 'That's the problem with new money, Amy. It spends fast and, well, when it runs out . . .' Colleen clicks her fingers. 'Then you're suddenly accustomed to things you can't afford, like Ronnie over there.'

'Till that day then,' says Amy, and moves on.

. . .

# THE DREAM

THE FOLLOWING MORNING, Amy drives across the border to Saint Andrews Catholic Church. Inside the chapel, she finds the priest, Father Frank Hanlon. He's sitting alone in the pews. For no reason other than instinct, Amy slips into the row behind him. 'You got a minute, Father?' she says.

Frank nods. 'I was thinking I might run into you.'

'Yeah. I saw you at the service. I forgot that you knew Victor.'

'I wanted to make sure the coffin wasn't empty. You fancy a drink?'

'Sure.'

Frank gets up and goes to the altar. He pours communion wine into two coffee mugs and brings them back. 'To new beginnings,' he says.

'Amen to that.'

'Now, what can I do for you? Have you come to repent?'

'Something like that.' Amy takes the envelope from her pocket. Victor's job contract, his dying wish. 'I don't know what you've heard, but my father put me in charge of his estate. He has a son, it seems. A living son. I couldn't care less about managing the family business, but if I find this kid, he'll be set for life.'

It was true. Victor's secret son was set to inherit a stake in Fantasyland, something Amy held on to despite Buddy Winters inheriting the park. It worked out well for Buddy. He had one silent partner now, instead of three, and all Amy had to do was make sure no one ever caught wind of what almost happened. They announced the grand opening in the paper last week.

'What about you?' says Frank. 'You'll be looked after too, I imagine?'

'Never mind me. This kid's my brother.'

'And the mother is?'

'You remember that girl I came in here with a couple of weeks back? The one I took to Adelaide.'

'Sarah.'

'That's right. I think it's her kid. I'm on my way down there to find out. Has she been in touch?'

'She might have. What makes you think Sarah's baby is the one you're after?'

'My father says so. He hired her with the express intention of getting her knocked up. He made movies of it. Home movies. She's in them.'

'It can't have been easy being that man's daughter.'

'He's dead now . . . so who gives a shit.'

Father Frank swirls the wine around in his cup. 'You know, people say Sarah's boy is Robert Emmery's bastard, not your father's. It was a whole thing a few years back. A lot of people got hurt because of it. I assume you know Emmery? Talk is, your boss keeps Emmery in line by threatening to expose the child, or worse.'

'I don't work for Colleen anymore. Like I said, I work for my father now.'

'I work for mine too,' says Frank. 'Here's to aligned interests.'

'So, you'll help me find the kid?'

'It's the right thing to do.'

'Is it?'

'Destroying Colleen Vinton is God's work, Amy. It's his plan for me.'

AMY OWENS DRIVES for a full day into the bush and scrub, along straight empty roads out into the country's flat dry centre. She keeps the radio down. Just the engine and her thoughts, and a fresh pack of smokes.

At dusk, as the sun finally loses its sting, she pulls over.

She's in the middle of nowhere. Red earth. A near-treeless plane. The highway is so quiet that Amy sets up her camera and tripod on the empty bitumen, in the centre. She sets the timer for five seconds.

It's enough.

*Five.*

She scoots around.

*Four.*

Takes the spot.

*Three.*

Stands tall.

*Two.*

Tries to smile.

*One.*

The aperture opens and the dying light washes in, capturing a new image.

# BRUNO
## The Strip, Surfers Paradise

LIFE GOES ON. BRUNO and his siblings put their father's house on the market. Buyers start sniffing around. Danny considers it a done deal and starts talking about moving out, telling everyone he's off to university. He keeps calling it a fresh start, asking the same question over and over, 'Are you going to be okay on your own?'

'I'll be fine,' says Bruno.

For the first time in a long time, he believes it.


WORK IS STILL A MESS. After the events at Fantasyland, the Joke is rattled. The Surfers Paradise police station throbs with paranoia. There are no congratulatory drinks for Senior Constable Bruno Karras after closing the O'Grady case. No promotion pending. He may have solved a double homicide, but everyone knows there's a tranche of missing evidence and everyone can guess who has it.

To keep Bruno in line, Internal Investigations ask difficult questions, all of them veiled threats.

*How did you end up at Fantasyland that night, at just the right time?*

*How did Mike Nichols end up with a gun during the siege?*

*How does Amy Owens figure into this?*

Bruno lets his union rep do the talking, and it's no comment all the way. There's only so far they can push it because the God Minister was there as well, and he's not saying a word either.

The murder of Allan Watts is swept under the carpet. No one wants to look too hard at Allan, not with his connections to the Force. As such, Amy Owens walked away, unscathed.

Everyone else, not so much.

Mike Nichols is dead, evaporated in the helicopter fire.

The O'Grady family, dead.

Bill Webber.

CIB detectives found Webber and Sunny in Fantasyland, their bodies not five metres from each other, pummelled and broken on the bank of the canal. Webber's involvement with the Gold Coast bank robberies was never publicly disclosed. They buried it. Couldn't have a detective seconded to the Robbery Division named as a culprit. The embarrassment to the Force would be too much to bear.

The deal put to Bruno is to let sleeping dogs lie, or get fired.

Or worse.

But at least he's not alone in the ether. Every other night, Pete Reynolds comes to the house and the two of them sit around Bruno's kitchen table and look at everything O'Grady had in his sick bunker. It's grim work, but they can handle it. They do it to honour the dead, for the victims guilty and innocent. They stay on it. They collate leads. They work the case, refusing all censure. But they don't rush, either. It's a long game and some nights—lonely, hopeless nights —they just talk and keep each other company.

UNFORTUNATELY, they're still on the books with Colleen Vinton. But there's hope on the horizon now. A new deal in play, a way to get out from under, because of the helicopter crash that killed Mike Nichols.

The wreckage presents conflicting stories.

The official one is that Mike Nichols effectively killed himself, and the pilot, by discharging a firearm inside the cabin. The bullet taken from the impacted skull of Samson O'Grady lends some credence to this.

But the unofficial story is that this is the handiwork of Deputy Commissioner of Police, Arthur Sorensen. It was his private helicopter that went up, and everyone who saw the thing come apart in the night sky knows the truth: it was loaded with explosives.

Colleen wants her revenge.

Bruno and Reynolds tell her they can deliver.

*We're sitting on something that can give you Sorensen's head.*

*But we need to keep our jobs to do it.*

*We need you out of our hair.*

*We need time.*

She agrees.

Nonetheless, dark days are coming.

'I might just throw it in,' says Bruno on one of those long nights at the house.

'Oh yeah? What are you going to do?' says Reynolds. 'Open a bakery?'

'Surf shop,' says Bruno.

Reynolds loves the sound of it.

BRUNO FLOATS in the dark ocean, out past the breakers where the quiet water is. Another morning— just him and two other blokes further down.

In the distance is the Strip.

Still not much action there. A city still in recession. A construction site, biding its time. But progress can't be far off. The money is coming.

But not today.

Today's Monday. Mid-October 1982. The start of another work week, another stretch of endless complications and their impossible balancing act and—

A long shadow passes beneath his feet in the water.

Bruno stays in place. There's no thrashing around in the surf and screaming *shark* this time. He stays on his board with his legs out in the sea, waiting.

The shadow passes again, a little further out.

Then, nothing.

No dolphin diving from the waves.

Just the slow undulation of the tide. An ocean filled with unknowns.

Bruno rides it back to the shore.

HE PUTS his surfboard in the back of his ute and slips behind the wheel. It's a balmy day and the interior of the ute is blisteringly hot. He reverses out and puts the thing in gear, and there it is, tucked under the wiper.

Another envelope.

The same white half-page business stationery.

His name written in the same blue biro, facing in.
*Bruno.*

He reaches around, puts his hand in. It's a document of some sort. A list of names and dates and figures. There's a Post-it note attached: *From Mike Nichols, RIP. PS: Turn it over.* Someone has written, *Under Sorensen's tennis court*, in pencil on the back. Bruno doesn't know what it means, but there's more inside the envelope. He reaches in a second time and touches the glossy surface of a photo.

# VICTOR

SOMETIMES WHEN I DREAM, I find myself wondering if I've already passed over to the afterlife. In the dream, I'm wandering through some strange moment—along some landscape formed out of the real and surreal—and I find I can stop the dream momentarily. I can stop the procession of scenes and think to myself, 'Is this it? Has it happened already? Am I dead?' Because at some point, my body will slide away and my last memories will not be memories at all, just the first tentative steps into the never-never. Electrical current in my brain petering out, showing me some vision or representation. An image that happened or never happened, with barely a moment to comprehend.

I just pray that when I go, I'm young and happy in my dream.

I pray for fantasies to usher me away.

When I go, I aspire to be with people I find agreeable. I hope I'm mid-sentence or mid-thought when I realise—like an absolution of reality—that I'm finished. That it's all over.

*Let me float away, happy and free, knowing my descendants will bear the load going forward. I built them a paradise and now they need to learn how to live in it.*

**END**

# Subscribe

Subscribe to my newsletter and get free stories, book reviews, and discounts on my new releases.

iainryan.substack.com/subscribe

# Contact The Author

To contact Iain visit IainRyan.com.

# About Iain Ryan

www.iainryan.com

Iain Ryan grew up in the outer suburbs of Brisbane, Australia. He predominantly writes in the hard-boiled/noir genre and his work has been previously published by Akashic Books Online, Crime Factory, Kill Your Darlings and Seizure.

His novella, *Four Days*, was published in November 2015 by small press Broken River Books (Portland, USA). The following year the book was shortlisted for the Australian Crime Writing Association's Ned Kelly Awards (Best Debut Fiction). It didn't win. Then Broken River Books folded, and the book fell out-of-print. On a roll, Ryan wrote and self-published a trilogy of grimy *romans durs*, all set in the Queensland tropics: *Drainland* (2016), *Harsh Recovery* (2016), and *Civil Twilight* (2017).

Disillusioned with self-publishing, Ryan submitted the manuscript for *The Student* to a single editor (Angela Meyer, an acquaintance) and the book was published by Echo Publishing. In 2018, *The Student* was shortlisted for The Australian Crime Writing Association's Ned Kelly Awards (Best Novel). In 2021, Echo Publishing and Bonnier Zaffre (UK) published Ryan's third novel, *The Spiral*. Virtually no one liked it, except Ryan himself. In 2023, Ultimo Press published Ryan's sixth novel *The Strip*. A QBD Book of the Month, *The Strip* is Ryan's highest selling book to date and will be followed by sequel, *The Dream* (2024).

# ALSO BY IAIN RYAN

**Six unsolved murders.**

**Two detectives.**

**One chance at redemption.**

When Detective Lana Cohen is assigned to investigate a brutal murder on the Gold Coast, she has no idea that she's about to uncover a scandal that will rock the city to its core. Partnered with Henry Loch, a detective haunted by his own past, Lana must navigate a complex web of lies and corruption to uncover the truth behind the killing.

With six unsolved murders already casting a shadow over the investigation, Lana and Henry find themselves in a race against time, facing mounting political pressure, and battling sinister police corruption. In a place where ambition and greed reign supreme, no one is innocent, and everyone has something to hide.

*The Strip is a gripping crime thriller inspired by real events that will keep you on the edge of your seat until the shocking final page.*

## PRAISE FOR THE STRIP:

'Page-turning from the start, this book ratchets up the tension tenfold as the pieces fall into place and the novel reaches its thrilling pinnacle.' - **Books + Publishing**

'The Strip is bingeworthy reading – a gritty crime thriller reeking of corruption, murder and sex. If you like your heroines flawed and kick-ass and your cops dirty as hell, you'll love Ian Ryan's gripping foray into the underworld of the Gold Coast. Hardly took a breath from first page to last.'

**Kate Mildenhall,** author of **THE MOTHER FAULT** and **THE HUMMINGBIRD EFFECT**

'Fast paced, gritty, sharply observed noir that goes hard into the sleaze and corruption of the moonlight state.'

**Andrew Nette**, author of **ORPHAN ROAD** and **GUNSHINE STATE**

'Steeped in the bitter lore of old-school policing and backlit by the gaudy neon of the Gold Coast streets, The Strip is hands down one of the finest Australian crime novels you'll ever read.'

**DAVID WHISH-WILSON** author of **LINE OF SIGHT CUTLER**

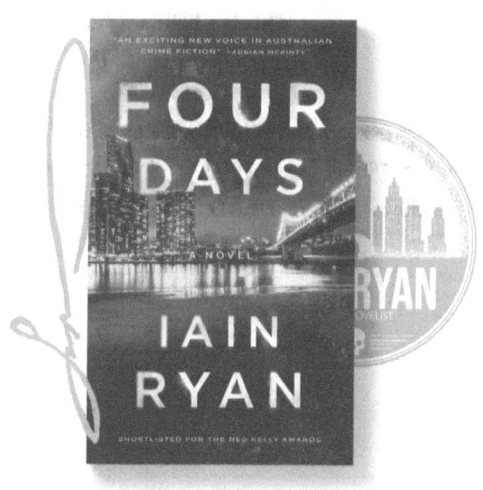

## FOUR DAYS by Iain Ryan

### Shortlisted for the Prestigious Ned Kelly Award

*NEW EDITION contains bonus material: four collected short stories + a new story written entirely for this edition.*

Four days to locate the killer.

Four days to take revenge.

Four days to find redemption.

Jim Harris is a hard-drinking Australian detective on his way to a nervous breakdown. Every day, he works alongside corrupt police and dangerous crooks. That is, until a brutal murder case unravels his career, bringing past indiscretions to light. Alone, afraid and out-of-control, Harris makes a pact with himself: solve the case or die trying.

SHORTLISTEAD FOR
THE NED KELLY AWARDS

# THE STUDENT

A NOVEL

## IAIN RYAN

"A TERRIFIC NEO-NOIR"
—ADRIAN McKINTY

## THE STUDENT by Iain Ryan

### A Twisted Tale of Murder, Drugs, and Deception in the Heart of Small Town Australia

In the quiet town of Gatton, a shocking murder rocks the community to its core. Maya Kibby, a young student, is found dead, and no one knows who killed her.

Nate, a student and part-time weed dealer, finds himself caught in the middle of the investigation when his friend and supplier goes missing. As he delves deeper into the mystery, Nate uncovers a suitcase that holds the key to unlocking the truth behind Maya's murder. But with the killer hot on his heels and his own life on the line, Nate must navigate a treacherous web of secrets and lies to survive.

Set against the stark beauty of regional Queensland, The

Student is a gritty, fast-paced thriller that will keep you guessing until the very last page. As Nate confronts the dark underbelly of his seemingly idyllic town, he realizes that evil can lurk behind even the most familiar faces.

**Can Nate unravel the twisted truth behind Maya's murder before it's too late? Or will he become the killer's next victim?**

~

## PRAISE FOR THE STUDENT:

"The Student is a terrifically dark tale, set in a part of Australian that seldom features in local crime fiction, with clean, sharp prose that wonderfully evokes atmosphere and moves the story along at a fast place."

**Andrew Nette**, author of **ORPHAN ROAD** and **GUNSHINE STATE**

"Hits hard and keeps you enthralled until the very end."

## THE HERALD SUN

"*The Student* is a scrappy delight of a second novel from the Ned-Kelly-shortlisted Ryan.'

**Fiona Hardy, READINGS**

"Iain Ryan's punchy prose draws you in..."
## THE SYDNEY MORNING HERALD

"A terrific neo-noir from an exciting new voice in Australian crime fiction."

**Adrian McKinty**, author of **THE CHAIN** and
## THE ISLAND

"The Student takes the campus novel and mines within it a

dark seam of violence, deception and suspense in prose that
burns with a fierce propulsion."

**David Whish-Wilson** author of **LINE OF SIGHT**
**CUTLER**

Erma Bridges' life is far from perfect, but entirely ordinary. After years of dedication to academic research, her career is falling apart, all because of a mysterious workplace complaint. So, when she is shot twice by Jenny – a vindictive colleague who has seemingly disappeared – her quiet existence is shattered in an instant.

With her would-be murderer dead, no one can give Erma the answers she needs to move on from her trauma. Why her? Why now?

Panicked, overworked and on the verge of a nervous breakdown, Erma begins her quest for the truth – and a dangerous, thrilling journey into the heart of darkness. As a web of brutality unfurls around her, Erma uncovers a dark series of crimes on campus and discovers a side of herself unimaginable within the polite world of academia.

NEW RELEASE

**WHAT LIVING AND DYING IS LIKE**

IAIN RYAN

"An exciting new voice in Australian crime fiction"
ADRIAN McKINTY

An ex-con circles back to L.A. and knows it is a mistake. Elsewhere, in Vegas, a restless kid buys a mysterious, stolen guitar. Two characters, worlds apart, but drawn together by the same buried history. Spread across two connected stories, Iain Ryan's *What Living And Dying Is Like* is about regret and hard-won recovery.